GOING TO SEE THE ELEPHANT

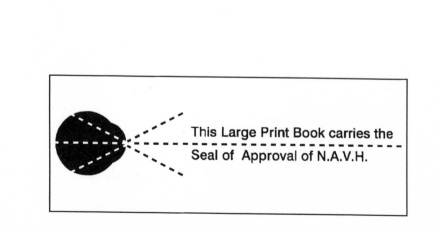

This Large Print Book carries the
Seal of Approval of N.A.V.H.

GOING TO SEE THE ELEPHANT

RODES FISHBURNE

THORNDIKE PRESS
A part of Gale, Cengage Learning

GALE
CENGAGE Learning

Detroit • New York • San Francisco • New Haven, Conn • Waterville, Maine • London

GALE
CENGAGE Learning·

LIBRARY OF CONGRESS CATALOGING-IN-PUBLICATION DATA

Fishburne, Rodes.
   Going to see the elephant / by Rodes Fishburne.
     p. cm. — (Thorndike Press large print laugh lines)
   ISBN-13: 978-1-4104-1574-5 (alk. paper)
   ISBN-10: 1-4104-1574-0 (alk. paper)
   1. Reporters and reporting—Fiction. 2. San Francisco (Calif.)—Fiction. 3. Large type books. I. Title.
PS3606.I7685G65 2009b
813'.6—dc22
                                          2009007719

Published in 2009 by arrangement with The Bantam Dell Publishing Group, a division of Random House, Inc.

"Things can happen in San Francisco."
— Frank Norris

A NOTE ON THE TITLE

In 1858, if the reader had lived in New York City, or Abingdon, Virginia, or Hayes, South Dakota, or any other large or small town in the United States, and a friend had stopped by one afternoon to inquire into your whereabouts, your mother *might* have said: "He's going to see the elephant."

This meant you'd headed west to participate in the gold rush. The elephant was fame, fortune, and with a little luck, luck itself.

Later, when the gold rush in California had mostly died down, you were considered "off to see the elephant" if you embarked on a trip to India, Africa, the Orient — any sublime experience would do.

For our purposes this nearly forgotten expression is meant to identify those rare souls interested in making contact with the story of a lifetime.

7

For Lindy
From Dumbarton to the Fog
314

PROLOGUE

All good first sentences have a kind of energy, wrote Slater Brown in his yellow notebook as he was being pedaled erratically down Market Street.

And all good first sentences have a kind of sincerity, he continued, adjusting his pencil as the wheels of the rented rickshaw bounced beneath him.

But what kind?

Soon enough the oncoming cars began slowing, their passengers staring hard at the young man standing in the back of the bicycle taxi, writing God-knows-what, while being driven the wrong way down the busiest street in San Francisco.

A-l-l GREAT s-t-o-r-i-e-s contain within themselVEs SOMEthing . . . faMiliAr, he scrawled as his driver swerved between a delivery truck filled with Tomales Bay Oysters and a rental car filled with wide-eyed nuns from Fargo.

11

As if, sOmeHow, we're nOt reaDing thEM for the first TIME!

He chewed his lip. It hadn't come through this clearly in days, weeks even. Just then the driver of the three-wheeled chariot steered back across the trolley tracks dividing Market Street and oblivion, and settled calmly into the correct lane.

All great writing sounds as if one solitary voice were behind it, throwing itself across the chasm of eternity! Having sensed this, having t-a-s-t-e-d this, having understood this in the very fiber of my being, it would be ridiculous not to follow suit. I only ask that my

—

WHOOOOOOOOOOOOOOOOOOOOO-OOSH . . .

A bright red electric trolley, passing inches away, blew the yellow notebook out of Slater Brown's hands. So deep in thought was he that he simply pulled a fresh one from his jacket pocket and turned to a clean page.

For San Francisco's most recent arrival, there was so much to capture: the city's bright streets, the shimmer of water just beyond the tallest buildings, the clangor of the cosmopolis. He wanted to see it all — everything — first. Fast and messy. Like running through a museum of great paintings. There would be time to circle back

12

later, to double-check, to consider thought-fully. But just now he wanted to eat the city.

Preferably with both hands.

All down the boulevard he tapped the driver's shoulder every time a particular view, or landmark, or spectacle revealed itself: the clots of people walking along Montgomery Street, speaking into tiny phones.

Together and alone, he wrote.

The buses whizzing past, their tops con-nected by long arms to electric wires strung high above the street.

Like a modern-day Indra's net!

At Lotta's Fountain he was particularly enthralled to see two men playing checkers, each atop a unicycle.

After stopping and starting for twenty minutes, the bicycle taxi coasted to a halt in front of the majestic Ferry Building. *Like legs of a visiting giant,* he wrote while peer-ing out over the Bay at the ironworks of the great bridge, only partially visible through the clouds.

A city of infinite magic! A city of synchrony, he wrote, spinning in a slow circle, taking everything in like a passenger on a private merry-go-round.

A city where fate and luck collide in an explosion of destiny!

13

He inhaled the salty October air.

I want to write something that will last forever. Something future generations will read with great delight. As if putting their fingers on the pulse of a ghost!

He exhaled.

He'd been in San Francisco for exactly forty-seven minutes.

After soaking in the downtown atmospherics Slater Brown put away his notebook and returned to the padded backseat of the bicycle taxi, pointing down Market Street with the confidence of Achilles circling Troy.

"Take me to the city!" he shouted above the street noise as the wheels lurched into motion. "Take me to her!"

■ ■ ■ ■

BOOK ONE:

■ ■ ■ ■

Make Happen

CHAPTER ONE

Perhaps the bicycle taxi driver spoke no English. Or perhaps he was the trickster Loki in disguise. Or perhaps he was simply tired of pedaling around a passenger with a 250-pound trunk full of first-edition nineteenth-century novels. But after a fifteen-minute ride Slater Brown's luggage was deposited on the curb in front of TK's Bar in the Mission District and he was presented with a bill for eighty-seven dollars.

As the bicycle taxi jingled off into traffic Slater Brown smoothed his suit and stepped inside. Upon first review TK's wasn't exactly the literary place he'd hoped for. In fact, the only book any of the residents were reading was the Bay Meadows racing form.

Nevertheless, it was at TK's Bar & Simmer (it wasn't licensed as a grill, but they kept a hot plate next to the cash register), beneath a faded photograph of Joe DiMag-

17

gio holding a stringer of tiny silver fish, that Slater Brown first sat down and made the round wooden table talk.

The talking table — christened the "noisy fecker" years ago by the sour-faced Irish barman known as Whilton — had first exhibited its propensity to thump during an after-hours dice game of "Ship, Cap'n, Crew." The game, a not-to-be-missed ritual at TK's, had been played every Thursday night since the Nixon administration. During one particular game, Sideways Sal had pounded on the table so hard as he was losing that one of the spindly table legs had inexplicably become shorter than the others.

"I wish't I'd me a furnace," said Whilton at the time.

But he didn't, and tilting the table sideways through the door and out into the open street was too much hassle for an aging man with a bum back, so he simply slid the round wooden table to the farthest corner, where the extra glasses were stacked below the pay phone, and forgot about it.

Tonight the talking table, having finally found its muse, was impossible to ignore. It vibrated madly, sending up little explosions of dust and pencil shavings from the linoleum floor like hot grease, as Slater Brown filled his yellow notebook with observations.

It was the kind of thumping conversation that held no interest to the tired faces gathered alongside the bar. If they had lifted their heads to listen to the frantic sound coming from the corner, they would never have understood the language. Transcribed, the talking table told a secret, unknown to anyone else, for Slater would never share it:

Twenty-nine, twenty-nine, twenty-nine . . .

The very idea of it beat down on him with the weight of a thousand steel hammers. There was a kind of numerological destiny to twenty-nine.

If you haven't anted up the chips of imagination by twenty-nine, then what are you? Just a professional mourner, looking back, pulling away on the wrong train, your voice caught in your throat, unable to attract the attention of the impatient conductor.

By the age of twenty-nine James Baldwin and Saul Bellow and T. S. Eliot and Fitzgerald and Rilke and —

The pencil point crumbled. He'd been pressing too hard against the page.

As Slater Brown paused to resharpen with his pocketknife, blowing the cedar shavings onto the floor, he couldn't help but look over his shoulder to see if anyone was watching.

By the age of twenty-nine Hemingway and Chekhov and O. Henry had pulled themselves together for the world to see, walked to center stage, forgotten the lisp or canker sore, the bunched-up underwear, their mother's stink-eye, and killed — killed! — the audience.

Yet here he was at twenty-five, rising each morning, trying to pull forth some kind of original writing that would stand without support. There had been the one poem, published in *The Bartleby Review.* But that had been in the special issue devoted to dyslexic writers. And he'd even faked that!

For him, the worst part was the loathing.

No, actually the worst part is the panic. Turning each breath into a battle . . .

Actually, the worst part was that he didn't even have the courage to admit to the world that what he wanted, more than anything, was to be a writer people would remember.

He'd read the masters. He'd reread the masters. James Joyce had been quite explicit in *A Portrait of the Artist as a Young Man:*

Welcome, O life! I go to encounter for the millionth time the reality of experience and to forge in the smithy of my soul . . .

But despite repeated attempts, Slater

20

Brown found the smithy of the soul a lot harder to locate than Mr. Joyce had ever let on.

The idea that you simply read everything — from the Bard to Balzac, from Cervantes to Conrad — picking up clues on how to write your own masterpiece is just bullshit. Because it leads you to believe that by following their footprints you can learn the route in advance. But it doesn't work that way!

Behind Slater Brown a jubilant cheer went up at the bar as the residents watched a televised home run float out of the baseball park — a lonely, predestined comet on its way to illuminate the inky darkness of the Bay.

The talking table had gone quiet. The faces at the bar were quiet too, turned upward like geckos, basking in the muted glow of sporting highlights. When the ninth-inning home run was replayed on the eleven o'clock news, they cheered again, like drunken sailors who had forgotten they'd already seen land. By now Slater Brown was standing, hunched over the talking table in a kind of masturbatory clinch, unconsciously holding his breath as he tried to force himself down the tiny aperture of the pencil point and spread his thoughts across the page.

His mind reached for something to write. He could locate the right ideas, always in fact, but it was impossible to put them onto paper exactly the way he thought of them.

It's not my fault, he promised himself. *It's the words' fault! The English language, in all of its elastic, indeterminate obstinacy, is to blame!*

He had every confidence in his ability to communicate his deepest philosophical thoughts and feelings (and sense of humor!) if the words would just present themselves. *In the correct order!* That was important, because a lot of what Slater Brown had identified as bad writing was not bad thinking or bad observation or bad feeling but simply bad order. *Case in point,* he wrote in his yellow notebook: *A dictionary. Every book ever written comes from words in a dictionary. But it isn't the words that make a book interesting. It is the ORDER of the words. Otherwise, people would go around reading dictionaries!*

Pleased beyond reckoning with this digression, he touched pencil to paper and soon the wooden table leg began pounding along again, a manic telegraph sending out a midnight S.O.S.

He'd come to San Francisco expressly for

the purpose of writing something that would last forever. Only he didn't feel he could share this personal ambition with just anyone. They would think what? That he was a fruitcake! That he had lost contact with reality? It was a tricky situation, having a plan you couldn't share. Nevertheless, for the first three days he exerted the plan flawlessly and with maximum concentration from his perch in the back of TK's. In the evenings he would reread what he'd written by the bar's dim light. Nobody paid him a scintilla of attention.

By day four he began to flounder. By day five he couldn't even look at himself in the cracked bathroom mirror. After flogging and thrashing through the catalogue of ideas in his mind, seeking a theme, or character, or even a single word that would last forever, Slater Brown began to change his mind. Irrespective of the fact that this self-assigned task was harder than anticipated, he was slowly but surely running out of money and for the first time it occurred to him that writing for eternity didn't pay very well. At the outset, this had seemed like a future problem. But on the morning of day six, given his diminishing cash reserves, it revealed itself to be a problem very much set in the present. So, with a pendulum's logic, Slater Brown decided to forget about forever and instead write something successful. You couldn't have it both ways.

For God's sake, as so many of the dead masters have shown, you can't shine and illuminate at the same time.

So there it was. Write something successful.

Simple.

CHAPTER TWO

The morning of his twelfth day in the city Slater Brown lay in his bedroom in a state of paralysis while the pages of the *San Francisco Sun* covered his naked body like a funeral shroud.

Piles upon piles of books stood in four-foot-tall towers around the room, making it look like a library bereft of shelves. Along the windowsill rested three decades of *The Bartleby Review,* salvaged from the dumpster of a decommissioned library. Propping up a three-legged mahogany wardrobe was a seventeen-pound untranslated, unexpurgated, and unread edition of *Don Quixote.*

The desk next to the window was covered by bound sets of Icelandic sagas and Russian short stories, while the major Irish poets, interspersed with a random selection of South American magic realists, occupied the only chair.

Simply moving around the room required

tiptoeing down serpentine pathways and around the pulpy stalagmites, or risk sending the greatest names in literature crashing to the floor. Only the small sink and the tiny bed remained uncovered by the bibliomania.

That Slater Brown wanted to be a writer was obvious. But it was more than that. He wanted to be the very best writer in the entire world. To one day have his work included in the company of the classics that surrounded him. But even this secret had a false compartment: By his calculation, he already *was* the best writer in the world. In the history of the world! He knew things, saw things, *heard* things that would blow people's minds!

He just hadn't gone through the irksome task of writing it down yet.

In the correct order!

It is not easy to maintain the idea you're the greatest writer in the history of the world when you haven't actually published anything yet. Yet there are ways this can be accomplished, and Slater Brown found one of them without benefit of instruction. Remarkably enough, if one were to imagine oneself the greatest writer in the history of the world, then it logically followed that one did not, *per se,* have to suffer through the dross of lesser scribes. This dross turned out to include almost all of known literature.

This philosophy was reinforced because Slater Brown believed that he could tell, straightaway, if a book was any good or not by simply reading the first sentence. Hopped up on double espressos and small pieces of Turkish halva, he passionately wrote and rewrote the familiar sentences in his yellow notebook:

All good first sentences have a kind of energy. And all good first sentences have a kind of sincerity. But what kind?

Outside his window came the echo of a distant foghorn. It was as if the city were agreeing with him. He took this as synchronistic coincidence of the highest order and pressed on.

Thanks to the Sincerity-Energy principle, more than one of the books in Slater's room had been opened and inspected before being thrown unread into the corner. The ratio of unacceptable books to acceptable was a dozen to one.

Feeding this unique reading habit was a second streak of compulsive behavior. Before Slater Brown dismissed the offending book — with the confidence of a pharaoh handing down a death sentence — he would invariably flip to the back of the dust jacket and read the author's biography. In its own way this little slice of information was more important to him than the book itself.

He mined each of these miniature life stories until he'd done the mental mathematics necessary to figure out how old the authors were when they'd first written The Big One. This was how he'd come to the horrifying conclusion about the terrible importance of the number twenty-nine, and furthermore how he'd convinced himself that, at the age of twenty-five, he was being left behind in the great parade of literary history.

Reading the first sentences of the greatest books in the English language in order to feel superior, and then reading the author's biography (which invariably caused him to feel terrible and inferior and, finally, terribly inferior), was not a pastime that ever caused Slater to get much writing accomplished, and seemed to be responsible for his current state of stasis. It was like watching a bee sting itself over and over again.

Suddenly there was a knock on his bedroom door.

"Who is it?" he said, lurching to cover himself with the crumpled newspaper.

"Who do you think it is?" said the voice.

"Just to let you know, your breakfast is getting cold."

"Than . . . thanks, Mrs. Cagliostra," he said, scrambling from bed.

Mrs. Cagliostra, a fifth-generation San Franciscan, had rented her guest cottage to him provided he sign a contract that stated he would keep an eye out for burglars, didn't play any musical instruments, was not in possession of a Himalayan longhair cat, and ("absolutely, positively!") allowed no sleepovers. Such was Mrs. Cagliostra's Catholic disposition that encounters with strangers latching her sidewalk gate at six in the morning had proven detrimental to her digestion. She'd also demanded a month's rent and a deposit, which Slater had been able to satisfy only by turning over a bejeweled silver snuffbox once belonging to his great-grandmother. "I'll just hold on to this until you find steady employment," she said, slipping the family heirloom into her apron pocket.

The renter's cottage sat in the rear garden of the big house, among the slugs and calla lilies, and looked like a miniature red-and-white shoe box, with a sloping slate roof and two wide windows that overlooked Powell Street. One entire side of the cottage was covered with tiny pink climbing roses, which Mrs. Cagliostra tended to every day and affectionately called "my girls."

He'd found Mrs. C. (as he came to call her) on his seventh day in San Francisco by perusing rental advertisements on a giant rain-spattered cork bulletin board in front of Generosa's pastry shop in North Beach. His first nights in the city were spent sleeping in a eucalyptus grove underneath the stars in the Presidio, which had seemed like a perfectly reasonable plan until the fog rolled in and made all his clothes, even his packed ones, smell like sour milk.

Besides, Mrs. Cagliostra's house had seized Slater's imagination the moment he read the street address: 135 Joyce Street. It might as well have been named "Finnegans Way," or "Smithy of the Soul Drive." Regardless, it was clearly a synchronistic co-incidence.

Mrs. C. stood five feet three inches tall and wore her hair in a huge neo-beehive hairdo that forced her sharp face to compete for attention. All of this made her already suspicious hazel eyes even more intimidating. She suffered no fools gladly, and her husband, Frank Cagliostra, being no fool himself, had sensibly passed away ten years earlier at the age of sixty-seven while recuperating from a mild stroke.

Yet for all of her fierceness, Mrs. Cagliostra possessed the rare ability to transcend the reflexive guffaw, as evident the day she opened the front door of her two-story Victorian and saw Slater Brown standing there, her address written on his hand in permanent marker. He wore a thrift-store linen suit, carried an ash walking stick, and had a white Panama hat tipped rakishly over one eye. If the linen suit hadn't been missing an outside pocket, or his walking stick hadn't been three inches too short for him, or it hadn't been clear that his shoes each belonged to the wing tip genus but not quite to the same species, he would have cut a very dashing figure indeed.

However, none of this mattered to Mrs. Cagliostra. She'd already read his face, like the opening lines of a promising story, and saw buried there both energy and sincerity.

At breakfast later that morning Mrs. Cagliostra burst in and out of her dining room bearing dishes: two kinds of toast, a bowl of sliced mangoes, sausage, coffee, juice, and sparkling water. She made a show of doing these things because they were included in her rent price and she had been raised to be exceedingly fair. Stingy, yes. Suspicious, absolutely. But fair, always.

Laying down a bowl of cereal in front of Slater, she sat down across the table and asked in the direct way of hers what he was doing for work.

"Not sure," said Slater after a moment. "Thought I'd peruse the paper."

Mrs. Cagliostra put her teacup down with a bang.

"I don't like the sound of that," she said. The word "peruse" had always sounded a little fishy to her. "What do you want to do, anyway?"

"Hmmm . . . don't know," he said.

"When I was your age we didn't have time to say things like that!"

"Well," he said, choosing his words carefully, "I want to be a writer." But he choked a bit on the last part so that it came out hoarse and wispy. What Mrs. Cagliostra heard was: "I want to be a waiter."

"Why didn't you say so!" she shouted. "I'll call Salvatore and see if he's got any openings over at DaVinci's Cellar. It's a first-class operation."

"No, no," said Slater, finally smoked out of his reticence. "Writer, writer, I want to be a writer!"

She tilted her head as if what she was looking at was so lopsided that it needed to be addressed on its own terms. The cereal in his bowl crackled like artillery.

"What for?" she asked.

He left the house soon after breakfast, herded out by Mrs. Cagliostra, who waved off his promises of finding work "right away" and "expecting success shortly." She had heard it all before. In her experience, men, particularly young men, would rather tell you, endlessly and without interruption, what they were going to do rather than just going out and doing it.

"It's one of the leading problems in the world today," she told her bridge group later that afternoon.

CHAPTER THREE

Shortly after noon, Slater Brown found himself sitting in a frail aluminum chair opposite a glass wall. It had been a rough morning. Getting lost four times in the city had not helped. Nor had getting kicked off the trolley car for not paying (pretending to speak Swedish had not fooled anyone).

Fortunately, his inherent romanticism allowed him to believe that a small, authentic life-pathway (with carefully orchestrated coincidences and time built in for lengthy epiphanies) was being rolled out just in front of him. At least that was how he thought it should work, how it worked in every novel he'd ever read, and how he'd written about it working the night before in his yellow notebooks. For just this reason he was keeping track of all observable synchronistic coincidences for a possible book on the subject.

Today's first synchronistic coincidence

was an advertisement in a newspaper he'd found folded faceup on the bus seat next to him:

Do You Enjoy Reading?
Leading business seeking creative types for interesting editorial position. Must like to read and have excellent comprehension.
Application available at
133 Clementine Street, Suite 405

Slater bit his fingernails as he considered the advertisement. This was not the perfect job, but it wasn't altogether bad sounding either. In a pinch it might work. Mrs. Cagliostra's voice echoed in his mind. It was definitely worth checking into.

Twenty minutes later he found himself in the lobby of the temp agency, a place with all the charm of an airport currency exchange. There was a tiny sitting area surrounded by a three-foot border of yellow carpet branded with dark circles where long-dead potted plants had once wilted.

The far wall was made entirely of what appeared to be bulletproof glass except for an aluminum vent cover the size of a large Band-Aid where applicants spoke to the receptionist. Taped to the vent cover was a note that read "No Use." Behind the glass sat a round mass of imperial brunette curls so dense they obscured both the vision and nose of their owner. She wore a headset attached to a thin black wire that ran over the front of her blouse before disappearing underneath the desk.

Every few minutes a red light would blink on the switchboard and the woman's mouth would move. Because he could not hear her from behind the glass, it took Slater a few minutes to guess at what she was saying. It was either:

"Yellow, lethal flower, waiting on my knees."

or

"Hello, PeoplePower, can you hold, please?"

He turned his focus to the application. A single line at the top proclaimed it to be "Official and Binding."

1) Name: Slater Brown
2) Age: 25
3) Address: 135 Joyce Street (in the back)
4) How many days in the last two years have you missed work, not counting illness, jury duty, vacation,

or paid holidays? N/A
5) Please explain fully any gaps in your employment history: N/A
6) How does your potential future work with PeoplePower help to further your career? N/A
7) Please list a local reference: Mrs. Cagliostra
8) Address of reference: 135 Joyce Street (in front)
9) Connection to reference: financial

By the time he'd finished the question-naire he began to feel a little self-conscious about how seriously he was answering such serious questions.

What could you honestly tell about a person based on such a ridiculous starting point? he wrote on a small corner of the application page before tearing it off and popping it into his mouth.

The truth was that the "editorial position" he was applying for — reading Sunday newspapers from around the country looking for stories with the words "powdered milk" in them, which he would be responsible for cutting out with scissors and putting in an envelope per the instructions given by the Federal Dairy Company Newsletter (9–5 M–F; 30 min lnch brk) — didn't exactly suit him.

It wasn't that he wasn't qualified. It was much more fundamental than that. It wasn't what he could imagine a writer doing. The more he thought about it, the more depressed he became. What kind of writer was he? Kneeling — kneeling! — down in a temp agency office, writing on a useless table the size of a waffle iron, being ignored by a two-toned troll behind bulletproof glass? What did it mean when the people you wanted to work for operated behind bulletproof glass? He began to sweat. Wiping away the sweat, he began to grind his teeth. He stood and approached the glass wall.

"Excuse me," he said, tapping on the window. The woman stopped her telephone conversation midsentence. Her lips glistened with freshly applied gloss and she radiated annoyance from every finely plucked hair in her furrowed eyebrow.

"I was wondering," said Slater, "if you had any writing jobs?"

The receptionist casually cupped her hand around her ear and made a wrinkled face of incomprehension.

"I WAS WONDERING," said Slater Brown, raising his voice, "IF YOU HAD ANY WRITING JOBS?" Slowly she reached toward the row of dials and switches in front of her. Each of her fingernails was painstakingly painted with a different national flag. He watched as Jamaica inched forward and flicked a switch.

Her voice bellowed at him from a recessed speaker in the ceiling above him. "Wha?"

"Right," said Slater, shifting his gaze up to the speaker rather than continuing to stare at her moronic face through the glass.

"Sorry to bother you. I was wondering if any of the positions you're trying to fill involve actual writing of some kind?"

"Nada," said the voice from above. "Only openings we got is scanners, clippers, proofers, spoofers, and pasters."

Spoofers, thought Slater, beginning to retreat — he didn't even want to know what that was.

Perhaps it was the epiphany at the temp agency, or perhaps it was the memory of Mrs. Cagliostra's parting look at breakfast, or perhaps it was the fact that when he walked through the door of TK's Bar, one of the residents glanced over his beer mug and said, "Thumper's here," to everyone's general amusement. But by the time Slater Brown sat down at the round table in the back, he'd slipped into a prodigious funk.

He'd been coming to TK's, like an orphan returning to his only known point of origin, for nearly two weeks. It had turned out to be an ideal writing place, so long as he was tucked away in the back and everyone else was focused on the blaring television above the bar.

Isn't something supposed to have happened to me by now? he scribbled in his notebook. *A story? A surprise? A synchronous explosion of fate and destiny? This is what I want to know: Is the city listening to me? I'm listening to her!*

And he had been listening, with a kind of fierce devotion, waiting for a message to reveal itself. Slater Brown was not just awake but alive to the city. He absorbed the sounds with the intensity of a monk: the *ring-adingding* of the trolley car, the basso profundo of the foghorn, the blurt of night voices on the street on their way to where? A party? A séance?

On and on his hearing extended, stretching outward like the tendril of an exotic plant seeking the sun. Those first nights after he'd unpacked at Mrs. Cagliostra's he sat cross-legged on his bed and listened as people passed on the sidewalk outside his back window. They spoke about jobs they hated, or girls they'd dated, or about the

40

secret supper club in the Haight:

"Say 'Dolores is bananas' at the purple door," chirped a female voice from the dark street.

Dolores is bananas. Slater Brown wrote that down in his notebook.

There was no question the city was letting him in on her secrets. *But these are just surface secrets,* wrote Slater. *The bigger ones come later. As soon as she gets to know me.*

Yet despite his optimism, and despite his monomaniacal listening skills, the days were slowly gathering themselves into weeks with no big news from the city.

He must have looked especially forlorn because a voice from the end of the bar called out, " 'Ut'll you 'ave den?" It was Whilton, squinting in his general direction.

"Nothing," said Slater, trying not to look at him.

"Jaysus, kid, you sit in here all day, marking down who knows what into your notebooks, least you could do is buy a drink. These lights don't pay themselves."

"Water," said Slater Brown, shamefaced. "Water's fine."

Whilton nodded and grunted "eedjit" as he threw his wipe rag over his shoulder and bent to scoop ice into a clean glass. Slater would have liked to order a beer or a liquor drink. But he couldn't. Today was a day he'd been dreading all along even as he'd convinced himself that it would never happen. Now that it had happened, he felt a sense of unexpected recklessness.

As the glass of ice water was placed in front of him, Slater pushed forward two quarters he'd been obsessively clicking together in his pocket and leaned back with a smile of perverse satisfaction. He'd just spent his last fifty cents on a glass of ice water and was officially dead broke. A wave of ecstasy overtook him.

Like flipping off the gods, he wrote. *Something's bound to happen now!*

He was distracted by the arrival of several regulars filing in after work. He turned over a new page in his notebook:

They fluttered in and settled like moths adjusting their wings on an evening lamp.

He watched them intently for a moment longer but nothing else came to mind. He closed the notebook and reached into his bag, where he kept a little book, a kind of touchstone that he turned to whenever he doubted himself. He could open to the title page and see his name, front and center, in black and white. He'd written it in college.

Technically it was a not a novel but a

novella. Or as one of his professors had called it, an "overlong short story." He'd written it in four days, actually four feverish nights. The title of the book was *Terminal Moraine,* after an entry he'd come across in an open dictionary in the library: a dead-to-rights synchronistic coincidence, certainly. At school, when he was asked who had published the book, which he carried with him in public, he would say he had decided to have it published privately, in the manner of Wordsworth et al.

The truth was he'd discovered an old Klugelman letterpress in the basement of the English department and had, after much trial and error in the art of mirror writing, taught himself how to print *Terminal Moraine* one sentence at a time.

In this way the entire book, all thirty-six pages, was printed in eighteen-point Dauphin font with drop caps, marbled endpaper, and leather binding. He had made two copies, one for himself and one for the girl he was dating at the time, Amy Horny, who was teased mercilessly for her last name but whom Slater Brown charmed by pronouncing it Hornée, with a French accent. He'd wrapped the book in gilded paper and written a gushing inscription that owed something in phrasing and rhythm to an Irish wedding toast:

My dearest Hornée,
May the wind be at your back,
May your luck be strong,
And may this book rise up to meet you.
All my love, S.

Terminal Moraine told the story of a young man who, at the exact moment of orgasm, believes he hears the voice of God. Or at least a few divine words before the orgasmic glow fades and, despite his best efforts, God's voice becomes harder and harder to hear. This development leads to incessant masturbation as the main character, Jack, tries to piece together God's revealed message one stroke at a time. Slater composed the novel during a period in which he was reading Philip Roth and Franz Kafka exclusively. On the frontispiece of the book was the inscription:

For Philip R. and Franz K. We ride as one.

Despite the presentation and the sentiment involved, Amy Horny never actually got around to reading, or even opening, *Terminal Moraine.* This was made evident one Friday night, as they lay in a tangle of sheets, their bodies still flush and sweaty, when Slater thought it opportune to ask what she'd thought about "it."

"Oh," she'd said, trailing a finger down the center of his back, "harder's always better."

Harder? he thought. Like what? More allusions, more metaphor, more double entendres?

As Slater sat in TK's, flipping through the pages of his book, it dawned on him for the first time how catastrophically bad the story was. Or if not bad, how simply unfinished.

He put his head down on the table.

What was he doing? Writing all day for an invisible audience, trying to put something wild and true down on paper?

From above him came the sound of a throat being cleared. Slater looked. It was Whilton again, his dirty bar apron drawn tight against his belly.

"Hare," he said, tossing a bundle of crumpled and creased newspapers onto the round wooden table. Slater looked carefully over the well-thumbed pages of a week's worth of the city's newspapers before turning back to Whilton.

"I can't pay for those," he said finally. "I'm

— I'm out of ducats."

"Eh?"

"I'm out of money."

"Who said nuttin' 'bout money?" growled the barman. "I seen you was a scribbler, is all. I thought you'd be needing scribblesheets." The grumpy Irish barman had barely acknowledged his existence before, much less struck up a conversation. Slater was so surprised he forgot to say thank you. Whilton turned to go, and then, as if a thought had suddenly occurred to him, he turned back.

"You true broke, kid? Flat-out, or just between-checks broke?"

The residents of TK's had given Whilton a lifetime of experience with the subject's nuances.

"Flat-out," muttered Slater.

"Fecking hell," said Whilton. "It's a faraway basket of kunkel, it is." This was Whilton-speak for "sorry-to-hear-you're-shit-outta-luck."

"Next thing I know, you'll be sleeping in the gutter, begging me ketchup to make 'mato soup!" he wheezed. Slater couldn't tell if it was genuine concern or a kind of macabre glee that caused Whilton to smile. He looked at his feet.

"Aw, feck off with your mullacker self,"

46

said the man from County Cork. "Work it through, is all. No man ever lived but by his wits. Shite, where do scribblers like you find work anyway?"

Whilton waited for the answer, and when it didn't come he screwed up his face into a fearsome look of annoyance and roared as he pointed at the answer.

"The place for scribbling feckin' stories is in the feckin' newspaper. You feckin' wanker!"

Slater stared at the pile of newspapers in front of him. As he did Whilton muttered a few more choice curse words before snapping his fingers. A flash of silver shot forth, striking Slater in the forehead before clanking to the floor. By the time he'd collected himself and reached down to pick up the mint silver dollar, Whilton had shuffled into the back room to change the taps on the domestic beer.

The evening crowd at TK's had thinned. Tonight's obscure televised sporting event, advertised to start in five minutes, was the world championship hurling competition, live from Scotland. Among the remaining residents the gambling had already begun, despite collective ignorance of the subject. "It's from medieval times," said Sideways Sal, the resident know-it-all. "The point is to grab your wife by the hair and throw her as far as possible." The other patrons considered this practically for a moment before returning to their beers.

Quiet as a nave, wrote Slater as he rose from his chair and clamped on his fedora. It was late, Mrs. Cagliostra would be asleep, and he could temporarily escape the inevitable inquisition.

As he passed the end of the bar a voice called out, "Say, kid, did'ya see the race today?"

Slater stopped and turned. It was the old man, the one they called Moon. He sat on the barstool, straight as an arrow. His eyes were sad and rheumy and he studied Slater Brown unblinkingly.

"What race?" asked Slater.

Just then the entire row of barflies — twenty strong — lifted their heads in unison and shouted, "The human race!" in one long, well-practiced chorus.

Slater Brown smiled at their noise, tipping his hat in their direction, before stepping out the door and into the fog.

Walking home from TK's, their laughter still ringing in his ears, Slater pondered Whilton's suggestion. He knew he couldn't get a writing job until he'd published something,

48

and he couldn't publish anything until he'd found a writing job. This double-ended line of logic filled him with a familiar dread.

Rounding the corner onto Stockton Street, he passed a newsstand open late for the theater crowd. Inside the narrow glass booth a Chinese man known to his customers as Qi sat motionless, listening to an extra-innings ball game from a radio hidden underneath an open newspaper. Slater's eyes drifted easily across the racks of magazines as if appraising a row of racehorses lined up at the starting gate.

On the bottom row, tossed in haphazard fashion and still bound to one another like prisoners by strips of thin white packing tape, were the literary magazines. The middle row held the glossies from Europe, their covers featuring women with scornful gazes and ruby-colored lips. The top row, the row he could barely stand to look at, were the biggies. His heart glowed with envy at the thick typefaces and sophisticated covers drawn by Continental cartoonists. If he could only get their attention. He already knew the names of all the writers. He'd written all the editors too, even the fact checkers, a dozen times with story ideas and inflated writing experience and . . . and . . . nothing. It was like being introduced to a beautiful woman who turned away the instant she heard your name.

Slater Brown stood there slowly sinking into the sourest of sour moods. He had the sickening feeling maybe San Francisco wasn't the right place for him. Maybe he'd have to go somewhere else before his fate and luck could collide in an explosion of destiny. He glanced at Qi, catching sight of his own faint reflection in the glass between them. He looked different. Thinner, more furrowed. As he stared at his reflection he noticed something hovering next to his face. A blue blob flickered with vibrating edges. Next to the blue blob was a white blob. Slater leaned in, toward the apparition, until his nose was pressed against the glass. Qi ignored him. The voice on the radio said, "Strike two."

Slater's eyes tightened as he studied the hovering shapes. They were words, that was plain to see, but they were confounding, both familiar and mysterious. As his eyes adjusted, the blue blob to the left of his face became nэqqsH. On his right, the white blob became эʞsM.

He swiveled slowly to see where the message was being transmitted from.

Across the street a luminescent storefront

lit up the night. The name stenciled into the glass read "Scrivener's Copy Shop" and underneath, a blue-and-white neon sign read, "We **Make** Ideas **Happen.**"

"Sweet Jesus," whispered Slater as soon as he'd solved the riddle, "nəqqɒH əʞɒM is *Make Happen* backward." Inside Scrivener's Copy Shop a half dozen men and women wearing red smocks spun in busy circles.

He stepped into the street. This was what he'd been waiting for. The city had finally revealed herself. He looked back at Qi's newsstand, where hundreds of publications stood staring at him like a compromised jury. If this wasn't *synchronistic coincidence of the highest order,* thought Slater Brown, then such a concept simply did not exist.

"Excuse me?" he asked Qi, the idea for what to do next already perfectly crystallized in his head. "Can I borrow two magazines and a newspaper for just a minute?" The old man just shook his head without looking at him.

"I'll be right back. I promise," pleaded Slater. Qi shook his head again and rose from his stool to go. The baseball game was over. Slater winced as the iron grate in front of the newsstand closed with a clang. As Qi departed he dropped a cardboard box onto the curb and patted his pockets, confirming the presence of wallet and keys. Slater waited until the man had walked down the block and turned the corner before crouching down to peer inside the box. It was a week's worth of unsold magazines and newspapers, waiting for pickup. He looked back at the sign across the street: make happen. The city had finally broadcast a message to him. She was listening! He pulled out his notebook.

When the gods speak, they do so with great cleverness, he wrote, balancing on one leg.

I will get myself invited to the party. I will write my own goddamn invitation. Then he dropped to his knees and dipped his hands inside the box of rejects.

CHAPTER FOUR

It's often been noted that a city isn't yet a City unless a healthy number of newspapers are available to cover it. At different points in San Francisco's history, it housed as many as twenty-seven newspapers. In 1854, the *Alta California, Town Talk, Evening Bulletin, Daily Dramatic Chronicle, L'Echo du Pacifique, Tong Fan San Bo, Prometheus,* and *Staats-Zeitung* all rubbed up next to one another seeking readers. Some were printed in editions no larger than a paperback book. Alongside these city stalwarts, the occasional journalistic meteor burned for a brief moment before fading from view. The memorable *Paris-Francisco,* a joint operation between the two cities circa 1878, published Bordeaux wine reviews, Dungeness crab prices at Fisherman's Wharf, and editorials denouncing the insipidness of the world's newest gadget: the telephone. *Paris-Francisco* had been a lively, well-edited journal, but the twenty-three-week round-trip delivery by tramp steamer went a long way toward dampening subscribers' initial enthusiasm.

Times changed, tastes changed. It was no longer fashionable to print the lead editorial on the front page using seventy-six-point leaded type. Nor was it standard to print the names and addresses of the prostitutes (and their clients) arrested the night before along Maiden Lane. But this was still a city of newspapers. So much so that two papers vied for the title of the City's chronicler — the *San Francisco Sun* and the *Sun of San Francisco.* They'd been separated, like Siamese twins, by a federal judge to prevent a monopoly.

Stretched between these two pillars of the community was a web of secondary newspapers that covered all sorts of unique slices of city life. For the religiously minded there was the *St. Francis Topical,* distributed free by nuns on the steps of St. Patrick's Cathedral. For those who made their living on, or around, the water there was the *San Francisco Fog Horn.* For lawyers, *The Green Bag.* There was even an irregularly printed newspaper for traveling circus performers known as the *Hup! Hup!*

Somewhere near the bottom of this long

list was *The Morning Trumpet.* The *Trumpet* was a gold rush holdover (some called it a hangover) that had survived for over a century and a half on eccentric prose and one instance of business genius. Recently, when the *Trumpet*'s own reporters had launched an internal investigation hoping to better identify this institutional intelligence, it had been revealed to be nothing more than good old-fashioned dumb luck.

At the apex of its popularity, in 1885, *The Morning Trumpet* had been printed three times a day to meet the needs of sophisticated San Franciscans. It was loved especially for its snappy pen-and-ink illustrations and brimstone editorials. The phrase "It's a sad commentary on humanity" had actually been coined by one of the *Trumpet*'s earliest columnists, T. T. Figgins.

Since then, despite its illustrious beginning, the *Trumpet* had been traveling down one of the longest slides in the history of publishing. At present, *The Morning Trumpet* didn't even have a Web site. Such expenditure, explained its editor, Maynard Reed, was superfluous.

"People read newspapers with their HANDS!" he shouted whenever the topic came up. "HANDS! HANDS! HANDS!"

However, the real reason for the *Trumpet*'s

reluctance to join the digital revolution was much less philosophical. There simply wasn't the cash. In fact, the *Trumpet* couldn't afford most things — including a stable of regular reporters — and the things it could afford were typically third-rate.

Currently the newspaper was printed on paper so thin it was not uncommon to see people trying to read it in the shadow of a building or the corner of a bus shelter — anywhere to keep the sunlight from bleeding through and running the stories all together.

Yet despite its imperfections, the *Trumpet* survived. It was like a weathered nag spurred over an endless series of approaching hills: year after year, headline after headline, correction notice after correction notice.

Had its loyal readership ever been polled, they would have said they were attracted to the *Trumpet*'s spirit of survival, and to the fact that it was the only place in the world where you could read certain kinds of stories, and of course because the price — fifteen cents — hadn't changed since 1962.

At 10-1/2 New Montgomery Street, on the corner of Market, stood a seven-story building coated with untold layers of city soot. It was one of the few downtown survivors of the Great Earthquake of 1906, and among its architectural flourishes were the individual faces of the nine muses delicately sculpted in Tuscan marble above each window eave. To the careful eye, however, there were nine places, but only eight faces. One was missing, fallen away in an instant and subsequently forgotten.

How a third-rate newspaper like *The Morning Trumpet* managed to stay in operation in one of the most expensive cities in the world was a question only this building could answer. The peculiar circumstances that led to this arrangement could be traced back to 1857 and involved the nascent *Trumpet's* own T. James Mawson (editor 1851–1861), Wild Bill Hickok, several local businessmen, and the hard-to-square appearance of two royal flushes in one hand of poker.

After the card game was halted, the man with the false royal flush, Rufus Shiflett, was summarily shot in the leg by Wild Bill. To avoid being shot again — this time, Hickok implied with a wave of his Colt .44 pistol, it would be somewhere above the shoulders — Mr. Shiflett immediately signed over the deed to his sole asset, 10-1/2 New Montgomery, which was currently being used as a wig factory, to the rightful inheritor of the pot. This turned out to be the *Trumpet's* very own T. James Mawson. Hickok had been so pleased by this spontaneous outburst of frontier justice that he and Mawson (and whoever came into their orbit) celebrated at the Palace Hotel's redwood bar for the next three days.

Four years later, while on his deathbed from pleurisy, editor Mawson, bereft of family or romantic attachments, left the building to his successor, Mr. Virginius Hobsgood (editor 1861–1866). One balmy spring evening, after single-handedly consuming a bottle of Hungarian absinthe, Hobsgood considered his own destiny after having recently lost twelve thousand dollars at the blackjack tables in Sausalito, of which he had only eight thousand dollars in hand. After discussing the matter with his personal bankruptcy attorney, Hobsgood signed over the *Trumpet* building to the newspaper itself in order to protect the paper's longevity. "So that it shall be listed, from this day forward, as part of the *Trumpet's* working assets." It was a bold gesture for two reasons: first, he had written these instructions on the back of a linen napkin using his mistress's lipstick, mistakenly left in his coat pocket; and second, when his wife found out about both the mistress and the use to which the mistress's lipstick had been applied, she shot him dead during his afternoon bath.

Nevertheless, this single act of munificence was to provide *The Morning Trumpet* a safe harbor during economic storms that were to lash other struggling publications into oblivion during the next century. To this day, whenever somebody did something unintentionally helpful at the paper, it was called "pulling a Hobsgood."

Unfortunately, as *Trumpet* staff learned in the years that followed, safe passage into Hobsgood harbor did not automatically inoculate them against stiff competition, scandals, litigious action, advertising droughts, poor management, rotten morale, and just plain terrible reporting.

In 1957, after endless procrastination by previous *Trumpet* administrations, the decision was made by Staige Davis (editor 1932–1959) to generate some extra income by renting offices in the *Trumpet* building to outside tenants. This was an unpopular decision, as it meant that every junior editor, reporter, copyboy, and dogsbody would cease to have his or her own personal office. Bernice Adler, the head copy editor who had gone so far as to convert the *entire* third floor of the building into her own personal residence, threatened to boycott the building in protest of the rental plan until someone pointed out that she lived in the building.

Nevertheless, the decision to rent offices immediately stabilized the *Trumpet's* hemorrhaging bank accounts, as well as provided some money for long-delayed repairs. Staige Davis's first response to these pressing repairs was to tell his overworked staff he was "repairing" to Puerto Vallarta, where he stayed in the penthouse of the Hotel Espléndido for two weeks and played bridge every night with Clark Gable and Doris Day, who were shooting a film nearby.

Since 1957, the revolving tenants of the *Trumpet* building included a steady roster of lawyers, businessmen, poetry magazines, Fibonacci experts, independent salesmen, and inventors (the self-rocking hammock was developed there). The rented offices were on the third and fourth floors of the building, each frosted glass door stenciled, like a raised eyebrow, with the occupant's name. The *Trumpet* maintained offices on the fifth and sixth floors. The seventh floor was reserved for the newspaper's library, where several metric tons of the *Trumpet* sat in piles of moldering yellow newsprint overseen by the staff librarian, or archivist, as he preferred to be addressed, Alistair Macintosh.

Mounted to the outside corner of the building, an old brass clock with an aquamarine patina read "The Morning Trumpet," and, underneath, "The Sound of News." Though no living person knew this, the clock had stopped working shortly after the Great Earthquake of 1906, when a violent aftershock knocked the ninth muse from her perch. Her face fell at precisely 10:16 A.M., striking the clock and loosening the machinery inside. The paper's management had intended to fix this problem immediately, but over the years it never quite happened. In the 1970s the bank across the street installed a temperature clock, with a digital display, and the *Trumpet,* having other things to do, decided to simply let time go.

It was underneath the "Sound of News" clock that Slater Brown officially panicked. How could he be nearly an hour late for such an important job interview? He spun on the heels of his freshly polished shoes in a tight pirouette of regret. Being late was not how a professional writer made a first impression! His panicked eyes finally focused across the street, where the correct time blinked on the bank's digital clock: 9:20 A.M.

"Ah!" he shouted, grasping his mistake. Above him the eight muses shared a stony wink as the morning crowd of bicycle messengers and businessmen spilled over the sidewalk. Slater Brown was a blur as he spun through the revolving doors of the *Trumpet* building and stepped into the elevator. His appointment with the editor in chief of *The Morning Trumpet,* Mr. Maynard Reed, was in exactly ten minutes.

As the elevator doors parted, Slater Brown's first impression was that the newsroom seemed to vibrate with activity. It was unlike any room he'd ever seen before. Every square inch was covered with discarded paper.

Paper on the floor, hiding everything but the little pathways between desks. Paper on the walls, pinned up or crushed into place. And paper on the top of the watercooler in a great leaning tower of regret. There was even paper in the bathroom, where he'd gone to collect his wits before the interview. Old office memos were stuffed behind the radiators, in the sink the current issue of the *Trumpet* sat darkening beneath the leaky faucet, and at the foot of each toilet stall lay little square subscription cards, all that remained of the glossy magazines consumed there.

Slater reflexively ran his hands over his belt and looked at himself in the bathroom mirror. His last interview, three days earlier, had never really found its footing. The editor at the *Sun of San Francisco* opened the interview with a line so crippling even Slater Brown's enormous smile could not sustain itself:

"Do you always attach your suspenders to your boxer shorts?"

This time he made sure his suspenders were attached to his trousers and he carefully retucked his freshly ironed shirt around his waistband. He looked at his face in the mirror again before sticking out his tongue. He'd scrubbed it well before leaving the house. In his right hand was a brown manila envelope with crisp black-and-white copies of his brand-new writing clips. His interview with the *Trumpet* would be different.

Maynard Reed was sitting behind a large redwood plantation desk reading a single sheet of pink paper. A cup of coffee sat steaming at his elbow. Even in repose he projected the worried visage of a busy man. His pomaded hair was combed back in thin orderly strips and his shirtsleeves were rolled to his elbows. All that was missing was a green eyeshade.

"Sit down, Mr. Town, sit down," said Maynard.

"Brown, sir," said Slater, making sure to sit carefully on the tail of his blazer in order to give his shoulders that extra zip.

"Right, Brown. I understand you're here to interview with us?" said Maynard, finishing with a small, distracted smile while shuffling papers on the surface of his desk.

"Yes, sir, I'm looking for work as a writer."

"Clips?" said Maynard, bringing his fingertips together.

As Slater leaned to hand over the envelope, he had the very clear impression this simple act was going to change his life forever. In his mind a curtain opened and behind it he could see himself, a new and improved self, dressed in a brand-new three-piece suit, waving to a crowd of indeterminate size. The curtain was the greenest of velvet greens, with wide, generous pleats and silent pulleys. Everything prior had been about arriving at this place; everything after would owe itself to this moment.

"Make Happen," he murmured under his breath.

Maynard placed the envelope on his desk

64

without opening it, reclined again into his overstuffed chair, and fixed Slater with a long penetrating stare.

"Hmmm," he said.

Hmmm is good, thought Slater, as he stared back unblinking. Hmmm is so much better than Ummm.

But Maynard Reed wasn't thinking about the young man sitting in front of him. He was thinking about Doris Lester, his pit bull circulation manager, and the pink sheet of paper she brought him every morning with the previous week's page count and sell-through rate listed in four neat black rows. These numbers told the complete story of *The Morning Trumpet.* In 1887, the *Trumpet* had been a daily newspaper with no fewer than fifty pages of six columns each. In 1925, thanks to a brief appearance by H. L. Mencken as national correspondent, the *Trumpet* was regularly at forty-two pages and holding. The sixties and seventies maintained an average of twenty-eight pages (Truman Capote had been an advice columnist for eighteen months), but by the turn of the new century — like a party balloon three days after the party — the *Trumpet* had lost buoyancy. After months of back-and-forth, the difficult decision had been made to change from a daily newspaper to a weekly. This "adjustment in frequency," as management directed in a memo, ensured a nearly perfect lugubrious aura for years to come. To go from a daily newspaper to a weekly newspaper was to write your own eulogy in block letters on your forehead.

Maynard Reed's dream had always been to take the *Trumpet* back into daily circulation, chewing up the competition and expanding down the coast until there was only one name anyone ever meant when they said they'd "read it in the paper."

But this idea had lain fallow from the moment of conception. There simply wasn't enough talent at the *Trumpet* to generate advertiser enthusiasm, and without advertiser enthusiasm they couldn't climb out of the page-count cellar. Even now, as a wretched weekly, they were a scant twelve pages on average. This included the four-page color advertisement insert for Judy's Nudies, which broke their hearts to run. "Prosperity follows talent," thought Maynard, though he couldn't remember if he'd read that somewhere or if he'd just thought it up himself. He leaned forward to write it down as a possible column idea to pass along to the staff when he encountered Slater Brown's face again.

Case in point, the young man sitting

across from him. He looked like a nice boy, with the reporter's notebook lying open in his lap. Yet the expression on the lad's face . . . it was as if he were trying to mimic the seriousness of a television anchorman covering a natural disaster on location. But he was just a baby. He'd probably worked on his college paper covering student council intrigue mixed in with sports scores and local politics. And the haircut! It looked like it had been performed with sheep shears! No, what the *Trumpet* needed was a star.

Maynard cleared his throat and thought about what to do next. Not a few of the best minds ever to pass through the *Trumpet* had racked their brains trying to figure out the calculus by which Maynard Reed made decisions. He appeared the most whimsical man in the galaxy. Monumental decisions about the future of the *Trumpet* were made without a moment's reflection and no discernible concern for consequence. But Maynard's mode of decision-making wasn't actually that complicated. Whenever he was faced with a situation in which he, personally, had no idea how to respond, he simply imagined what one of his heroes would do.

In his own way, he was addicted to biographies, and not just any biographies, but preferably those that explained in clear

67

detail not only how the titular subjects had arrived at their station of celebrity, fame, or accomplishment, but especially how they'd overcome all the obstacles along the way. Every wall of his office was filled with rows and rows of neatly organized biographies. Just the C's included Custer, Caesar, Calamity Jane, Caligula, Capone, Capra, Carlyle, Carnegie, Columbus, Crockett . . . The list went on and on.

And so, still not having opened the manila envelope lying on his desk, Maynard renewed his steely-eyed stare at the young man across from him and asked, "Where did you go to school?"

"Back east, sir."

"Ah, yes," said Maynard contemplatively. Perhaps this kid could be molded. He glanced at his bookshelf: What would Hearst do?

Fancying himself the same sort of improvisational student of people, Maynard swiveled in his chair away from Slater and looked out his large office window onto a brick alleyway where several stolen bicycles lay in an abandoned tangle.

They sat this way for five, ten, and then finally twenty minutes. Slater Brown eyed the manila packet on the desk and wondered if it was too late to reach across and snatch it back. He could always go back to TK's and keep writing. But it was too late, because Maynard Reed had already made up his mind and, like Churchill, decided to take a nap.

The following Monday a newly hired Slater Brown stood at the end of the long hallway on the fifth floor of the *Morning Trumpet* newsroom. It was lined with the framed front pages from years past. Stories about five-alarm fires, ship collisions, stagecoach robberies, stranded whales, home runs, bank runs, and bridge construction all competed for attention. At the very far end of the hall the first black-and-white advertisement the *Trumpet* had ever printed — for "Sperm Oil" — was lacquered to the front door of the newsroom. Next to it, framed under glass, was the linen napkin Virginius Hobsgood had used as a legally binding document, with the words "Trumpet Building to Trumpet" in his mistress's maraschino-cherry-colored lipstick. Slater passed slowly down the hallway, pausing to savor each item.

For the most recent major earthquake, a front-page story on the wall read:

Last night the City shook for thirty-eight

seconds. At Candlestick Park lovers clutched one another in the upper deck, while beer vendors bent their knees to keep the merchandise from spilling. When it was all over, a twelve-year-old batboy sitting on the third-base line was overheard to say, "Man, that was some train!"

The byline read Niebald Peters. Slater nodded appreciatively as he walked into the newsroom looking for his new desk.

In the center of the newsroom was a large black table where a group of people were gathered around the next week's layout, each with scissors in hand. *"Bonjour,"* Slater called out as he passed, looking for the *Trumpet's* managing editor, Robert Motherlove, with whom Maynard had said to check in. Slater wanted to see what his first assignment would be, though he already had ideas of his own.

Motherlove was standing next to the watercooler talking to a man in a wrinkled tan suit about the rising cost of paper.

"Gonna kill us, gonna stop us cold," said Motherlove, sighing deeply. The heavy man said nothing, merely lowering his chin in agreement.

"All because of a damn bird!"

"Not just a bird, an owl!" replied the fat man in a mocking tone.

"I don't care if it's a fucking bald eagle. It's killing the newspaper business."

"Hello, gents," said Slater Brown, interrupting. "I'm looking for Mr. Motherlove."

The first thing that caught their eye was the cant of the black fedora. But before a first impression could be fully formed a three-piece gray pin-striped suit begged attention, although it was difficult to discern its full shape, as the suit's wide lapels were hidden beneath a white cashmere scarf. Below the scarf, caught on the outside button of the jacket, was the thin gold chain of an antique watch fob. All of this was just a warm-up, however, for what lay below the ankle: a pair of caramel and cream two-tone wing tips, with little brass eyelets that sparkled like freshly polished teeth. Invisible to all eyes was the name tag first sewn inside the suit twenty years ago — "Frank L. Cagliostra."

As they finished the full-body scan the two men were snagged by one last outrageous detail: The buttonhole on the lapel held a white carnation as big as a tea saucer, with a sprig of holly twined round the base, boutonniere style.

"Fuck'r you?" said Motherlove in a growl

71

curiously lacking malice, for that was how he spoke to everyone. The heavyset man studied the situation wordlessly.

"Slater Brown. I'm looking for my desk, actually."

"Desk?" said Motherlove, as if intoning the long-forgotten name of a friend rumored dead.

"You work here?" asked the heavy man.

"Yes," said Slater Brown, leaning in to shake hands. The heavy man offered the limp handshake outsize men often allow.

"Name's Niebald," said the man.

"And what is it, *exactly,* you've been hired to do?" asked Motherlove.

"I'm a writer," said Slater.

"Well, pardon me. I had you pegged as a bit of a pipe welder myself!" cackled Motherlove, elbowing Niebald.

"What have you been hired to do *here,* kid?" asked Niebald.

Slater shrugged. "Write for the paper."

The two men turned toward each other, erupting into laughter, as they performed a shoulder-shrugging pantomime.

"Where are your clips, kid?" asked Niebald, cleaning his fingernails with the end of a letter opener.

"Clips?" squeaked Slater.

"Yeah," said Motherlove in a tone sug-

72

gesting they'd finally found a dangling thread in this image of sartorial splendor and only needed to pull it in order to make the whole effect disappear.

Slater slid Frank Cagliostra's toffee-colored leather valise from his side and unsnapped the two brass buckles holding it together. He hadn't even had time to remove the old tax returns stuffed inside. After several moments of fumbling silence the manila envelope was located. Motherlove snatched it from him, ripped off the top, and blew a puff of air inside. He handed half the clips to Niebald. With the practiced ease of professionals who have spent a lifetime reading things quickly, the two men scanned the copied articles bearing the banners of some of the country's most notable newspapers.

"How old are you, kid?" asked Niebald.

Slater cleared his throat. "Nearly thirty."

"Well, son, these are real impressive," said Motherlove, handing back the clips. "But who hired you?"

"Mr. Reed. Friday morning."

"I see," said Motherlove, a look of disgust rippling across his face. It was another one of Maynard Reed's famous ambush hirings, which he'd been springing on them with increasing frequency in recent months. But even still, something wasn't adding up. On the other hand, Motherlove wasn't entirely sure it was worth expending the energy to make it go away.

"Well, I'll tell you what, we don't have a desk for you at this very moment, but how about we make a little table for you right here." Motherlove picked up an abandoned piece of cardboard from the floor, swept aside the stack of paper resting on top of the watercooler, and secured Slater's new desk in place with a heavy stapler.

"Ta-da!" he said when he was finished. "Think of it as one of those fancy standing desks."

But Slater Brown didn't notice. He was too busy looking around, convincing himself he was really there, anchoring the moment with details.

"Oh, and the editorial meeting's in my office in ten minutes," said Motherlove, his green eyes twinkling. "You're very invited."

Motherlove started the editorial meeting by clearing his throat and dispatching a short fart.

"Ladies and gentlemen, let's keep our pie-holes closed for the next twenty minutes," he said before running down the day's assignments. A sallow-faced Russian named

Nurgev was told to write about the fire that had burned down the famous Hotspur Theater the night before, and a dour young British woman named Fenton Foote, wrapped in a black trench coat with a pencil between her teeth, was told to go over to City Hall and "find out who, what, when, or how the mayor is fucking up tomorrow's election" and so on and so forth. Although Slater Brown didn't know it at the time, both Fenton Foote and Nurgev would be gone by the end of the week, just more bodies rotating in an endless carousel of people who used the *Trumpet* as a kind of minor springboard for bigger things. Sometimes they redefined the concept — one particularly debilitating tale going round was of the young reporter who'd recently resigned his post in order to pursue a career as a meter maid. Either way, the frequent departures were just more salt in the open wound that was the *Trumpet's* institutional ego.

Next to the radiator, Niebald surveyed the latest crop of reporters before tipping his chair back on two legs, dipping his chin to his chest, and dozing.

Slater waited. He was sure Motherlove would be introducing him any second. He weighed whether it was appropriate for him to say a little something directly to the staff, or if it would be better, in the long run, to let Motherlove carry his water this first time.

"We've got another letter from Benjamin Franklin," called out Motherlove as he shuffled his papers looking at the day's business. "It's a real doozy."

Benjamin Franklin, or B. Franklin, as he signed his letters, was one of the greatest letter writers in the history of English-speaking newspapers. His most recent letter dealt with the upcoming mayoral election. In carefully worded prose that frequently made reference to Greek poets and Heisenberg's Uncertainty Principle, he wrote:

"We cannot, it seems, know where the mayor is and what the budget is doing AT THE SAME TIME!"

He had endeared himself to the newspaper staff by remembering to write in and mark odd anniversaries — the 132nd birthday of the *Trumpet,* for instance — and by not allowing a week to go by without penning another long letter to the editor, often replete with footnotes. These letters were especially popular during slow news cycles or when the *Trumpet* was short a reporter and they needed to fill up column inches.

After finishing the B. Franklin letter Motherlove adjourned the meeting. As the staff filed out Slater raised his eyebrow.

There'd been some sort of mistake.

Motherlove sat on the edge of his desk scanning the most recent editions of the *Sun of San Francisco* and the *San Francisco Sun.* Slater approached cautiously. After standing there for several moments he shuffled his feet.

"What?" said Motherlove without looking up.

"I was just wondering about my first assignment, sir?" said Slater.

"Assignment?" asked Motherlove as if he'd never heard the word before. He fixed Slater with a hard look. This kid was greener than new money, no matter what his clips said. But was it really worth warring with Maynard Reed over? Two chair legs hit the floor. Niebald was awake.

"Niebald," said Motherlove, "what should our young flaneur's first assignment be?"

Rubbing his eyes with the back of his hand, Niebald flipped through the *Trumpet*'s assignment calendar on his lap. "The hundredth anniversary of the fortune cookie is coming up."

"What else?"

"That hot-shit inventor's giving a speech tomorrow over at the Palace of Fine Arts."

"And?"

"And," said Niebald, his thumb running

down the entries, "the mayor's election's tomorrow."

"It's already assigned, and besides, we're not sending *him* out on *that*," said Motherlove, scowling. "By the way, I'm getting down on my knees tonight and praying to Jesus Christ our Lord and Savior that our very own public pissant, Tucker H. Oswell, does not get himself reelected." Motherlove was not especially known for his religious disposition.

Niebald closed the assignment folder.

"Well, he's such an ace reporter, Bob. Remember those clips? I say we don't hold him back. A real wolf-scout like this oughta hit the ground running." Niebald's weary eyes stared at Slater for a few moments before he tipped his chair backward again.

"My thoughts exactly," said Motherlove, nodding.

"Kid," he said with a generous smile, "go find us a story."

They might as well have told him he'd won the tristate lottery. He was stunned. He'd bum-rushed the palace gates only to find them unlocked.

"Go find us a story and you might be our lokul-item man," Niebald called from the corner, invoking ancient newspaper slang for the man-on-the-street beat before clos-

78

ing his eyes again.

"Eh, eh," said Motherlove, waving an inky finger. "Junior lokul-item man."

"Actually," said Niebald, warming to the fun, "technically he would be the junior lokul-item factotum."

Slater listened to them going back and forth. He knew they were fucking with him, but he also knew if he acknowledged their condescension he might as well pack it all in and go home.

"Kid," said Motherlove, his smile fading. "What's the point really? What do you plan on doing here, anyway?"

Slater surveyed Motherlove's face. To speak was to offer an answer he didn't yet have. He flipped on his Biltmore beaver weave hat with a roll only recently mastered and left.

Years later, after Motherlove had retired and was much requested as an after-dinner speaker, he would always respond honestly, if a little flatly, "We never thought we'd see him again."

CHAPTER FIVE

The first thing Slater Brown did upon exiting the *Trumpet* building was to throw his hat high in the air. Next he stomped out what passed for an Irish jig as the stream of pedestrians adjusted their flow around him.

A story! They want me to go find a story! How hard could it be to find a story? Stories are everywhere in a place like this. All you have to do is walk down the street and look and LISTEN.

The greatest unknown writer in the history of the world tilted his head. Hemingway had started out as a newspaperman. So had Orwell. And Dickens. And Balzac. The list went on and on. Newspapers were where writers of promise found their footing.

As long as you shine, what does it matter which lantern you use? he wrote in his yellow notebook.

Even if the lantern is a Trumpet!

Looking around the main thoroughfare,

he caught sight of the afternoon light. It stopped him cold. In a trance he stepped into Market Street to get a better look.

It was four o'clock in the afternoon and Market Street was bathed in a peculiar end-of-the-world light known only to San Francisco. All up and down the boulevard the afternoon sun fell in heavy angled columns that cast the buildings in a bronze glow and caused the trolley rails to shine like silver tears.

Anyone who has been in San Francisco for longer than a day recognizes the light is different. Some think it's because she is a north-facing city, and some think it's because of the salt mist in the air, which clings to everything, even the light, and gives it a texture, and some more mystical minds think the light is different because the city itself is straddling two worlds: the visible world of stars and sun, water and edges, and the invisible world, which can only be felt. The light from these two spheres mixes in San Francisco, they say, the way an eddy in a great river mixes not only water, but also fish.

Sunbeams with a curious texture, wrote Slater in his yellow notebook, just as the first car swerved to miss him, the words "muuther foooker" hurled out the window as it sped past.

The next car slammed on its brakes, resulting in a slow-motion domino effect down Market Street, past the Civic Center, the Hibernia Bank, the *San Francisco Sun,* the curbside chess games, the *Sun of San Francisco,* a conclave of pogo-stickers, the Farmers' Market, until it had caused a traffic backup all the way to the intersection of Van Ness Avenue.

Slater Brown was unconscious of his impact on the traffic. For a moment the city had become timeless, like a photograph that moved, even as he slipped into it, walking around her streets, dancing down her marble stairs, across her glassy surface. He stared at the movement around him, thinking "*That,* I want to capture *that.*" It didn't really matter if he did it in a book, or story, or newspaper. It wasn't so much what was happening — although goodness knows the *what* was interesting — but it was the movement that enchanted him. Without movement a city would be nothing but a yellowing photograph. It was the living, breathing city he loved. Like a woman he loved her. Like a sister and a mother and a beautiful girl all wrapped into one. And she had her eyes on him, of that much he was certain. Her voice called out to him, vibrating up from beneath the pavement.

At the very moment he was about to be run over by a beer delivery truck, a human sacrifice in the name of commerce, a heaving monolith whooshed to a stop across the street. A fleshy black face appeared, framed in the driver's window.

"Child, you best be removing yourself from this thoroughfare." He looked up at her. In his glassy eyes was the reflection of the invisible world.

"C'mon now, don't be a heartache tonight."

The honking cars heckled him all the way across the street, until he'd stepped onto the sidewalk, and the bus, lowering itself to the curb with a pneumatic wheeze, folded its doors open, like a beckoning hand.

CHAPTER SIX

Milo Magnet was wearing his favorite sweater on the day he was to address the Society of Newspaper Editors at the Palace of Fine Arts. It had crisscrossed splotches of color that stretched from underneath his armpits and converged in the center before bouncing away toward the edge of his belt. Milo had knitted the sweater himself in order to demonstrate to his many admirers how a prism diffuses light. "I'm a professional inventor and an amateur explainer," he told people when asked what he did for a living.

Only a year earlier at Buckingham Palace Milo had engaged in a lively debate with Prince Charles about the mathematical origins of game theory. He had stunned onlookers when he reached into the billowy pockets of his pants and pulled out an article written in 1952 by the mathematician John von Neumann to support his argument. The prince was considerably flustered. He'd never known a man to bolster his argument by reaching into his "nethers," as he put it later to friends, but there was the article, and shortly after hailing the butler to provide him with a pen, Milo circled the paragraph he was looking for, folded the paper at the correct page, and handed it to His Royal Highness.

But it was not the sweater, nor the enormous trousers, nor even the red headband that measured Milo's heartbeat, breath rate, and pulse (wirelessly beaming the results to a computer in the toe of his shoe that calculated what he should eat for dinner) that attracted most people to Milo. People were attracted to Milo Magnet because he possessed the quiet confidence of his place in the world — the knowing air of a know-it-all.

Under the average balding pate of a late-middle-aged man, his was not a memorable face. His eyes were a little larger than usual, but of no special color or distinction. His only tic involved a small patch of silver-blond hair riding high on his head that he patted down just before saying something important. He was known to pat his head a lot.

The event Milo was to address, "Hot

Type," was held each year in a different city as a means of drawing journalists from across the country together to talk about the state of the publishing industry. Typically, the speakers were outrageously handsome television anchormen or self-important publishing big shots who commanded high speaking fees, but who, it was customarily observed, always offered to give their speeches at Hot Type for free. The prevailing wisdom among the big shots was that they were addressing influencers, opinion makers, and the right-hand men of the world and it was savvy to give them something for nothing. The something would be remembered and rewarded later. The nothing was simply nothing.

At least that's how the conventional wisdom went, but Milo Magnet would have none of it. When he learned from Alice, his personal secretary, that his speech was expected to be delivered for free, he was furious.

"I don't do charity! I don't talk about my ideas gratis!"

The very notion offended him and he rejected it as easily as a change machine rejects a phony twenty-dollar bill (he'd invented the latest anticounterfeit design of all U.S. currency).

A man who lives in his head, who cares not a whit about food, or clothes, or comfort; a man who doesn't know the difference between Spam and sacrapantina (or care) believes the real world is the universe of the *mind* and ideas the coin of the realm. Such a man would not simply give away his precious thoughts any more than he would toss change into a beggar's cup.

Milo doubled the price of his speech. Or rather Alice called that year's head of the Hot Type conference, Mr. Maynard Reed, and diplomatically suggested that because of Milo's schedule — his invitation to the World Economic Forum in Switzerland, the sultan's request for him to speak at Brunei Polytechnic, the tutoring of the first daughter in trigonometry — he could not possibly attend the Hot Type conference as planned. Maynard Reed took a deep breath before crumbling.

"We've got to have Mr. Magnet speak," he said. "It's been printed on all the advance programs, it's been confirmed by the schedulers, and —" he went on, unable to stop himself, "it's all anyone can talk about."

Alice suggested that perhaps things could be straightened out if he would only sweeten the pot. Though Alice, being Alice, let Maynard Reed arrive at that understanding all

87

by himself.

The day of Milo's speech, cloudless pastel blue skies stretched from one end of the city to the other. The Palace of Fine Arts looked both sturdy and elegant. When, at noon, the sun was directly overhead, a Renaissance glow attached itself to the Palace's sandstone columns as tourists from every nation mingled in the shade and rubbed their tired feet.

Five hundred folding chairs were arranged around the open-air Palace and the area cordoned off to preserve exclusivity. A light breeze ruffled the crape myrtle blossoms surrounding the pond. In the background the uppermost joints of the Golden Gate Bridge pinched the sky.

Taxicabs slowly filled the parking lots as journalists clad in either blue jeans or polyester trousers got out to point at the bridge, or search the horizon for the famous prison, or simply find a patch of sunlight to stand in and try to forget that someplace, somewhere, a deadline loomed.

Milo's entrance was neither showy nor calculated. He bolted out of the passenger seat of the car Alice was driving (he didn't have a driver's license) and walked toward his audience. His multicolored sweater gave him the air of a veteran housepainter on lunch break.

Maynard Reed glowed with the satisfied flush of a boxing manager bringing his slugger to the ring, stepped onto the makeshift stage, and turned on the microphone.

"Ladies and gentlemen, it's easy to introduce our keynote speaker. He's the most creative, ingenious, and educated man in the world. Hailed as the last great polymath, he's the inventor of wildly popular software, the man behind Diffused Number Theory, and the holder of one thousand seven hundred and forty-nine original patents. An internationally sought-after lecturer, he puts the 'vision' in visionary. Without him our world would look very different. Please give a hearty Hot Type welcome to Mis-ter Mi-lo Mag-net!"

The clapping was long and sustained. Milo walked briskly from the back, head down. As he stepped to the podium a small polished black cube accidentally fell from his pocket and landed on the ground, where it captured everyone's attention by righting itself and rolling beneath the stage under its own power.

Milo's customary opening was to begin by thanking his host for the opportunity to speak, then pausing to look upon the audience for a few moments, scanning their faces for some unknown signal that triggered him to start talking about whatever came to his mind. Today that signal came in the form of a twenty-foot banner snapping in the breeze above his head: HOT TYPE PRESENTS: WHAT COMES NEXT IN THE DIGITAL FUTURE?

"The only way to talk about history is to do it backward," said Milo, taking in the banner. "From Normandy to Moscow, from Heidelberg to Birmingham, we can only address history in reverse. There's not a person alive today who could have seen, at the time of the Gutenberg press, the impact that delightful invention would have on the world. Six hundred years of change in religion, culture, politics, and business . . . We simply had to wait for these things to emerge in the great progression of human life. It's only by looking backward that we see the connections and understand their deeper significance." He paused to sip from a glass of water. "The same is true of the future. As any good Braudelian knows, we must look backward before we can glimpse what comes next."

Each face in the crowd went blank. After a moment, as if uncomfortable with idle hands, they reached instinctively for the notepads they carried in their pockets. Some even tried tapping out notes on their BlackBerries. Milo looked up at the banner again.

"Let's begin our backward thought process with the title of this lecture. 'What Comes Next in the Digital Future?' First the last word," said Milo, pausing for effect. "Future. At the moment of the Big Bang, three parts of time were created — past, present, and future. Since then, we have looked backward over our history in order to create the picture we wanted of our origins. Our world, our history, our lives are our own creations, limited and unlimited by our imaginations. 'He who controls the past,' said Orwell, 'controls the future.' Our future will be shaped by the imagination that cries out with the loudest, most patient, most fearless voice. Thus it is in the past that we create the present that creates the future."

A few more notepads were opened in the audience.

"The next word, digital. The idea of digital is merely that of translating the world into two symbols, zero and one. Every culture in the history of the world has always been bilingual. That is, they have been able to understand more than one language form and the cultural implications of those languages . . ."

There was a slight stir in the crowd as the remaining journalists in the audience who weren't taking notes leaned forward in their seats and borrowed pens from their neighbors.

"With the new digital language, we are securing, for all time, a permanent change in the way humans communicate. The entire world will be translated into this new language form — each book, art image, and physical act. We ourselves will become digital formulas. We are at the end of the bilingual era; the age of one digital language is upon us. Ideas previously thought best suited to the realms of comic books and darkened cinemas will be unleashed on an unsuspecting world. The science fiction stories of yesteryear are the business plans of tomorrow!"

Milo continued, even though nobody in the audience was looking at him anymore. They were too busy writing down everything he said in hastily scrawled shorthand. They hadn't a clue what Milo was talking about, but they knew they couldn't afford to ignore it. Behind the podium the afternoon sun cast a dazzling display across the surface of the tessellated pond. The swans were alert, paddling for open water.

CHAPTER SEVEN

Just like other municipalities in the country, San Francisco held a mayoral election every four years. Unlike other municipalities, however, over the last sixteen years San Francisco had reelected the same person, Tucker Oswell, each time.

His reputation as a political force was not widely known beyond the confines of the West Coast, but inside the state his tenacity, charm, and willingness to win at all costs were envied by even his fiercest enemies. Oswell, whose early critics labeled him with the nickname "Tucker the Fucker" during a hotly contested race for fourth-grade class president, was remarkable for his natural ability to make the most politically astute decision possible regardless of its moral implications. Like a warped divining rod, he always found the dirty water.

His mayoral career had started well. He'd been a force for progressive politics, reforming the police department, cutting dead-wood on the school board, and announcing ambitious plans to "restore civility." But as each of his successive four terms dragged on, he seemed more and more entranced with the perks of the job rather than the job itself.

Perhaps, it was whispered, he should have simply gone back to practicing law at Oswell & Oswell, the firm he'd started out of law school (when asked why he had doubled his own name on the firm's letterhead, he retorted, "Because I'm twice as smart"). Each time he considered returning to private practice, some exciting project or initiative or lobbyist came along to wrestle away his attention and fire his ambition.

But in the months leading up to his fifth mayoral race, Tucker Oswell was remarkably absent from the campaign trail. It was as though his staff thought papering the city with posters reading "Oswell That Ends Well" would be enough to carry the day. And yet people still packed into his infrequent fund-raising dinners, where his speeches were prefaced by a nine-piece horn band breaking into "You Are the Sunshine of My Life" as he bounded to the stage waving to the audience and flashing his trademark grin.

His ability to stay in office, flouting the established term limits (the mayor's office called this a "term irregularity"), was tolerated for the simple reason that the mayor had handpicked the district attorney's office, the board of supervisors, the school board, the traffic board, the park board, and the waterfront board. Not to mention the entire Election Department office down to its security guard, Duane Oswell, the mayor's not-very-bright stepbrother. To dissuade pesky questions from the press, he kept the city charter in his office, under lock and key in a redwood chest underneath a five-hundred-gallon saltwater aquarium filled with miniature barracuda.

For a bureaucratic organism Mayor Oswell's administration could move with lightning efficiency, as demonstrated by the construction of a new cycling velodrome on Alcatraz that a) both specifically and immediately benefited Cannoli Bros. Construction, the mayor's biggest campaign contributor, and b) was part of a plan to entice the International Olympic Committee to consider San Francisco as a host city. Alternatively, when requested to provide an independent investigation into its own term limit scandal, the Oswell administration moved with what the mayor's longtime press secretary Pinky Beale liked to call "exceptional prudence" and "thoughtful scrupulousness."

Even so, Tucker Oswell's long reign appeared to be drawing to a close. Sitting in a hot tub in Aspen, Colorado, surrounded by a coterie of former stewardesses, whom he playfully referred to as his "jet hags," even he could feel his accrued power waning. While previous reelections had come with the sort of easy momentum afforded to all things that appear inevitable, the last two years had seen him withdraw from the daily task of running the city in order to pursue "official business" in Las Vegas, New York, and Dubai. If he was going to be reelected, something special would be needed this time around.

The smart money around town was not as befuddled by Tucker Oswell's winning track record as they were by his opponents. Oswell had the unbelievable luck of consistently running against opponents who were, as one memorable *Trumpet* editorial put it, "more full of shit than a Christmas goose."

Oswell's current opponent, nicknamed Loco Larry, had run on a platform promising city-sponsored alien abduction insurance and had thrilled scornful New York City papers with his press conference antics.

It was a measure of Mayor Oswell's waning power that in the most recent polls he led Loco Larry's campaign by a mere 4-1/2 points.

Slater Brown was only vaguely conscious that Election Day was upon the city, having seen a few "Oswell That Ends Well" posters plastered to bus stops, but not really registering them. His entire concentration was bent on satisfying his first assignment for the *Trumpet.* The truth was he didn't know exactly what to look for. He knew what constituted a newspaper story. A wharf strike, for example, was on the cover of today's *Trumpet.* But wharf strikes, politics, crime, business, and sports didn't particularly interest him. What he wanted to write was a story that would capture the life of a city in clean detail and reveal something so true about its residents that they couldn't bear but to read it. He stopped writing in his notebook and rolled his eyes upward in thought.

A story that would grab the reader by the throat and say "This is how it is, don't look away." A story so strong it wouldn't fade, or pop upon closer inspection. A closer of a story.

He looked up to see the number 5 bus bearing down on him. He glanced at the driver's face as he climbed the stairs. It was bone-tired, with navy blue bags under each eye and two warts perched like archipelagos on the end of a wide nose. Slater slid his quarters into the change taker and waited for the *chink, chink* to register deeply within the purring machine. Details, thought Slater as the bus accelerated, pushing him down the long aisle toward the seats in the back, what my story needs are details.

Soon enough he got off next to Golden Gate Park and began to wander around the city. He sucked up everything he came into contact with like an anxious anteater. In the first two hours he covered only six and a half blocks.

First he compiled a list of interesting haircuts: *dyed wedge with pearl highlights; reverse-bleach Mohawk; widow's peak with finger mullet curls.*

To round out this stockpile of minutiae he made a note of the arresting smells he encountered:

Honeysuckle and Brunswick stew at the bottom of Green and Church

Oysters and acrylic at the top of Bush Street

Sourdough and tequila on Noe and Market

Standing at the top of the Lyon Street Steps, he noted of the world's most famous bridge:

Its color not gold, but burnt orange. Her beauty comes from the feeling that opposing forces are at work here. Muscle and balance. Both solid and poised. Like a shot-putter cast in the Nutcracker.

On the corner of Mason and Turk he was stopped in his tracks by the clacking of an old-fashioned typewriter drifting up from beneath the street. It sounded as if somewhere beneath the city a writer was composing the stories that would become tomorrow's headlines. Lifting the lid of a metal plate in the middle of the street revealed a thick, greasy cable moving noisily across a series of interlinked cogs. He reached down to touch it as a bell sounded and a voice shouted above him, "Get outta da way!" Slater rolled to his feet and watched as the cable car, packed with tourists, coasted to the top of the hill. From the back, a buxom woman holding a shopping bag and wearing a T-shirt that said "Nurses Call the Shots" waved enthusiastically at him before disappearing.

That particular day happened to be the kind of day when the sun was unimpeded by fog and thus cast itself around San Francisco with impunity. In any given year there were usually five such days when it was so hot and windless and fog-free that the entire city emptied itself from offices and class-rooms and coffee shops and nail salons and spilled out into parks and beaches and outdoor cafés so the sunlight could marinate their bodies. On days like this, the elderly would open up their garage doors and sit in battered lawn chairs on the sidewalk just to soak in the golden glow.

That afternoon Slater Brown expanded his walking tour, marveling at the coiling streets that ran straight up and down San Francisco's seven hills at angles only a Swiss ski-lift operator could love. He interviewed Croatian shopkeepers and Peruvian dog walkers and schoolchildren playing hooky in Golden Gate Park. He watched the clouds move across the sky like *vessels from a distant mooring* and he tried without success to capture in writing the smell of eucalyptus in the air. Along the way he was spun around many times in the wake of pretty girls on Rollerblades.

On and on he walked and listened as the city's careening streets took him in unexpected directions.

As he wandered through the Mission District, he came upon a line of people standing in front of San Jose's Taqueria Espectacular. What they were waiting for was unclear; there were thousands of Mexican restaurants in the city. Could the salsa really be that good here? Maybe there was a story in it. He could only imagine Motherlove's face if the greenhorn reporter actually discovered a culinary delicacy that had been under their noses all this time. Slater walked closer until he noticed a small piece of paper taped to the front door:

Señor de las Respuestas
Para preguntas que pocos entienden
Abierto todos los días por 50 minutos
durante el almuerzo

Below, written in the scrawled hand of a child:

Answer Man
Specializing in questions few
understand
Open daily for 50 minutes during lunch

He joined the back of the line and listened carefully to the conversations around him. Two Latina housemaids were speaking rapidly in Spanglish, anxious for romantic advice. Behind them a tugboat captain muttered about losing his nerve navigating the tidal sandbars beneath the Golden Gate Bridge. Next was a businessman clutching his briefcase to his body. It wasn't difficult to imagine what he wanted to talk about.

Slater took this all in, making a few notes on the stray details around him as the line inched toward the dark doorway where a waterlogged telephone book propped open the iron security gate. Inside the taqueria a group of lunch customers sat eating gorditas and guacamole with the satisfied look of people who have had their innermost questions answered.

By the time it was Slater's turn to be received it was almost 1:00 P.M. The two Latina women came out of the back room and brushed past him, laughing. He stepped up to the entryway and waited for some kind of signal.

Answer Man's full-time job wasn't answering questions, but rather this was what he chose to do on his lunch break, at Fourteenth and Valencia, in the back of a Mexican taqueria owned by Chinese people (which accounted for the throw rugs and wood-block paintings on rice paper that covered the walls). By day, A.M., as he was sometimes known, was an accountant for a Spanish insurance company, but during lunch he . . . what was he? He was a person capable of being asked a question, any question — love, life, marriage, hemorrhoid-reduction time line — and he would give back a simple "yes" or "no" answer.

There seemed to be a difference in quality between his answers and those of Madam Sooth, the porcine-faced woman with the fake Scottish accent and velvet housecoat who, for forty-five dollars, would peer into her crystal ball over in North Beach. At the very least, A.M.'s answers seemed to be more consistently accurate and did not start with the preface "Darlings, let me tell you something very important," so that little by little people had started talking about the man who could answer your questions. Any questions.

Nobody was entirely sure exactly when A.M. had started providing his service, but it had not taken long for news to spread and it was now common for a line to form outside of San Jose's Taqueria Espectacular well before his fifty-minute lunch services began. Today, with the beautiful weather, people's minds were on other things, and so the line was shorter than usual. Payment was made discreetly in a small wooden tithing box that had been found outside a demolished church on Ninth Street.

A.M. always stood in the back room, usually by the door, so that he appeared to be on his way toward leaving. This posture had the intended effect of making people talk faster and not linger too much on the irrelevant details of their questions. He had come upon this tactic after realizing that women, in particular, seemed to have difficulty formulating a yes-or-no question in fewer than two hundred words.

At first what amazed A.M. was that what people wanted to know about their lives was not *what* was going to happen to them, but *when.* Everyone seemed to understand that a good measure of everything was in the cards: a little love, a little pain, a little forgery. But when? *¿Pero cuándo?* He was asked this question so often he considered putting it on his business cards. Answer Man: ¿Pero Cuándo?

When Slater was finally called back, A.M.'s session was nearly up. Coming face-to-face with the man, Slater was a little disappointed. He was a diminutive fellow, with carefully combed hair, modest glasses, and a sparse, trimmed mustache. On his left hand was a large turquoise ring.

"Hola, amigo," said A.M., his eyes cast downward.

Slater noticed that a card table behind A.M. was covered with items that would not be out of place at a picked-over yard sale: a pickle jar full of broken sand dollars, a curling iron, three black shoes, a book called *Famous Lawn Bowlers 1943–1945,* an ornamental hookah pipe, and a scratched pocket radio with headphones wrapped around itself.

"*Hola, amigo,*" said A.M. again.

"Oh, hello, thanks for seeing me. How does this work, exactly? You want me to ask you —"

A.M. held up his hand. "*¿Cuál es la pregunta?*"

"Well, I'm working on a story, and it would be great to ask you about that, but I have some other questions too, about myself and —"

A.M. held up his hand again.

"*En español, gracias.*"

Slater's mind went blank as his face betrayed his monolingualism. A.M. rapped twice on the desk in front of him. A beautiful young Latina, her black hair held up in a red bandanna, appeared from a door leading to the kitchen. A.M. spoke rapidly to her in Spanish. She looked at Slater. "*Señor* takes his questions in *español* only. No *español?*" Slater shook his head. The girl conversed with A.M. "He says he is very tired and that if you have a question please make it short."

"OK, OK, OK, um, let's see . . ."

105

"Remember," said the young woman, holding a chopping knife in one hand, "yes-or-no questions are preferred."

"OK," said Slater, screwing up his courage, "ask him if I'm a writer."

The woman turned to A.M., who replied instantly, clearly irritated.

"Please, *señor,* he says he is very tired and would prefer answering questions you don't already know the answer to."

"OK, OK. Ask him if people will read my writing in the future?"

A.M. smiled, not unkindly, at Slater and waved his hand before speaking to the woman. "He says what makes you think people will read in the future?" Slater Brown was incredulous. He couldn't tell if they were joking.

"OK, *terminar,* last one," said the woman, carefully wiping the blade of the knife on her apron.

"Ask him what my story for the *Trumpet* should be."

The woman looked frustrated. "Yes-or-no question, *pór favor.*"

"Should my story for the *Trumpet* be about San Francisco?" asked Slater.

"Sí," said A.M., his eyes suddenly shining brightly as he focused intently on the young reporter for the first time. Slater said *"Gra-*

cias" before looking away. The session was over.

A.M. turned and began putting the miscellaneous things on the card table in a cardboard box at his feet. "Are these things he sells on the side to supplement his consulting business?" he asked the young woman.

"Some of his clientele cannot afford to pay. They bring in whatever they can," she said before nodding good-bye and slipping between the kitchen's swinging doors. A.M. stared at Slater again in a way that made him thoroughly uncomfortable.

"Es tarde," said A.M., tapping his watch and moving toward the door, the cardboard box tucked underneath his arm. Slater nodded and moved out of his way. As A.M. passed, he reached inside the box and pulled out the battered pocket radio. He pressed it into Slater's hands and stared at him. Slater noticed that one of his pupils was white.

"Para su narrativa," he said quietly before leaving. *"Para su narrativa."*

CHAPTER EIGHT

In the early evening, as the sun was beginning its slow pink good-bye over Ocean Beach, Slater Brown climbed back onto the bus heading home. His pockets bulged with his notebooks, each filled with details — glorious, sublime details he'd collected during his walk across the city. Taking his seat in the back of the bus, his finely tuned ears became enchanted with how much hidden music came from the hulking mass of metal and gears. At first it was nothing but discordant rumblings and squeaks, but after a few minutes of the bus's lurching movement he started to piece together a melody from the anti-cacophony.

It started with the note A, which was the sound produced when someone pulled on the bus's plastic cables to signal an upcoming stop to the driver. Slater noticed different people caused different notes to chime. Elderly Asian ladies, hands clutching beaded bags in their laps, would reach up and grab the cord firmly for a long chime: *dinnnnk*. While young men would casually lean over and flick the cord as if swatting a fly: *dink*. Mothers with children would tentatively, but often impatiently, reach over: *dink . . . dink*.

When the bus rolled to a stop, two pieces of metal in the undercarriage that were supposed to shake hands only grazed fingers and a *whomp, whomp, whomp* occurred. Delighted by his discovery of this hidden symphony, he wrote down the sound of the bus's compressed music. This would make an excellent beginning for my story, he thought.

#38 Bus, Symphony in A Minor
Hisssssssssssss
Cachunk,
Muuve, Muuve, Chunk
Grange, *dink!*
Hissssssssssss
Cachunk,
Whomp, Whomp, Chunk.
Grange . . . *dinnnnk*

After getting off the bus he passed Cool-brith Park. It was a hidden gem of green grass with an Italianate fountain surrounded by hedgerows. Only locals knew of it, as its single unmarked entrance was easy to miss. As he passed the long wall of hedges, he heard someone singing softly on the other side. He listened to the lilting voice, tracing the words in his head:

"*Árboles lloran por lluvias,*" the voice rang out in a clear unselfish melody, "*y montañas por aires. Ansí lloran los mis ojos. Por ti, querida 'mante.*"

He parted the hedgerow to get a better look at the singer, and when he still couldn't see anything he edged a few feet into the bushes. Instantly he found himself entangled by a nest of inch-long thorns, which forced him to stand frozen in place, as if at gunpoint.

"*Árboles lloran por lluvias . . .*"

The singing was closer now, so close he felt its delicate vibrations buzzing around him like benevolent bees, but he still couldn't see who was on the other side of the hedge. He decided to retreat to the sidewalk, but the moment he moved, a hidden thorn pierced his stomach as hard and fast as a hornet.

"Balls!" shouted Slater, unable to contain himself. He reached to remove the offending spike, but this only caused him to lose his balance. Before he could stop himself he crashed through the underbrush into a quiet cove of Coolbrith Park.

The singing had stopped. Spread out on the ground, not far from where he'd exited the hedgerow, a little red-and-black blanket lay beneath a pair of black sandals. He rubbed the sore place on his stomach and rose to his feet.

Finally a voice called out, "You've got some leaves in your hair." Slater nonchalantly ran his fingers through his hair while turning in a slow circle.

"Up here," the voice said.

Above him, in the lower branches of a giant elm tree, stood a young woman leaning gently against the trunk.

"What do you want?" she asked, arms folded across her chest.

"I was, uh, looking for the — singing," said Slater, realizing how ridiculous this sounded.

The young woman waited.

"I hope I didn't startle you," he said, suddenly aware of what she was waiting for.

"Well, you did," she said. "It sounded like a wild boar running out of those bushes for all the noise you made."

He judged her to be about his age. Her eyes, quick and intense, glistened like black agates.

"What's your name?"

"Tim," he said quickly.

"No, it's not," she said, her nose wrinkling at the deception. "What's your name, your real name?"

He thought for a moment. "Slater," he said finally, meeting her gaze.

"Slater what? I like Slater. Slater what?"

"Slater Brown."

"Hmm," she said.

"What's your name?" he called back, knowing intuitively that a conversation like this must not be allowed to drag.

"Callio," she said.

"Callio what?" he asked.

"Callio's fine," she replied as she swung her arms around the tree trunk and dropped lightly to the ground.

As she approached he felt the edges of his stomach tighten. She was prettier than he'd realized. Her skin was pale, even alabaster, which contrasted with her black hair and eyes so finely that it seemed to create another dimension around her face, like a ring around the sun.

"Slater Brown," she said, lingering on his name, "you should be more quiet."

After the first rushing thrill, after he allowed himself to be taken in by the sight of her face, he felt euphoric. Actually, it was

112

only partly euphoria, the sense of being momentarily out of control; coupled with it, like a weight on the end of a druggist's scale, was a tiny kernel of pain.

"What were you singing?"

"Oh, just an old Spanish love song. Do you speak Spanish?"

"Do you?" he asked, acutely aware that each of them was now answering a question with a question.

"Well, someday you should learn it," she said, parrying his query with a thrust, "and then you can know what the song was about."

His cheeks were starting to ache from all the smiling he was doing. "I'd like that very much," he said. "It was nice to listen to."

They stood this way, suspended for that rare moment when impressions are made into memory and refined as if by a sculptor's thumb. He noticed her full lips; she noticed the blotches of ink on his much-bitten fingers; he noticed her short black haircut, which ended at the nape of her neck like a flame; she noticed his large eyes were those of a dreamer, which was altogether not a bad thing; he noted that she was not beautiful in the establishment sense of the word — there was no angular cheekbone, no marzipan nose made for the cover of a

113

cosmopolitan fashion magazine. Yet there was something remarkable there. A kind of boundless self-possession she radiated so purely he could feel it surrounding them both.

He struggled as the moment emptied itself; she let it slip away without worry.

"I must go," she said, stepping onto the red-and-black blanket as delicately as if it were a diver's platform and piling her things into a small canvas backpack. Slater Brown scanned the backpack for a college logo, or a plastic gym membership card; anything that would give him an extra piece of identifying information. But there was nothing. He was doubly annoyed to realize he was unfamiliar with the title of the only book she was reading: *Nine Moves* by Ivor T. Stravinofsky. She is a dancer, he decided. She must be a dancer. She even looks like a dancer. But why nine moves?

"This was interesting," said Slater, trying to revive the conversation.

"Good," said Callio as she stood.

"Perhaps we shall meet again?"

"Perhaps," she said, handing him an empty green soda bottle.

"As of tomorrow I'll be a lot easier to find."

"Oh?"

"I'm the new lead writer for *The Morning Trumpet.*"

If the beautiful young woman with the black agate eyes had never heard of *The Morning Trumpet* she had the good manners not to show it.

"Excellent" was all that was offered as she shouldered her backpack and began to move toward the park's gate, leaving him clutching the green bottle in both hands as if Venus herself had handed it to him.

"What do I do with this?" called Slater.

"Recycle it!" she said over her shoulder before disappearing from view around the hedgerow.

He stood holding the green bottle for a full minute before the truth of the matter showed itself. He didn't want to leave the scene. He looked at the spot on the grass where her blanket had been. Had she really been there? Or was he dreaming? She was so beautiful that it hurt him a little just to think about her. As he moved across the park a patch of fog passed in front of the sun and the air turned cold.

How was it possible to hurt just by thinking of her? he wondered. Was the hurt because in thinking of her he confronted something much finer, much more perfect, much more elusive than himself? Or was the hurt coming from the fact that he did not have her, could not have her, would in fact probably never see her again? Was the hurt only his future loneliness reflected back at him? Or was it simply the sting from the thorns?

Young men faced with incomparable beauty cannot wash it from their minds as easily as older men, who have seen these things before and have turned away so that they can live without regret. For young men the image sticks much longer, or rather the feeling of the image sticks much longer. Left with nothing to accommodate the feeling, no other information, or facts about age, or whereabouts, or inclinations, or even a last name, Slater did what young men have done for thousands of years — he imagined her life and her world, and then he went another well-worn step, and imagined himself in it.

But as Slater Brown settled into a canvas chair at the Avalon Café in North Beach he decided to put her from his mind and finally focus on his story for the *Trumpet*. First, he spread out in front of him all the notes he'd taken during his tour through the city. The last was a slip from a fortune cookie he'd been given at lunch:

"The fortune 'May you live in interesting times' is a curse."

He concentrated on these haphazard scraps of paper like a scientist who imagines he can conjure up a chemical explosion by staring at the periodic table. His first attempt at writing the story for the *Trumpet* owed something to James Joyce:

In the fogsphere, a row of shiny faces appeared, rattling on about the sandywind of San Francisco . . .

The next had a touch of Hemingway:

The city was quiet. The streets quiet too. I walked until the nails fell out of my shoes and the soles began to slap the ground like applause. It was good.

Finally, as the sun lowered itself over the western edge of the city, and the people began to pull on sweaters and woolen hats and reluctantly slide inside, he tried out his Old Testament voice:

In the quiet hour just before the sun set . . .

Each imitation sputtered out after a sentence or two, each crumpled piece of paper its own private monument to failure. For once, it wasn't the writing that was the problem. Or the translation. Or the order of the words. It was the fact that he couldn't keep his attention from his stomach. His earlier encounter had left the edges still taut, like the skin of a drum waiting for the inevitable thump.

CHAPTER NINE

The next day at precisely 2:12 P.M. Motherlove read Slater Brown's inaugural story out loud at the staff meeting, milking the situation for everything it was worth.

"Wait a minute!" howled Motherlove, hushing the room as he came upon another riotous section. " 'In a city of endless noise, it's something of a shock to find a symphony of sounds coming from the number thirty-eight bus'!"

Here Motherlove could not contain himself as his mouth feasted on Slater's descriptions.

" 'Muuuuuuuuuuuuuuuuuuuuuuuuve . . . dink,' " he shrieked like a wounded guinea hen.

" 'Schlink, schlink, schlink'!" he cried, hotfooting across the room, moving his hand back and forth as if conducting a swing band. The laughing was loud and sustained and by 2:19 P.M. Slater had been fired. Niebald clapped him on the shoulder.

"Good luck, kiddo," he said, turning the ex-reporter, weak-kneed and crimson, toward the door. Niebald's stony face betrayed no signs of suppressed sympathy. There were no parting words of solace. No offer for a consolation lunch "sometime next week."

As Slater rode the bus home, dreading the conversation with Mrs. Cagliostra, the city's landscape flipped past like frames from a strip of film. A woman wearing a wedding veil, the languor of pigeon flight, two skateboarders flicking themselves high into the air. It swirled around like a gentle storm only he could apprehend. The story of life! Of his life! Faces, people, a ripe city ready for harvest. But nobody wanted it. They couldn't bear to read it the way he'd showed it to them! Too raw, too painful! Too something!

It's still literature, he wrote, pausing to turn up the collar of his jacket before sinking lower into his seat. *Even if it's unread.*

From his jacket he pulled out the pocket radio A.M. had given him and put on the headphones, happy for a chance to finally stop listening to the world around him. WGGB was in the middle of a marathon Hank Williams tribute.

"Your cheating heart," wailed the plaintive voice, "will make you weep."

Slater touched his head to the side of the bus and began to doze.

"You'll cry and cry and try to sleep." The music played on for a few more moments. A wounded angel singing a lullaby to a weary imp. As the number 9 bumped along, he drifted asleep, his head resting gently against the side of the bus. Just then a pair of strange voices broke open within the song:

"And then I told Cath, look, you're being difficult just for the sake of being difficult, and I think that's really unfair."

Another voice bounced through.

"And then what happened?"

"She said she thought *I* was the one being difficult and that all of this started at the party with Rory and that penis flytrap from Brazil . . ."

Slater blinked one eye open. He took off the headphones. Nobody else was on the bus except two mothers in the front row tending to their babies, and they certainly weren't talking about penis flytraps from Brazil. He put the headphones back on. The voices had slipped away. Slater touched his head back to the window frame. Just your imagination, he assured himself.

"Heh-hey good lookin', whatcha got cookin'?" sang Hank Williams.

"First you get fired," thought Slater, "and now you're hearing voices." The decline had been swifter than he'd anticipated. He closed his eyes and thought about crying. A few seconds later a new voice came through the headphones.

"Bob?"

"Yeah."

"Bill here."

"Yeah."

"How's it going?"

"Can't complain, you?"

"Well, actually we're sweatin' it out over here, looking for a little clarity on the Mc-Clusky account."

"Right."

"Understand?"

"Crystal."

"What's the latest?"

Slater jerked awake again. "What's the latest?" he whispered as he fumbled with the radio's controls. "Where's Hank is what I want to know."

He studied the pocket radio. The voices stopped. He clicked the controls off and on, cleaned out his ears with a pinkie, and took a deep breath. The number 9 bus was turning onto Van Ness in front of the opera hall.

Slowly Slater touched his head to the window again. His eyes were open and alert. This voice was new. And it was agitated.

"And all I'm saying is, it's that time again, and we've got to take care of a little business. So don't wait any longer, just bury them. That's the only way that things really ever go away. Jimmy Hoffa, right? So make a little trip to the park and find our buffalo friends and do what needs to be done."

As the bus lurched onto Market Street the conversation started to fade out. Slater Brown pressed his headphones so hard against the side of the bus he looked like a man trying to eavesdrop on a conversation in the next room.

"Damn r.ght. Y.u play your cards r.ght you g.t a.yth.n. y.u w . . ." The voice faded away completely. Slater lifted his head and looked out the bus window.

For over forty years in San Francisco wires had been stretched overhead, down every avenue and thoroughfare, so that the fleet of buses and electric trolleys could touch the taut lines for a volt of electricity. This cat's cradle of wires had been overhead so long most of the citizenry had mentally erased it from their vision.

By making the mass transit run on electricity, the city had eliminated the need for combustible bus engines, greatly improving the city's air quality. But unbeknownst to anyone, the wires had the unintended effect of acting as a giant, sprawling antenna that covered the entire city and served up individual phone conversations to anyone with the right receiver: in this case, a pocket radio with faulty headphones pressed just right against the metal frame of the number 9 bus.

Slater Brown touched his head to the frame of the bus window again, hoping the headphones would pick up more of the conversation. But the agitated voice was gone, lost to the ether. What had he meant, "take care of business"?

For the first time all day Slater Brown smiled. His disastrous meeting at the *Trumpet* fell away like a dirty shirt.

"Who can't find a story?" he said aloud as he pulled the cord — *dink* and then again — *dink dink* (in honor of Motherlove) as he stood to get off at the next stop.

CHAPTER TEN

It had taken six hours and four phone calls to convince Niebald to come meet him in Golden Gate Park. When he'd finally pulled up in his convertible MG with the broken top, he still wasn't happy about it. But by the time Slater explained the situation and walked him over to the freshly dug hole next to the buffalo paddock, Niebald's face cracked into a rarely seen smile.

"Motherlove, we've hit the motherfucking mother lode!" he shouted as they marched triumphantly through the doors of the newsroom, each carrying a cardboard box full of an equal mixture of paper ballots and buffalo dung. All Tuesday night, as Niebald and Slater holed up in Motherlove's office writing against the printer's deadline, the *Trumpet* remained in a state of ecstasy not felt since Lindbergh buzzed the building.

Maynard Reed was particularly rapturous. Not so much with the message as with the messenger. The kid had delivered news. Real, hard, honest-to-goodness news and not some airy-fairy literary shit that sounded good but didn't mean anything. A scoop this good hadn't come along in living memory. It couldn't have happened at a better time. "Put the headline in sixty-two-point font, and make it BOLD!" he shouted for all to hear. "BOLD! BOLD! BOLD!"

THE MORNING TRUMPET
⋆⋆WORLD EXCLUSIVE⋆⋆
STUNNING MAYORAL ELECTION SCANDAL!
Election Count "Unusually Irregular,"
Says District Attorney.
Votes "Missing," Announces Election Commissioner.
Something's Fishy, Says Man On The Street.

BY SLATER BROWN AND
NIEBALD PETERS
San Francisco — Ms. Kerri Lyn of 234 Gough Street; Mr. Lawrence Strong of 197 Bush Street; Mr. and Mrs. Holden Keller of 2989 Fulton Street; Mrs. Merlin T. Peabody of 1200 Fell Street, you and 917 other citizens deserve an apol-

ogy from City Hall. It seems your un-counted votes were misrouted to a ma-nure pile in the buffalo paddock at Golden Gate Park after the general elec-tion . . .

The only person who was noncommittal on the whole phoenix-rising-from-the-ashes experience was Motherlove. He had over-seen the proceedings from the center of the newsroom like a moody bull. It was true that "The Kid," as Slater was now officially being called around the *Trumpet,* had needed help writing his story. Help that Niebald was happy to provide. But it wasn't as if he'd written the story *for* Slater. The instincts were intact, just under layers of inexperience. It was something else that didn't feel right to Motherlove. Not that the story wasn't true; he'd gone out to the buf-falo paddock and seen the hole himself, even pulled from the dung with his own fingers a few stray ballots Slater and Nie-bald had overlooked. And it wasn't that he couldn't imagine the mayor's office involved with such shenanigans; he'd covered Tucker Oswell for his entire political career and could fill a thick book with stories of that cretin's capers. It was about Slater that his doubts persisted. His friendly smile and quick eyes and that anxiousness to impress disguised underneath all that goddamn fancy clothing . . . the kid didn't smell like any kind of newspaperman he'd ever come across before was all.

Slater Brown remained mum about the "particulars of his discovery." That was the phrase Maynard used when he encountered Slater in the long hallway outside of the newsroom.

"Helluva piece of reporting you've done here."

"Thanks, Mr. Reed."

"What're your ways and means?"

"Excuse me?"

"The particulars of your discovery?" said Maynard.

"I'm sorry?"

"How'd you do it?"

Slater swallowed hard. In all the excitement he had not anticipated this line of questioning. Maynard watched him for a moment and then waved him off with both arms as violently as if he were an approaching aircraft.

"Whoa! Say no more! Reporter's privilege, right? Never disclose a source, right?"

"Right," said Slater.

"You pulled a Hobsgood, kid. And I mean that in the best possible way!"

"Thank you, sir, it all seemed meant to be."

"You know where this story's going to end up, don't you?" said Maynard, flicking the layout with his finger.

"Tomorrow's trash can," said Slater without thinking, for that was a joke he'd heard Niebald use around the office.

"No!" said Maynard, shocked. "This baby's going to take its rightful place out here," he said, spreading his hands to indicate the Hallway of Fame. Slater looked around, stunned.

"This story is putting us back on the map," said Maynard, clapping his arm around Slater's shoulder. "Actually, this story *is* the map. The map that's leading us out of the wilderness," said Maynard, looking at Slater lovingly, as if he'd just discovered a Thoroughbred colt nibbling grass on the median strip.

For one long, dark afternoon, as the fog rolled in off the Pacific and obscured the city by the Bay in a whiteout, it appeared as if *The Morning Trumpet* had done the impossible. The official word from the mayor's office was "no comment," but the off-the-record whispers ricocheting around town were of a pending investigation, of FBI interviews, of a handover of power. Of imminent collapse.

■ ■ ■ ■

BOOK TWO:
WHIRL IS KING

■ ■ ■ ■

CHAPTER ELEVEN

It had snowed only once in San Francisco, in 1887, which was not altogether a bad starting point for Milo Magnet. He'd been holed up in his studio for three weeks, exercising considerable thought about what to do next. What interested him — what always interested him — was figuring out the most elegant way possible to alter the course of human history. He'd done it before, first in the late 1960s with the invention of the PortoCalc, a kind of early computer that was used by scientists at NASA to calculate the trajectory of the Mercury moon landing. And he'd done it in the 1980s with his invention of the Neptune satellite. More recently he was being hailed as the godfather of the Internet. "I didn't invent the World Wide Web," he liked to tell reporters, "but my ideas begat the ideas that begat the Internet."

On the whole Milo found too much media

excitement about any one of his contributions to humanity tiring. He'd learned to avoid, at all costs, getting mired in the frisson of the crowd. There was something about convincing presidents, kings, and corporate executives to follow his lead that he found utterly intoxicating. But once he'd done the high-level conclaves — the European conferences, the social salons in New York, the Sand Hill road shows — he lost interest. By the time the top people shared the zeitgeist with their top people at some five-star "off-site," and those people had mentioned it to their lieutenants, who'd mentioned it casually at the Monday morning staff meeting, until finally it was the sort of thing you might hear about around the guacamole bowl at a bank picnic, Milo Magnet was long gone.

For this reason, and a million others, he enjoyed working in absolute and total privacy. He preferred to think of it as protecting his curiosity. But there was a practical nature to his seclusion as well. Everyone wanted a moment of his time. Having Milo Magnet's name associated with your project added the ultimate intellectual legitimacy to an endeavor in need of money, talent, or media attention. His admirers cornered him at scientific conferences, purchased his books in bulk, and dropped unsolicited folders brimming with strange equations into the mailbox at the end of his unmarked driveway. In an online auction, his private e-mail address had recently fetched $7,900.

The only downside to maintaining such privacy was that if he went into radio silence for too long the media would inevitably start making up ridiculous stories — "Milo Magnet developing levitating sneakers that will change the way cities are designed." What irritated him most about these stories was not that they were universally untrue, but that they were always *less* interesting than what he was actually working on.

There were no shortages of ideas for his next project. In fact, the bulk of his time was spent simply sorting the good prospects from the bad. On the large steel table in his workshop (a giant cog salvaged from the inner workings of a long-obsolete steamship) were reams of proposals, business plans, and scientific breakthroughs sent from around the globe by investors, former students, and past rivals.

Milo snapped the most recent fax in front of him to keep the scattered crumbs of his coffee cake from obscuring the words. It was a preliminary sketch by an old MIT pupil, Foy Wang, who claimed to have developed a working prototype for a device that could "rearticulate harmonious fragments from plus minus atmospheric conditions." Foy went on to explain:

"Nothing ever said is truly lost. Sound particles vibrate in spatial dimensions forever, even if we can't hear them. I have developed a device that retrieves sound fragments hibernating in the seventh dimension and restores them to their original condition. This is unprecedented. We can retrieve anything we want. Nixon's eighteen and a half minutes? We can get that! What Pontius Pilate said to Jesus? We can get that, too!!"

He'd signed the fax "Meet me in Boston," but Milo paused. Foy was brilliant, but no mention of funding meant there was no funding and, frankly, the thought of lassoing sound fragments from the seventh dimension left Milo nonplussed.

He crossed his arms and looked out at the western slope of San Francisco. A storm was rolling in over the Pacific. Farther out, halfway to the smudged outline of the Farallon Islands, crepuscular rays shot like golden lasers from the clouds. The only noise in the otherwise breathless laboratory came from the fans cooling the racks of computers running algorithm simulations.

Milo Magnet had the luxury to consider what to do next because he'd recently published, after a decade of secretive work, a 4,278-page book titled *Theory of Everything*. The book, known as TOE among the Magnetos (a cabal of large-brained science groupies who blogged MM's every move), explained how, in clear detail and deadly prose, the entire physical world could be reduced to simple digital patterns. Everything from the recipe for snowflakes to the formula to Coca-Cola to the monthly fluctuations of the Japanese stock exchange was reduced to chapter-length digital pattern formulas inside the pages of *Theory of Everything*. Even the license plates on Milo's car read 011001.

The subsequent lawsuits from Coca-Cola, and the shareholders of the Japanese stock exchange, and everyone else who was furious that Milo had revealed their secrets (both political parties resented Milo's prediction of who the next ten presidents would be) had pushed the global media hive into a buzz frenzy and fueled book sales to the point that it was considered a sign of intellectual depravity *not* to have *Theory of Everything*, squatting like a fourteen-pound bullfrog, on your coffee table.

"If we can understand it, we can turn it

into a pattern formula," he'd announced proudly at the White House the day he went to explain to the president what the book meant to the future of the U.S. economy. That afternoon in the Rose Garden, while fielding questions from the Washington press corps, Milo did not refer to his summa as "TOE," but rather *Everything."* As in *"Everything* is the key to everything."

But despite the adulation, and the critical notices, and the headlines ("Einstein's Heir?" asked *Time* magazine; "Heir of Einstein?" asked *Newsweek*), the publication of *Theory of Everything* had not satisfied him. A book was a fine thing to have done, but for him it was rather like *talking* about doing something rather than doing the thing itself. For Milo Magnet, at a very basic level, elucidation felt like an elaborate form of procrastination.

A mind capable of teaching itself fluid dynamics in a weekend, dismantling particle physics on a long plane trip to Qatar (where he was teaching Sheikh Faisal to decipher his family's genetic code), and boiling down all of Western mathematics into a single page of equations was looking for something . . . new. Something . . . actionable.

"We've stopped rivers in their tracks," he'd enthused as Harvard's commencement speaker the year before. "We've reshaped entire ecosystems. We've conquered biology, psychology, and time! Why not tinker with genetic code? Why not splice the longevity gene from a redwood tree into human DNA? This is the age of cut-and-paste! The reign of the remix!"

But despite his public optimism, something was niggling at Milo Magnet as he circumnavigated the vast possibilities afforded men of his capability.

He looked out from his study over the Pacific. Windsurfers sliced the sea, their taut sails jumping like excited fish as they carved loops on the whitecapped water.

The proposals on his desk were piled in three-foot stacks: white papers on nanotechnology, patent applications for wormhole kits, even an offer to lead a New Zealand team on the verge of wholesale human cloning. The cloning project held his interest for an hour or so — the science behind it genuinely intrigued him — but for a man who cared so little for his own personal appearance, it was difficult to get enthusiastic about the prospect of making a physical duplicate of himself.

More important, as far as Milo could see, most people were unhappy, secretly or otherwise. Some were biologically unhappy, some were chemically unhappy, and some, he'd decided, were unhappy because they were just plain weird.

"It's not like people actually *enjoy* being human," reasoned Milo aloud. He often spoke aloud to himself when in the privacy of his laboratory as he found it helped him work out concepts in an uninhibited fashion. "It's not like human history is littered with examples of hundreds of millions of *happy* people succumbing to the joys of mortality!"

He rose from his chair and imagined himself at Madison Square Garden, where a standing-room-only crowd materialized in front of him. He straightened his posture and addressed their searching faces — tilted upward like sunflowers — with his vibrant public speaking voice:

"In all of recorded history, there are what, a half-dozen people who have 'mastered' the art of being human? Jesus, Buddha, Muhammad . . . The rest of the one hundred billion souls born are walking encyclopedias of doubts, desires, and fears — mixed in with a liberal dose of regret. Hardly satisfied customers if you think about it. My fellow citizens, the primary problem one encounters when thinking seriously about human cloning is 'Why make more unhappy people?' " He managed a small bow for the thunderous applause erupting in front of him.

No, Milo Magnet was searching for something bigger. He looked out the window. Something no one else had thought of yet. He wanted an idea as broad as the sky and as elemental as the stars. Not a small personal canvas. Not this time.

"Ideally it would be something I could develop without my having to spend tremendous amounts of time around pee . . . people."

There, he'd said it.

Now the storm was moving fast across the Pacific, riding low as it caught the tail end of the afternoon wind. He walked toward the enormous cathedral windows, squinting into the sun's glare.

"Curtains down," he said to the voice-activated rattan fabric he'd written custom software for.

"Curtains *down*," he said again.

"Curtains *down!*" he shouted before becoming distracted by a spider lowering itself from the windowsill, a thin translucent tendril twinkling in the sun. Each tiny leg of the spider contracted as it inched downward.

"Spider silk!"

Could he replicate that in his laboratory?
He shouted aloud the possibilities:

"Bulletproof vests!"

"Prophylactics!"

"Bungee-jump cords the thickness of
dental floss!"

The daydream suddenly darkened. He
opened his eyes. The afternoon sun was hidden behind the approaching thundercloud.
He counted the trailing puffs, each bruised
cloud carrying a payload of leaden rain.

Just then, a mile away, a finger of lightning
licked the Pacific's glassy surface. Intense
and deeply mysterious, the weather imposed
its personality on an otherwise placid world.
Milo watched it all, his bottom lip curled
underneath his teeth in an uncalculated
pose of maximum absorption.

How long had that storm been traveling?
he wondered. And what elemental forces
were involved? Had they come together in
the last ten minutes? Or had that storm
been wandering for days, weeks, upon the
open ocean, like a ship broken free of anchor?

"How exactly does it work?" he asked
quietly behind the glass as the storm ship
unleashed a crackle of thunder on its march
toward the Golden Gate.

Now, *this* was interesting. This actually

142

was very interesting. This was in fact the most interesting thing he'd come across in a good long while. And it was all the more intriguing because it hadn't been faxed to him under the header of "Urgent Proposal."

He absently patted his pockets for a pen before the equations flashing through his mind evaporated.

CHAPTER TWELVE

Five months had passed in San Francisco since the revelation of the mayoral election scandal and they had been busy ones. Every week, all through the wet winter and into the spring, a new intrigue was reported in sixty-two-point font on the front page of *The Morning Trumpet.* In March alone, two financial scandals, one dangerous liaison, a spate of no-bid contracts, and the true identity of a serial flasher were all the city could talk about.

At a traditional newspaper these stories would have been discovered by a series of reporters working as a team to break the latest scoop. But at the *Trumpet* there was no such team, and it didn't matter anyway because each and every story revealed itself to the same person, Slater Brown, sitting in the last seat of a bus, head pressed resolutely to the side as he deciphered the different conversations passing through his pocket radio:

"How'd the date go?"

"Fine, I guess."

"You sound weird."

"Well, what kind of man orders milk with fish?" . . .

"RJ's got the ball game at forty and a half, but I say we fix it at thirty-nine and say boo-yays." . . .

"I'm convinced the only reason my wife had children was to have grandchildren. Once that happened, I was a freakin' bachelor all over again." . . .

"Frank?"

"Yep."

"We just opened the kimono."

"Did you show them everything?"

"Everything, the assets, the financing. They were hungry for it all. We just finished voting ten minutes ago on the whole package. We'll have the title to the Transamerica building by Monday. Keep this on the down-low until the deal's signed."

"Roger that."

It's like listening to a theremin hooked to a CB

radio controlled by a caffeine-buzzed auction-eer, wrote Slater Brown in his yellow note-book.

Everyone's response to the outbreak of civic transparency afforded by the *Trumpet* was different. The little old ladies at the Church of the Holy Ghost saw it as irrefutable evidence of the Second Coming, and immediately added Slater Brown's name to their Tuesday night prayer circle (in addition to inviting him to address their congregation on Sunday), while the residents of TK's were furious. All the excitement in the city had stalled their long-standing betting pool around the number of weekly suicides off the Golden Gate Bridge.

"Even the goddamned jumpers are waiting to read the paper," lamented Moon overtop his beer.

Privately, Mayor Tucker Oswell was beside himself. Never before had his political dominion been besieged with such persistent inquiry. The "bullshit voting scandal," as it was known around his office, had been survived only by lying as low as possible. No press conferences. No lunch meetings at the big table at Pearl's. No motorcade down Van Ness on his way to his weekly haircut. After a couple of weeks tourists began to

146

think City Hall was closed.

The mayor had finally ended this period of self-enforced seclusion by giving an emergency "State of the City" address over the radio.

"Ladies and gentlemen, I come to you a humble and *angry* man." That line, "humble and angry," had tested well in focus groups. "I have never had my trust so betrayed by people who work for me. This outrage will not stand on my watch!" he bellowed to a crowd of handpicked loyalists who barked approval like sea lions at Fisherman's Wharf. Over the radio, this response played like a crowd three times its size. Pinky Beale couldn't help being pleased with himself.

During the next five minutes of the speech the mayor publicly fired everyone who could plausibly be counted on to take the fall for, in his words, "conspiring to commit a fraudulent act that I was unaware of."

After the radio address, the front doors to City Hall were thrown open and the mayor raged as he stomped back to his office.

"It's conspiratorial!" he said, popping the first of several chocolate-covered doughnut holes into his mouth.

"Goddamn it! That little pencil dick at the *Trumpet* must be getting this stuff from someone!" He looked around before yelling

147

for William Heck, his chief of staff.

"Is it Spider Garcia? Feeding that little puke stories? Tell him I've reconsidered those real-estate developer credits. I'm confident we can work something out."

William Heck, a slight man with the mind of an accountant and the morals of a shoplifter, shook his head.

"It's not Spider, boss, I checked."

"What about Crazy Charlie Fritz? Or his brother? Or his mother! That whole family hates my fucking guts for routing the subway under their funeral parlor."

"Them neither," said William Heck as the mayor slowly wound himself up, reciting his favorite enemies one by one.

"What about the Costello twins?"

"Nope."

"How about that birdbrain owns half of downtown?"

"You mean Mankiewicz?"

"Yeah, him."

"I don't think so."

"Lois Levering?"

"She's in jail."

"I got it. Of course. It's gotta be Schnittke! What was I thinking? He's been on a slow boil ever since I boinked his sister and still didn't give him the hot dog concession at Candlestick."

William Heck wrinkled his nose.

"Schnittke died three months ago."

"You're kidding me." The mayor paused. "Did we send flowers?"

"Yes, boss," said William Heck, for he never forgot a birthday or funeral.

"Well, goddamnit, who could have done it? Hey, you," said the mayor to a passing intern as he licked his fingertips, "get me another bag of these doughnut holes."

It was going to be a long night and they were still at the very top end of the enemy list.

"And make sure they're hot!" he screamed.

Publicly, Tucker Oswell couldn't praise *The Morning Trumpet*'s young cub reporter enough for bringing such inequities to people's attention. At the mayor's urging Slater Brown was given ribbons of commendation for his journalistic services by the Kiwanis, Elks Club, Oddfellows, and Samoans for Peace.

Finally in April, after much debate in the mayor's office on the pros and cons of trying to co-opt the young reporter, the decision was made to honor Slater Brown with the newly created "San Francisco Fine Citizen Award" at a special luncheon in the private gilded dining chamber at City Hall.

Everyone was there, including the mayor, the editors of the *Sun of San Francisco* and the *San Francisco Sun,* not to mention Mrs. Cagliostra (accompanied by her bridge club), Maynard Reed, Motherlove, and Niebald.

The three newspapermen sat like uncomfortable schoolboys, their freshly shaven faces above new regimental striped ties bought just for the occasion. Though Memorial Day was a month off, Maynard Reed insisted on wearing his seersucker suit.

"Must be reading F. Scott Fitzgerald's biography again," whispered Niebald to Motherlove as they rode the elevator up.

Inside the dining room, Niebald approached the center table with wariness. Having battled City Hall for years trying to flesh out a story or confirm a lead, he'd never in his wildest dreams imagined he'd be passing aioli to the mayor now. Accustomed to sitting at the margins of events like this, scribbling notes while dodging waiters, Niebald remained skeptical until he saw his name written in calligraphy on a little cream doily at the center table. Below his name were the words "Honored Guest." He reached down tentatively to touch it. When no one was looking he gently slipped the placard into the breast pocket of his suit.

After a brief lunch of leek soup and broiled chicken, the mayor tapped his water glass and rose to speak. He wore a resplendent dark blue suit straight from Savile Row and a white cotton shirt so bright it was best looked at from an angle. He was easily the best-dressed man in the room except for Slater Brown, who had cast away Frank Cagliostra's hand-me-downs and was now wearing dark green suits with lemon yellow pinstripes and a cream waistcoat. A Danish seamstress in Chinatown made the suits to his specifications.

"One of the proudest moments I have as leader of this city is highlighting the achievements of our fine citizens," said the mayor.

His fleshy small-mouthed face, typically so animated that in his youth caricaturists had been known to waive their fees, was unusually placid today. Niebald, Motherlove, and Maynard found themselves nodding along in spite of themselves.

"Freedom of the press!" shouted the mayor as he changed tempo. "Freedom of the press, and the transparency that freedom brings must be greeted in our fair city as we greet the morning sun: with gratitude and relief! We must never forget that government, unchecked by a free press, is not good

151

for the people! And that the people, un-checked by government, are not good for the press!" Maynard Reed rose first, clapping manically as the syllogism swept his deductive reasoning off its feet. His colleagues tried to restrain him, but it was too late. Soon a standing ovation spread across the entire room.

At the end of lunch the mayor presented Slater Brown with the "Fine Citizen Award," which turned out to be a large sterling silver bell engraved with the words "Merry Christmas," left over from the holiday party for big political donors. As the mayor shook Slater Brown's hand he issued a smile so wide and false it looked physically painful to carry. When, for the briefest of moments, the two men stood out of earshot of the hovering pack, the mayor clamped his hand onto Slater's shoulder and drew the younger man toward him.

"Chickens don't always come home to roost," he whispered. "But turkeys always do." With that he turned, bright, fresh smile resplendent, and began to pose for the gathering photographers.

CHAPTER THIRTEEN

In a darkened room at the top of the oldest sugar-baron mansion in San Francisco, a young woman sat at a large writing desk. Her closed eyes and faint smile carried with them the preternatural calm of a sculpted bodhisattva.

As a pinprick of sun leaked in from the drawn velvet shades and made a pool of light at her feet, her hands rested lightly on the book open facedown in front of her: *Nine Moves* by Stravinofsky. On the polished surface of the redwood writing table was a carefully measured blank square.

She lifted her hand slowly and made precise movements above the invisible space. Her slender wrists were unadorned, but a small emerald sphere rolled gently at the end of a golden chain in the curve of her neck. At her elbow lay a thick Russian-English dictionary.

Five minutes elapsed without the slightest

hint of agitation. When it did appear, it was only a tiny wrinkle in her right eyebrow. She raised her hand again and made a quick movement above the writing table. Three more times she did this, as the irritation played out across her forehead and the corners of her eyes, finally shifting to her lips, which she'd started to gently bite. Back and forth her hand flew from the arm of the antique chair to hover over the blank space. The pool of light at her feet grew in diameter as the sun began to pass over the city.

Finally she stopped. The faint feline smile returned. She rested her hand on the edge of the table and popped her tongue softly against her teeth: *tock.* Although the exercise was clearly finished, she did not open her eyes, but rather made a sweeping motion through the air above the desk, as if wiping chalk from a blackboard, before resuming her stoic position. From the corner of the room a deep masculine voice whispered in an insistent tone.

"Again. But faster. Much, much faster."

Chapter Fourteen

As the halcyon days of spring spilled into summer it became easier to judge the distance Slater Brown had traveled since arriving in San Francisco. The former unknown was now hailed on the street by bus drivers, mooned over by mothers with unmarried daughters, and watched by local trendsetters to see what fashion statement he would revive next. He'd single-handedly brought back the Panama hat and pocket silk and was currently attempting a one-man restoration of leather spats.

But no single entity had been more on the receiving end of Slater Brown's popularity than the *Trumpet* itself. Circulation was up 337 percent and the newsroom was in a state of spastic optimism. Maynard Reed had first decided to channel all new profits into "institutional improvements," which meant new desks, fancy orthopedic chairs, four-percent salary increases for all, and better-quality paper. No longer would long-suffering *Trumpet* readers have to worry about sunlight bleeding all the stories together.

On top of that, for the first time in living memory they had an executive meeting to talk about what to do with future revenues. It was as if a cool breeze were flowing through the place, freshening up everything it came into contact with. At the meeting it was decided that after a year of steady profits they would consider buying computers but *only,* Maynard stipulated, if a good case could be made for why they would be helpful.

"Who needs computers?" crowed Motherlove as he paced the newsroom. "Look how far we've come without 'em!"

The last improvement they'd all agreed upon. It had originally been Niebald's idea. He'd whispered it to Motherlove who'd passed it on to Maynard who dismissed it with a sour expression before bringing it up ten minutes later as if it were a bolt of personal inspiration. Niebald and Motherlove let it pass without comment. They had long ago learned this was the best possible method. Two days later an Arburo & McInnes repair van parked on the sidewalk in front of the *Trumpet* building to fix the

"Sound of News" clock.

The next edition of the *Trumpet* ran a small photo on the lower right-hand corner of the front page: Slater Brown, Niebald Peters, Maynard Reed, and Robert Motherlove standing on the repair scaffolding, their hands reaching out in unison to set the "Sound of News" clock to twelve noon. On their faces were the same blissful smiles as those found in photographs of the first astronauts upon reentering the atmosphere.

The city savored Slater Brown with the fierce adulation usually reserved for heavyweight champs and Nobel Prize winners and Michelin-ranked chefs — he was *theirs.* From the very beginning he couldn't pay for a drink or a meal, no matter where he was, but as he continued reporting eye-catching stories the city's good cheer spilled over to small, neatly tied bouquets of flowers tossed gently onto the doorway of the *Trumpet,* or onto the green grass on the inside of Mrs. Cagliostra's white fence (almost immediately he'd had to request an unlisted telephone number). The flower phase was superseded by the pastry phase: dark chocolate hazelnut brownies, coconut macaroons, sheets of peanut brittle stacked on top of one another like ice.

It was all done respectfully, perhaps too much so. On the odd occasion when Slater Brown opened the front door, the thwarted gift-givers would often freeze in their tracks, as if by being seen they were spoiling the intention: Don't mind me, they seemed to be saying, I'm just dropping off a wheel of Parmigiano-Reggiano cheese, or a pair of custom-made roller skates, or free tickets to the hit play *Ladies in Hades.* Over the course of the next two months, the citizenry bestowed upon him four cartons of Blackwing pencils, two ear wax removal kits (one was opened), a piece of the Berlin Wall, a pair of panties, two parakeets, a five-gallon tin of Turkish figs, a gift certificate for an above-ground swimming pool, one Jack Russell terrier, a skateboard with three wheels, two ferrets (which the Jack Russell immediately chased down a storm drain), a Wurlitzer filled exclusively with accordion music, and for months after he'd included a line of poetry by Rainer Maria Rilke in one of his stories for the *Trumpet,* the manuscripts of several hundred unpublished books of poetry. It got to be such a fuss that the *Sun of San Francisco* and the *San Francisco Sun* sent reporters around so they could do dueling photo essays on the subject, complete with sarcastic captions that reduced

158

the gift-givers to degenerate freaks and Slater Brown to a mysteriously lucky nutball.

But the mayor never got around to reading the captions. The photographs were enough to get his blood pressure above 150 and make standing in his presence all but unbearable. "Bro," said Duane, "what if we hassle anybody seen giving gifts to that wackjob? We can blacklist them. Or we audit them. Or fine them! What if we get the Board of Supervisors to pass a law fining the giving of gifts?" His suggestions didn't seem to be going anywhere. " 'Course," he said, reversing direction, "if we were to do that, he might catch wind of it and then we'd be hoisted on our own retard."

The mayor's eyes were so glazed over from a breakfast sugar buzz he hadn't been paying attention. He opened his mouth. Duane Oswell leaned in to listen: "The Christmas goose comes home to roost, but not before he calls a truce," muttered Tucker Oswell underneath chocolate caramel fudge breath. "Definitely not a good sign," thought his stepbrother as he tiptoed out.

For Slater the overall sensation was one of gliding. It was not hard to feel that somehow everything was happening at his direction.

If he'd once doubted that the city was listening to him, he did not harbor such thoughts any longer. She was listening to him, and he was listening to her, and everyone was listening to them.

"I've got the world on a string," blared the radio at Antonio's Barbershop, where Slater got his weekly on-the-house haircut. "I'm sitting on a rainbow . . ." When Tony finished, he spun Slater around to face his reflection in the mirror and stepped away to get the bottle of tropical aftershave he kept in the back for special customers.

"Got the string around my finger . . ." Slater studied himself. He could feel it — bouncing around inside, pushing to get out. He repressed it for a second, but the new haircut, and his permanent smile, and the overall splendidness of the image that he cut begged to be let loose. Finally he couldn't help himself any longer. He looked at his reflection in the mirror, settled on the eyes, and winked.

It was after he'd published his twenty-second story — revealing that British rock star Stomp Jackson had snuck into town for a midnight assignation at the Idyll Hotel with the wife of home-run king Max Mauler: *Steamy Stomp Tryst Twist* read the *Trumpet* headline — that Slater Brown found himself invited to dinner at 23 Pacific Avenue. This particular address belonged to Moorpark Mansion, longtime residence of Mrs. Gloria van der Snoot. When Slater told Niebald of the invitation, the older reporter waggled his head back and forth and pursed his lips in the universal sign for "hoity-toity," before walking away without a word.

Gloria van der Snoot was the oldest, and richest, and thus most powerful of the city's social doyennes, and her table, set Wednesday through Saturday with Waterford Crystal and Anastasia china, was where power came to sup.

These dinners were lit by six golden candelabras and exquisite portions of whatever was fresh: Dungeness crab, Alaskan halibut, Bavarian stuffed pork chops, and always for dessert, Gloria's favorite: a single large scoop of tangerine sorbet with raspberry frizzle.

An aged lioness of seventy-nine, whose Dutch ancestors had opened the first distillery in California in 1867, Gloria was a woman to whom problems were brought with the sole expectation that she would solve them. In this way her salon was ideal for both mixing and fixing, and she took delight in mastering both activities with an expertise that was impossible to measure. A

161

nod of Gloria van der Snoot's gray head could gain a guest instant admittance to the Social Registry, or relegate another to a lifetime of calling up friends on Sunday morning to ask about last night's party. It was whispered, but never confirmed, that she had played important backstage roles in many of the city's dramas over the past thirty years, from resolving labor strikes to luring sports team franchises. She had the uncanny knack of always being in the picture, but never in focus.

To be invited to Moorpark, as it was called, was a mark of high social distinction, but one's true social value was calibrated, instantly, by where one was seated for dinner. On his first visit Slater Brown failed to appreciate his placement to the right of Gloria. This was the traditional place for honored guests, but at Moorpark it was even more so because Gloria was stone deaf in her left ear, and anyone seated there was understood to be on their way out of polite society.

The evening Slater Brown came to Moorpark for dinner he'd been summoned early. After gonging the copper-plated doorbell outside, he'd been led up the curved marble staircase to Mrs. van der Snoot's boudoir. It was there Slater encountered the unflappable dame for the first time. She sat on a purple velvet chaise longue, her predinner face embalmed with a cucumber moisturizing resin recently flown in from Milan into which little slices of almond were embedded. In Gloria van der Snoot's hands unfathomable wealth had been transmuted into incorrigible insouciance.

"Young man," she said in a feminine baritone stained by countless Benson & Hedges cigarettes, "you have come to my attention."

Slater could only think to bow. She continued, her pursed lips struggling to keep from breaking the cucumber resin mask. "Every now and again this city needs a little slap. And you, my dear boy, are the most recent love pat to come down the pike," she said, chuckling at her own amusing turn of phrase.

"The pleasure's all mine," said Slater, rising from his bow.

"I like to surround myself with young people," continued Gloria without pause. "They give me vitality, a sense of life, and let me know all the things that a little old lady would never hear about otherwise." She turned for her cigarette, which sat smoldering in a jewel-encrusted ashtray.

"Now, before we go downstairs I should

give you some background on who will be joining us for dinner. Mr. and Mrs. Frampton Saunders, of Saunders Insurance." Slater Brown nodded. "Judge O'Sullivan and his wife, Margaret. Must try to keep her to two drinks tonight," she said, extinguishing her cigarette.

"The Goldfarbs, the Stubbses, the Strausses, and a few other odds and ends," she said, drumming her long red fingernails in mock contemplation on the richly lacquered Oriental dressing table. "Who am I forgetting? Oh, of course, my niece, Brooke van der Snoot. She's about your age. She's just back from a modeling — what do you young people say? gig? — in Paris."

Slater nodded.

"But before we get into the tedious bits of gossip about tonight's guests — all off the record, of course," she said, reaching out to clutch his hand in jest, "I wanted to have a little chat with you. Marquis!" She tinkled a little brass bell at her side. Presently Marquis, the van der Snoot valet, floated into view, a glazed look of perpetual patience on his face.

"Get this young man a libation to make him more comfortable."

Marquis left without inquiring what Slater wanted. At Moorpark you were not so much indulged as you were served. A few minutes later an icy cold Moorpark specialty known as fognog was served to Slater in a sterling silver cup. He sat next to his hostess. Her slightly bloodshot eyes clashed in a most unintentional way with the tan cucumber mask. Every time Slater said something she clasped his hands in hers and emitted a girlish giggle.

"Wonderful," she shouted. "You're a born storyteller. Why am I not surprised? Everyone speaks so highly of you. Slater Brown, the man-about-town. You must have pretty girls lined up around the block, mustn't you?"

"Well, I —"

"Oh, please. Don't be shy with me, young man. When I was a young woman I would not have rested until you were mine."

He blushed, which left precisely the desired opening.

"Speaking of stories, what, in your professional opinion, is the absolute best way in the entire world to find a story in San Francisco?"

He fingered the pocket radio in his jacket. Even its weight in his hand made him feel safe, a talisman that opened a secret world.

"Well, I can only speak for myself," said Slater, "but I find it most helpful to get out into the city and look and listen for stories. They're everywhere."

"True, true, so true," trilled the septuagenarian van der Snoot. "But how, exactly, is one able to locate the very *best* stories?" The emphasis on "best" was imbued with all the accentuation money could buy.

"Well, you know what they say about stories," said Slater. "They find the people best suited to tell them."

Gloria van der Snoot had not, in fact, ever heard this before, and its relevance resonated in her with a simulated authenticity.

"Well said, dear boy, well said," she murmured as she tinkled the bell again in advance of dinner.

The predinner confessional was over. It was just as well. The cucumber resin mask was starting to lose its grip on the almond slices and Slater was trying to put out of his mind that her face resembled the poached salmon he'd eaten the night before at the Avalon Café.

After dinner they sat around the oval van der Snoot dinner table as Judge O'Sullivan regaled them with details from his latest case, which involved a millionaire mugger targeting the homeless in the Panhandle District. The judge was a barrel-chested man who'd served thirty-five years on the bench and had the waistband to prove it. He wore his round bifocals halfway down his nose, which magnified his large green eyes, already sparkling with a sharp intelligence.

After the judge amused them, Frampton Saunders told of how his great-great-grandfather was the first person in San Francisco to open a brothel. Gloria, who had heard this story hundreds of times before, suddenly announced, "Well, I'm just glad our young guest wasn't around when your ancestors were starting out, Framp, or they might have found themselves splashed across the front pages of the *Trumpet*, mightn't they?"

Something about the incantation of the word "splashed" seemed to sharpen the evening's focus. Slater felt the eyes around the table brush his face like a spotlight. Embarrassed, he glanced at Brooke van der Snoot, looking for an ally. She was young and pretty and blond. He noticed how her tanned bare shoulders contrasted fashionably with her sheer green dress. For most of the evening Brooke had been quiet as she stared past Slater's shoulder at an orange moon slowly rising over the Bay. But just then she caught him looking at her and smiled with something close to anticipation.

"Yes, well, I don't know about that," said Slater into the silence.

"Come, now, sing for your supper, boy," said the judge to laughter.

For a split second Slater panicked.

"Is it a gift?" said Frampton.

"Or a gimmick?" said Gloria, turning her frail body and the evening's spotlight fully on him.

"Or is it simply luck?" said Brooke, fixing her drowsy blue eyes on his for the first time.

"Well, I'm not —" said Slater, pushing back from the table.

"Nonsense," said Gloria. She was not a devotee of self-deprecation.

"Are you saying you have no control over when you uncover these stories?" said the judge.

"It's just been kind of like a streak —"

"So," said the judge, the twinkle in his eye darkening, "if I offered you a friendly wager, say twenty-five hundred, to go find me a story worthy of the front page of *The Morning Trumpet,* you couldn't do it?"

The faces around the table tightened in an instant, as if by an old-fashioned sardine key. Yet this was not what Slater Brown noticed. What he saw was how flush the faces were with good food and the fragrant wine, and how the vacation sun still on their cheeks made them look positively vibrant. He thought of how effortlessly laughter had spilled from the table that evening, and the exotic taste of the 1978 Jayer Echezeaux Burgundy on the sides of his tongue, and how nice it was to be inside Moorpark.

Earlier, as he'd walked around the great house, passing the ancient Mayan wall hangings and the delicate azure orchids and the small glowing fires in each room, he'd had the distinct feeling of moving to music. A deep, quiet part of him purred with satisfaction at being invited to a place like this. Not only invited, he corrected himself, but sought after! It was not beyond him that when he spoke, people near him stopped talking in order to hear what he had to say.

"Well, Judge," said Slater, "I'd hate to take your money."

The room held its breath.

"Make it five thousand," said Gloria quietly.

"Ten thousand dollars," said Frampton, who never missed a chance to remind everyone in the room who had the most money. All twenty eyes glistened with anticipation.

"Very well," said Slater, folding his hands

in order to keep them from shaking.

"Excellent," said the judge. "In this age of equivocation I admire a man up for a challenge." He pushed away from the table and seized a steaming hand towel from a silver tray Marquis was carrying past. "Let us say, as of midnight tonight, you have forty-eight hours to turn in a stem-winder of a story."

Slater took a deep gulp of the port in front of him.

"And," said the judge to relieved laughter around the table, "it better not be about me."

"Slater, my dear boy," said Gloria, flicking her heavily made-up eyes toward the French doors overlooking the Bay, "there appears to be a full moon tonight. On a full moon my *Cestrum nocturnum* smell simply gorgeous. Would you be a dear and take these" — she produced a small pair of silver scissors — "and bring in some for us to enjoy?"

"Of course," said Slater, rising.

"Wonderful. You can't cut too much of it, it grows like wild. And Brooke, be a good niece and show Mr. Brown the way to the garden."

Once in the back garden, which was illuminated by several large alabaster globes partially hidden by the ivy, Brooke van der

Snoot immediately lost her faculties, dropping the elaborately sequined purse she'd inexplicably brought along with her into the flower bed. After stooping to pick it up, she rose slowly and Slater found her arms resting lightly on his shoulders. Her dreamy eyes gazed upon his face with subdued amusement.

"You're cute," she said. For young women like Brooke van der Snoot the world was divided not into black and white, up and down, or even rich and poor, but rather into cute and not cute. Slater felt her hands interlocking slowly behind his head and he realized that for the last two hours he'd wanted nothing more than to do what was happening right now.

She offered her lips, which he took as impulsively as he'd taken a second serving of tangerine sorbet. They stood kissing for several minutes underneath the giant orange moon before she stopped, holding his face in her hands.

"Everyone at dinner thinks you're amazing. You know that, don't you?"

Slater stared at her.

"You're all anyone can talk about. The way you've turned everything upside down. It's like you're from another planet," she said, trailing off. Her perfectly blue eyes glistened

171

like candy. "I always wanted to be a writer."

"You should," he said, taking her by the shoulders. "You should be a writer. I can help."

"You're sweet," said Brooke, shaking her head. "But I don't really even like to read."

For this he had no answer.

"Well," she said, "now I've told you a secret, I get to ask a secret. A secret for a secret."

"OK," he said, drawing her closer.

"Tell me, Mr. Writer, how do you get people to tell you their stories?"

"Oh," said Slater lightly, "it just comes to me."

"But how?" said Brooke, kissing him gently on the lips as if pressing a truth button.

"Can't say," he said as he watched the lines on her forehead furrow with impatience even as her soft gaze stayed locked onto his. She kissed him again, lingering.

"I don't want to go inside just yet. It's so boring in there . . . Let's play a game. Every time you answer a question I'll remove an article of clothing."

Slater Brown's eyes grew wide. "From me or you?"

"Good point. I think I should get to choose." He looked up at the enormous bay window. The dinner party was still seated, everyone laughing uproariously at another of the judge's stories. This could be fun, he told himself, kind of like charades with better prizes.

"OK, just to show you I'm serious, I'll take this off first," said Brooke van der Snoot, unwrapping a long cerulean silk scarf from around her neck.

"Your seriousness is not in doubt," said Slater as he watched her toss the scarf onto a prizewinning bonsai tree.

"First question. Do you find the stories all by yourself?"

"Yes," said Slater, staring at her silhouette in the moonlight.

"Good, now that wasn't so hard," she said, drawing him toward her. With precise movements her fingers carefully unbuttoned his shirt, leaving his tie on as a kind of padlock.

"Next question: Who is it that tells you these stories?"

This was going to be harder than he thought. He was already having trouble concentrating. His pants began to rise.

"Uh —"

"Come on, no stalling," she said with a coquettish smile. He was starting to feel detached, as if his mind could see his body standing in the garden all by itself.

"Tell you what, while you're thinking, I'll get a head start on my next piece of clothing." And she did, slowly wiggling out of the spaghetti straps that held up her dress. He watched as the sheer green curtain lowered past her collarbone and then her belly button. Even in the moonlight he could see she had a world-class tan.

"Ohh," he burbled in the tone of an outboard motor suddenly encountering shallow water. His eyes flitted back and forth between the dinner guests seated behind the plate-glass window and the nude nymph in the moonlight.

"I don't — I don't think —"

She wiggled one last little bit, dropping the dress onto the grass.

"Oh, come on, party boy. Don't freeze up on me now."

He couldn't take his eyes off her, even to blink. Her white panties glowed with a supernatural luminescence in the darkness.

"I don't know what to tell you."

She stepped out neatly from the circle of the fallen dress and came toward him, pressing her warm flat stomach against him.

"Oh, that's not true. Just tell me the truth. That's all. The whole truth and nothing but."

He closed his eyes.

"OK," he said. "OK, truth is, voices. I hear voices and that's pretty much how I get my stories."

"What kind of voices?" she asked. "Inside-your-head voices?" He could feel her hands on his belt buckle.

"Strange voices," he said, his own voice inching higher. "All over. Everywhere. I can't help it." His brain buzzed with a gentle roar. "They come at all times. I'm like a tour guide! A disc jockey, you could say, who facilitates . . ." It was no use, he was losing control. "I," he gulped as he struggled to reconcile the opposing forces at work in his body, each demanding total authority. "I," he said spasmodically.

"Yes!" shouted Brooke van der Snoot.

" 'I SING THE BODY ELECTRIC . . . THE ARMIES OF THOSE I LOVE EN-GIRTH ME, AND I ENGIRTH THEM; THEY WILL NOT LET ME OFF TILL I GO WITH THEM, RESPOND TO THEM, AND DISCORRUPT THEM, AND CHARGE THEM FULL WITH THE CHARGE OF THE SOUL!' "

Walt Whitman's poetry had never fallen on deafer ears. Brooke van der Snoot looked at him.

"What was that?"

"I was just saying . . . saying only . . .

175

explaining voices I was saying only just I." His brain and his tongue were no longer speaking to each other. A tiny and imperceptible feminine register clicked inside Brooke van der Snoot.

"I'm cold," she suddenly announced. Before Slater could respond, or adjust his trousers, she had scooped up her dress from the damp grass and darted inside the house.

"If you really want to write you need to read more poetry," he called out from the darkness.

By the time he reentered the dining room — carrying two priceless Turkish vases stuffed with night-blooming jasmine — the enormous grandfather clock was beginning its run toward midnight. The dinner party was gathered in the entryway with their coats.

"Tick-tock, grasshopper," said the judge from behind his glasses as the twelfth chime rang out. Brooke van der Snoot was nowhere to be found. Slater hastily bid everyone goodnight before running down Moorpark's long cobblestone driveway. It was late, but not too late to find a story.

Inside, Gloria kiss-kissed everyone good night and thank-thanked them for coming. As soon as Marquis shut the door she poured herself a tiny glass of sherry and retired to her chambers. Once ensconced she placed a telephone call.

"I should be tired of saying this, but you owe me one. Again."

"Gloria, you know you're my favorite."

"That's a dubious distinction, my dear boy, but suffice to say the trap has been set."

"Good. And you'll let me know what I can do for you."

"Oh, I shouldn't worry about that, Mr. Mayor. I shouldn't worry about that at all."

CHAPTER FIFTEEN

The twenty waterproof computers in the workshop were arranged in two long lines, each attached to its counterpart across the aisle by cords that ran like reins between them so that when Milo stood at the main keyboard and typed in his commands he looked as if he were overseeing a dogsledding team composed of beige boxes.

"Mush, dear boys!" he shouted when the work was going well. "Mush! Mush! Mush!"

This outdoor image was reinforced by the fact that Milo had taken to wearing a yellow rain suit of the sort favored by North Atlantic tuna fishermen. Though he hadn't stepped outside his compound for six weeks, the suit was slippery to the touch. Beneath the visor Milo could be heard to mumble incantations as he pushed forward, trying to unravel the codes he was after.

It was not the talk of an idle man. After the clacking keyboard faded away, the phalanx of computers translated Milo's latest commands into a series of rules representing a rough draft of a pattern formula. Once a diagnostic test was run, checking the computational validity of the pattern formula, the revised results were sent to a small red supercomputer at the end of the table. The supercomputer was the sine qua non of the operation. It contained specialized algorithms that could pull the pieces of the pattern formulas the lesser computers had generated and decide — within a trillionth of a second — which was correct and where to put it. After it assembled these pieces into a final proof, it flashed the results onto Milo's screen. Once he'd approved it (although this was a mere formality), the red supercomputer translated the pattern formula into carefully measured ingredients and expelled them out of a metal apparatus that looked remarkably like a microwave, but was actually a hydrogen lung. For all the scientific creativity that had gone into its creation, the final mixture resembled vapor from a teapot.

But this nondescript vapor had taken great mental effort to manufacture. At first he'd imagined the tricky part would be the ingredients. But trial and error showed that it was the mixture that mattered. After several minutes, the newest vapor cloud hovered above the floor, expanding until it was in the loose approximation of a circle.

As he stared at the steam organizing in front of him, Milo wiped his forehead with a damp towel. His intense work was about to play itself out. Either he was on the right track, or not.

The vapor cloud rose halfway to the ceiling as if seeking neutral buoyancy.

"Good," whispered Milo as the form expanded and retracted until it had grown to the size of a basketball, then a beach ball, and then finally an enormous bubble. Within the sphere the vapor seemed to thicken by its own interaction, changing in color from white to yellow to brown, and finally black.

Wherever the dark cloud moved Milo followed, muttering like a father watching a newborn's first steps. "Thatta boy!"

Finally, after Milo chased it around the room for fifteen minutes, the nebula, now quite thick, hovered above his desk and shuddered as if suppressing a long-held sneeze.

"Don't hold back," shouted Milo, lips glistening. "Let her rip!"

With that, the shudder transformed itself into a sustained tremor as the cloud's dark vapors puckered before expelling tiny drops onto the mass of papers on Milo's desk.

Milo Magnet, who had seen his share of astonishing things, couldn't believe his eyes.

He'd wanted to believe it. He'd believed he *would* believe it. But now that it was right in front of him it seemed impossible. There above his desk, of his own devising, was a perfectly good rain cloud unleashing a torrent of rain. Well, it wasn't technically a torrent, but it would be. It could be! Milo let out a long whoop of delight. His calculations had been correct. The proportions were perfect! He'd delved deeply into the weather arts and pieced together the correct pattern formula. It was the first known instance of man-made directed weather production in human history.

"Big!" said Milo, throwing his arms out in front of him. "Not nothing! This is definitely . . . something . . . big!" He stopped abruptly and turned around, one hand behind his back as he bounced lightly on the balls of his feet.

"Mr. President, it is with great pleasure that I humbly bring you the most astonishing discovery of our lifetime. We now have the ability to end hunger, to confound our fiercest enemies, to control the canvas of the heavens with the precision of a traffic cop."

He stopped and rushed to his desk to find a piece of scrap paper. He wanted to draft a speech now, while the words were flowing.

The raindrops continued, even as the cloud's menacing blackness began to drain to light brown. Fearing that the creation was stopping for some reason, Milo ceased writing, flipped his yellow visor back onto his head, and moved underneath the cloud to take a reading with his hygroscope.

CHAPTER SIXTEEN

Every day when he woke up, Slater Brown was convinced he'd heard all the secrets the city had to share, and yet every day that he climbed the steps of the bus with his pocket radio he heard something he couldn't have imagined the day before.

At first it's terribly confusing, like sitting at the knee of God. LISTENING TO EVERY-THING. (Not sure God exists, but if He does, I am impressed by how many threads of humanity He monitors simultaneously.) How does He do that (if He does in fact exist)?

Which is not to say that riding around San Francisco on a bus, listening to stories on a pocket radio, was a perfect science. Rain limited the transmissions. And conversations were all but indecipherable on windy days, when the wires swayed side to side and made every conversation sound as if it were taking place underwater. Not all of the bus lines were created equal either. It hadn't taken Slater long to develop a cheat sheet to help guide him on his daily journey. He carefully taped it inside the cover of his yellow notebook:

Bus Scouting Report:
#9 bus: good for financial information and nightclub gossip.
#12 bus: passes by both federal courthouse and bail bondsmen row.
#3 & #6 bus: Total dud. Avoid.
#17 bus: mostly Mandarin.
#5 bus: Very consistent. Route includes a double loop around City Hall. Especially good on clear days.

Even the most productive bus route didn't always deliver blockbuster material. There were only so many mayoral elections and secret assignations between the rich and famous and instances of high-level financial chicanery to reveal. But surprisingly, the smaller stories did more to endear him to the *Trumpet*'s growing readership than anything else.

"Peter, Peter the Meter Cheater!" touted the *Trumpet* after Slater discovered that the hour-long parking meters on Van Ness were rigged to expire ten minutes early by Peter

Maloney, the head of the Department of Parking and Traffic.

Or the secret meeting planned between the Pope and the Dalai Lama to discuss religious tolerance. He'd overheard a conversation between their assistants, negotiating where in North Beach to have lunch and who would pay for it.

"Pope Dines Dutch with Dalai!" revealed the *Trumpet*.

In order to find even these minor scoops he had endured endless banality: snippets of boring chitchat between shop-girls, of promises whispered between consenting adults to people they were not married to, of minor treason, of pathetic business schemes dreamed up by small-minded men, of unrequited love, and of terrible meanness. And that was just while passing the Transamerica Pyramid on the number 4.

In the beginning he wrote down everything he heard, unsure of what was worth keeping or what might turn out to be useful later. But after a couple of months he'd developed painful cramps in his wrists from filling up so many yellow notebooks. He'd also grown weary of the disbelieving looks from fellow passengers. One evening a group of medical students riding the bus home after rounds took turns staring at him

185

before whispering "hypergraphia" to one another with knowing glances.

As his career at the *Trumpet* progressed, he became more adept at telling what was good material from what wasn't, which allowed him the time to infuse his stories of San Francisco with as much literary emphasis as possible. For a piece about a Parisian bakery, he worked in mention of Gertrude Stein. His St. Patrick's Day story included a three-paragraph quotation from John Millington Synge. And a recent double murder in Oakland led off with a Capote epigram. In this way, he convinced himself, he was tending his own literary ambitions.

Each morning at eight A.M. sharp, Slater Brown would step onto the bus and wink at the driver — Willy or Sheila or Tubby or Marvin or Fiske, he knew them all — and slide into the last seat on the right, unwrap his headphones, and close his eyes. He'd become so skilled at picking up the city's voices he could tune in to different conversations by subtly adjusting the position of the pocket radio against the side of the bus, like a stethoscope pressed against willing flesh.

At the *Trumpet* they waited. Twenty-four hours a day, seven days a week. Whenever the kid returned, there was always some-body waiting for him. Maynard Reed had hired a doorman for the lobby of the building, in part to deal with the flowers and gifts left there and in part because, for the first time, they could afford to. He was instructed to call upstairs as soon as Slater Brown stepped into the elevator.

Maynard liked to greet the young man personally as the elevator doors opened onto the fifth floor, but if he wasn't available, he left specific instructions for Motherlove or Niebald to do it.

"No pressure, you come in from the field whenever you're ready," Motherlove told him after Slater appeared with a story about the Bartlett Twins, the city's most famous strippers. They were identical, but not, it turned out, identically female.

"Bartlett Babes X Why?" asked the *Trumpet.*

Even when Slater Brown wasn't at the paper, the newsroom was a hive of activity. There were plans to develop all sorts of new initiatives. "What we need are initiatives!" Maynard had announced at the staff meeting. "Initiatives and components!" Among the first of these initiatives was a raft of columns that covered topics the *Trumpet* had been forced to abandon years ago. "Up

Your Assets" was the new investing column, written by a twenty-eight-year-old Wall Street hotshot who had retired to live on a houseboat in Sausalito. The new restaurant review column was called "The Belly Pulpit" and was going to be written by the staff on a rotating basis.

"We'll cover the city's food scene like a rash!" said Maynard in a fit of excitement.

In fact, Maynard Reed had become so interested in the daily staff meetings that barely one went by when he didn't show up, interrupting Motherlove midsentence, in order to exhort them with a motivational quote — Teddy Roosevelt and Helen Keller were favorites — while the staff listened politely. When he wasn't "leading the troops," as he liked to put it, Maynard could be found standing in the middle of the room, a thumb hooked into the belt loop of his trousers, smiling broadly at the pink circulation sheet in his hand.

"What's it saying, boss?" called Niebald, in what was becoming a ritual whenever he passed with a stack of proofs.

"Up, up, up!" said Maynard, looking over the circulation numbers listed neatly in black. "The numbers, my friend. The numbers, they are improving!"

■ ■ ■ ■

With the ten thousand dollars he'd won from the Moorpark dinner party bet — he had picked up a conversation on his pocket radio between two city supervisors "exploring" the idea of selling the San Francisco Giants to the city of Anchorage — Slater Brown did not purchase a new suit, or eat out for a month at the finest restaurants in town, or even buy a case of 1982 Château Lafite as a hedge against middle-class mediocrity. Instead he did the most impractical thing possible for a young man making his living riding around on the buses of San Francisco. He purchased a car. It was a 1935 Riley Imp Roadster painted the iridescent green of a june bug's wing.

The car had sat unmoved for years in Mrs. Cagliostra's garage, and in her final paroxysm of spring cleaning, she'd unearthed it beneath a nearly complete collection of *National Geographic* magazines resting on the hood.

"I'll sell it to you on one condition."

"Condition met."

"You don't know what it is."

"Whatever it is, I'll meet it."

"Listen, smarty-pants, you gotta promise

me you'll get the brakes checked is all."

"Promise," said Slater as he slid onto the leather seat and tenderly depressed the ancient clutch.

"And don't drive this jalopy down Divisadero Street."

"Why?"

"It's too steep."

"Oh, you worry too much."

"I may worry too much, but I've been alive a lot longer than you and maybe all that worrying pays off."

"I promise."

"And I take cash only, no checks."

Slater smiled as he pulled out the wad of cash from his pocket and counted it slowly on the hood. From then on, he could often be seen wheeling around the city during his off hours. When people waved, and they did often, he honked with a bright cheery toot. It was not always easy parking a vintage car lacking power steering in tight spaces, but it didn't take long for the traffic cops to recognize whose car it was. Soon, when he double-parked on Lombard, or stopped in the fire lane in front of the *Trumpet,* there was an unspoken rule not to even chalk his tires.

Slater Brown had money in his tailored

pockets and the ear of all. After their feeble attempts to turn the city against him, the editors of the *San Francisco Sun* and the *Sun of San Francisco* had switched tactics and tried to poach him with fancy job offers ("Executive reporter — has a nice ring to it, doesn't it?") and signing bonuses that included a lifetime membership to the Pacific Union Club, a round-the-clock driver, and a monthly clothing allowance. "And you ever need a little companionship, you just let us know," they said to him sotto voce over soft-shell crab cakes in the two newspapers' identical private dining rooms.

He mulled all of this over politely while in their company, but there was no question of his actually leaving the *Trumpet.* It was where he'd started, and where he was staying. More to the point, he'd been told that the reporters at the *San Francisco Sun* and *Sun of San Francisco* worked in pairs and he didn't feel like drawing attention to why that wasn't going to be possible.

In the midst of his great accomplishment (or what looked like a series of great accomplishments to some, and to others like a kind of magic; to Slater it was both), he was approached by the reigning kingmaker of the New York literary world, superagent Bix Butterfield. Butterfield represented

191

more best sellers than any living agent (at the moment he had eleven books on the Top Ten list, two tied for first), and his roster of success stories was as long as the five-color brochure he carried in his pocket.

"We want you to write a book for us," he told Slater Brown when they first met, at a luncheon downtown in the Bison Room at the Palace Hotel. The way Bix said "we" made it seem like he was the sole proxy by which the desires of the known world were channeled.

"You keep this up, you're going to launch yourself right onto the best-seller list," said Bix. "You're so talented. You're a natural. You're fresh and natural and that's important," he said, flicking the ash from his Dunhill cigar onto Slater's shoe. "What do you say? Let's drum ourselves up a title, a little something to work with, shall we?"

This was standard play in the Butterfield book. Get the writer thinking about the creative part rather than the twenty-seven percent commission he was going to pay for the privilege of working with Butterfield & Co. Bix looked at his future client with a warm smile that belied the shrewd calculation going on inside his head. With a polish, two rounds of teeth whitening, and a word in the New York gossips, this lad could move a hundred thousand copies easy. Maybe two hundred thousand if they could gin up some kind of controversy.

The king-agent sensed Slater's vacillation. He used his fat tongue to move his cigar around his mouth. "OK, OK, let's see. Title. Title. We need something great for you. How about this:

"Downtown Brown: The Life and Times of an Ace Reporter!" He studied Slater's face.

"No? OK, OK. Gimme a second. Umm."

He threw his head back in mock contemplation.

"Ahhhhhhhhhhhhh . . ."

It was like sitting at the shoulder of a dentist.

"GOT IT!!" said Bix Butterfield, holding his fingers to his temple as if transmitting the idea via telepathy from his brain to Slater's.

"Ear Witness!"

He watched to see how that had landed. "See, everyone else is used to 'eyewitness,' but you make your living —" He stopped. "OK, I can see that's not literary enough. OK, I get it. I get it. I GOT IT!" He spread his arms as if preparing to take flight and waited for a moment to make sure he had Slater's undivided attention. *"The Unbearable Lightness of Listening: The Incredibly*

193

True Story of the World's Greatest Hotshot Reporter. You with me, sport? Has a nice ring to it. Whaddya think? And don't pull punches, I like a straight shooter."

The only wrinkle in the tapestry of glory unfolding before him was evident every time Slater Brown passed Coolbrith Park. Sitting in the back of the bus, as the afternoon sun reflected off the Bay, he slipped into a melancholy mood and reflexively turned up the volume on his pocket radio, wishing he could pick up the voice of a mysterious young woman singing. But there was nothing.

Maybe I imagined her? he wrote in his yellow notebook. *It happens. Someone flashes past in a red raincoat and disappears around the corner forever. Gone. And what you remember is not what you saw, but what you wanted to see.*

He got off at the next stop. There was just enough time to turn in a story for tomorrow's paper. He didn't have much, just a sliver of an overheard rumor about the Chinatown sushi mafia trying to pass off shark belly as Maine lobster tail using a special pressing technique imported from Bangkok. It wasn't great, but it would be enough for a slow news week in a city that worshipped food.

As he passed the Mermaid Tavern on Post Street, he glanced at the large plate-glass window. There, among posters for one-act plays, acoustical jam sessions, and children's ballet, was a small green postcard:

The San Francisco Pawns invite you to a special exhibition match.
Watch five men compete simultaneously against the finest female chess player in the world,
CALLIO
de
QUINCY

Slater Brown, man-about-town; his heart skipped a beat. He'd all but given up ever finding her again. He reread the postcard. This had to be her. And the book she had been reading that day, *Nine Moves*. She wasn't a dancer at all. It was chess she was reading about. How different, he thought. How interesting and charming and . . . different. When nobody was looking he filched the postcard and ran sixteen blocks back to the *Trumpet* to regroup.

CHAPTER SEVENTEEN

Callio de Quincy lived with her father in a grand house near the top of Pacific Heights. The de Quincys were originally from Turkey, via Cambridge and New York. Havram de Quincy was a short man with an immaculate haircut and the square face of his Moorish ancestors. He'd studied applied mathematics at Cambridge and worked in derivatives for a Swiss bank in New York for eight years before retiring to San Francisco to raise his only daughter. Everyone who met him marveled at all that he had accomplished: the wealth, the possessions, and the self-possession. That he had accomplished all of this while completely blind only increased their admiration. Even with one strike against him Havram was capable of training tremendous focus on whatever captured his attention.

"You must have an open mind, yes," he was fond of saying. "But an open mind with great strength."

By age four, Callio had been presented with many games and activities, the better with which to stimulate her new, open mind. But the only game that held her attention was chess. Her instructors at the time often mentioned, in one way or another, that she didn't appear to be learning the game as much as rejoining an old conversation. By the age of seven she was beating everyone in her chess club, even those twice her age. By the age of twelve she was the Western champion; by the age of fifteen she was the youngest (and only) female grand master in the United States. Through it all she remained not only victorious, but, even more impressively, undefeated.

Havram still smiled when he remembered the first time he sat down to test the depths of his daughter's mental acuity and found his king captured in four minutes. The next game it had happened in one.

That same year Havram made the decision that Callio would pursue her chess education at home, rather than in a European university. It was an easy decision on one level — what advantage was a traditional education for a young woman who dreamed of becoming the first female world champion? Besides, he made sure that she had a firm command of history, literature, and the sciences, and she already spoke three languages. No, keeping her close at hand was a much better decision, he reasoned to himself.

Havram, while not a true recluse, preferred to spend his time in his library, where his reading was slow and ran to the classics. Euclid, Aurelius; for a laugh he turned to Aristophanes' early plays. He used an expensive Braille glove that allowed him to decipher any text, regardless of whether it had been translated for the blind or not. The fingertips contained an optic eye that scanned the pages, turning each letter into a raised formation on the inside of the glove's padded fingers. Without the wonder glove Havram would never have been able to keep abreast of his daughter's chess education. Unbeknownst to either of them, Milo Magnet had invented the glove years earlier as part of a top-secret project for DARPA, for the purpose of disarming bombs.

As a young girl, Callio had often wondered about her mother, whose identity remained a mystery. All she'd managed to glean was that her biological origins were the result of a secret arrangement orchestrated by

Havram. On the rare occasion she heard her father questioned — at the passport checkpoint in the Paris airport, for example — Havram would proudly announce he had "never been married." Early on, Callio decided not to press him for details. On occasion she'd wondered if she were adopted, but that intuition had faded when she first saw herself in photographs standing next to her father. The resemblance was so striking that she could easily pass as his astonishingly beautiful younger sister.

Every morning at six-thirty Callio could be found at the Lyon Street Steps, running the stairs. She looked unusually beautiful there, with the morning light striking her face and giving her black hair — combed and wet — a relief that seemed impossible. By seven A.M. any number of young men would appear at the steps, wearing loose gym shorts with the yellowed lettering of eastern colleges printed on them, to see this leggy colt dashing up the stairs two at a time. If they were new to the city they would smile privately and begin to follow her, hoping to strike up a conversation at the top. But they soon learned several truths about Callio — she never noticed men who followed her, and she loved to run. Thus, eight, ten, twelve, fifteen laps up and down the vertical stairs never fazed her, with her rabbit pack of suitors in tow, each one of them trying to get close enough to whisper an invitation in her ear before bursting a blood vessel. If only they could catch her.

At home, although almost always in the same room with one another, Callio and Havram lived in clouds of great silence. The chess practice sessions lasted from shortly after breakfast, their commencement signified by a sharp rap of his walking cane, until lunch, broken only by a meal that was left outside the study by the Peruvian housekeeper, Camilla, whom they employed four days a week for cleaning and cooking.

After lunch Callio's father liked to converse with her for several hours, although they were not exactly meandering digressions.

"What was Klatchnivosk's seventh move of the second game in the 1979 World Championship match in Prague?"

"Knight seven, Father, and it wasn't Prague, it was Vienna."

"Excellent," Havram would grunt, his sightless eyes fluttering like hearts on a delirious slot machine.

At sundown Havram would excuse Callio for the afternoon to go out for a walk. She

200

was required to be home two hours later for dinner, after which she would study old chess matches from his complete collection of *Attack!* magazine in the library.

Havram's plan, as carefully constructed as a Steinitz gambit, was to let Callio develop her talents naturally, engaging her in local matches and tournaments before taking her abroad to conquer the European chess salons in preparation for making her run at the world championship. At twenty-three and already the most dominant female chess player in modern history, she was well on her way.

"The queen of the queen's game," he told her at night when he sat on her bed, brushing her hair with his fingertips.

CHAPTER EIGHTEEN

"What have I fucking done to fucking deserve this!" shrieked the mayor, lolling his tongue around his mouth like an epileptic with Tourette's.

"Nothing!" he answered himself, waving his hands in the air as if descending a roller coaster. "Fucking nothing!" He'd just been told Bix Butterfield was in town to court Slater Brown. They'd been spotted eating a dozen Olympia oysters apiece by one of the mayor's many spies. Mayor Oswell assumed, in a solipsistic rage, that the meeting's agenda was to encourage Slater to pen a tell-all book about *him!*

"God knows what dredged-up gossip, what hateful invective he will employ!" said the mayor, slipping into his professional orator mode, which he did only when genuinely vexed.

Each fresh report of Slater Brown's success had sunk the mayor into ever-finer pedigrees of funk. Among Tucker Oswell's many character defects, the most interesting was his ability to think that everything was about him, and if it wasn't good news, to take it remarkably personally. He frothed and fumed about the latest story in the *Trumpet* reporting that City Hall was working on a plan to rename the Golden Gate Bridge (which it was) in a secret initiative that would solicit the highest bid from a list of multinational corporations. The plan would bring in many millions, although, it was generally understood by those involved, probably not to the city exclusively.

Slater Brown's stories added up to one long nightmare for the mayor. After months of declining opinion polls, after having to rethink his entire political strategy every time another story came out — not to mention the ungodly amount of time he was forced to spend reassuring angry political supporters — the mayor had run out of ways to relieve his harried mind. In some ways, what had happened was only natural considering it was the sole thing that seemed to offer him no critique: eating.

The mayor was already a fan of the *boulangerie* on Jackson Square; it had become commonplace to see him with powdered sugar coating his lips, like the wipe-away from a Kabuki mask, at seven in the morning. Lunch had evolved into feasts that might include sweet-and-sour ginger ribs from the famous Happy Immortal Chinese restaurant and two medium-rare hamburgers with chanterelle mushrooms and Sonoma blue cheese crumbles ordered straight from the Paladin's Grill. A mid-afternoon snack might employ some handmade beignets from Babu's dipped in chocolate fondue and washed down with his new favorite drink, pomegranate juice over crushed ice.

So great was his anxiety about the stories Slater Brown was writing that the mayor had become a flame that nourished itself on the city's finest foods. It wasn't long before the considerable culinary resources of a very resourceful city disappeared down his gullet — at which point the flame only became stronger, and larger, and brighter. It was nothing for him to call the chef of the Origami Café, or the maître d' at the Dutch Oven, and order Peking duck or caramel soufflé at two o'clock in the morning. If anything, he considered these late-night phone calls a mark of affection.

So insatiable was his appetite that he arranged for an aquatic sanctuary next to Seal Rock to be raided for a fresh supply of silver abalone, an endangered mollusk rumored to be for sale on the black market at five hundred dollars an ounce. After the sanctuary raid William Heck, still dripping in his neoprene wet suit, stood beside the mayor holding a bowl of melted butter and watched in awe as his boss ate three pounds of silver abalone and four cobs of grilled corn, pausing only to wash it all down with two bottles of rare claret sent over by his personal tailor in London. When he was finished the mayor sat back in his leather chair and motioned for William Heck to come closer. The food had cleansed his mind.

"Get Butterfield out of town. That numbskull isn't going to make my life any worse. I don't care how you do it. Scare him. Send over Joey, or Duane, or somebody, and meet him when he's coming out of one of those fancy Nob Hill parties he's been going to every night this week and make it real clear that there's important business for him to attend to back in New York. Who does he think he is, coming out here, encouraging that little twerp? We gotta lotta problems, but he's not going to be one of them."

"What about pencil dick?" asked William Heck.

The mayor opened his mouth before holding up his pinkie as if in deep thought.

"Baaaaaaaaaaaaaaararrrrrrrrrrrrrrrrrrrrrr-rrrrraaaaaaaaappp!"

Two rooms away, his aides, busy unpacking a crate of lychee nuts flown in from Beijing, mistook the belch for a backfiring car.

"We're going to fix that little pimple, but one thing at a time. First you get rid of the mosquitoes, then you shoot the hippo."

William Heck nodded in agreement and moved toward the door.

"Oh, and while you're out, pick me up one of those roasted goat kebabs from Ali's over on Fillmore. And make sure they give you an extra serving of that fig sauce. And get one of those apricot kerfluffle things, too. The ones with the sesame seeds on top. Make sure they toast it. I like them best toasted. But not too much. Just a little dab of butter on the inside. Did I say one order of goat kabob? Make it a double."

"What in the world?" said Mrs. Cagliostra, reaching for her reading glasses, which dangled from a velvet cord around her neck. She'd opened the front door to find Slater Brown standing in a serge suit trying to close the front gate with his knee. In his clasped palms rose a stack of twenty-two books.

"Just some reading I need to do."

"You put any more books in that cottage I'm going to call the fire department."

"Oh, don't be such a philistine, Mrs. C," said Slater, edging past her toward the back door and the garden's safety.

She marched along beside him, reading the titles as they moved through the house.

"*The Black and White Guide to Chess, Hornsby's Guide to Winning Chess, Think Like a Grandmaster* — say, what are you up to?"

"Just developing a new hobby. The game of kings and all that."

"You're the only person I know who learns how to play chess by reading a book!"

"Well, I don't have anyone to play with, now, do I?" he shot back.

Ten minutes later they sat across from each other at the dining room table, a faded chessboard between them. Cups of herbal tea steamed at their elbows. From above the sideboard an oil portrait of the Virgin Mary watched over them.

"Frank adored chess," said Mrs. Cagliostra. "After he taught me how, we played twice a week. Right up to the day I beat the pants off him." Slater barely registered any of this pregame chitchat. He was trying to remember what he'd read about opening moves on the bus ride home.

Half an hour later Mrs. C. ended the game with a matter-of-fact "Checkmate." If she hadn't needed to put on and take off her reading glasses between moves she could have finished the game ten minutes earlier. She glanced at Slater.

"What're you staring at? Game's over."

"I'm trying to decipher what happened."

"Decipher away," she said, as she folded her hands in her lap and rested her chin on her neck. "What's this about, anyway?" she asked.

"Hmm," said Slater, his dreamy eyes popping to the surface.

"You don't know crapola about chess and I don't think you ever will. No matter how many books you read. You don't have the brain for it."

This blunt assessment stung him to his core.

"There's a —"

"I knew it!" She cackled. "It's about a girl, isn't it?"

He nodded.

"She plays chess, well, that's a good sign.

Chess-playing indicates a certain quality of mind."

He ignored the implications for his own mind.

"Look, is she any good?"

"I think so."

"How good?"

"I think she's professional."

Mrs. Cagliostra whistled quietly under her breath.

"Professional, now that's something. Professional lady chess player. Well, that settles that."

"What?"

"What can you possibly hope to achieve by playing her? I can tell you right now you're never going to beat her."

He nodded, carried along in the wake of her feminine logic like a water skier behind an oil tanker. What had he been thinking?

"And she's not going to be impressed because you can play chess. There's a million fellows can do that. Here's my advice, take it or leave it."

For one long instant he held his breath. It hadn't escaped him that her advice was usually the exact opposite of what he wanted to do.

"Forget chess, forget games. Take her away from chess. That's a woman's idea of romance. To be taken *away* from her life."

"Like where?"

She put her reading glasses back on.

"Like where? Come on. You must be joking! When I was your age we didn't have time to ask such silly questions." She took off her reading glasses.

"Ask her out on a date, you nitwit."

CHAPTER NINETEEN

As the months fell away it had gotten to the point where if you were even considering doing something bad, or illegal, or morally reprehensible within the city limits of San Francisco you planned it out of town and executed it with a whisper. Petty crime was down thirty-four percent in the month of June alone and priests all over the city were reporting an increase in attendance, not to mention more complete disclosure in the confessional booths. Adultery, purse-snatching, lying, finagling, scams, shams — flimflammery of all variety — seemed to be headed for a rout.

Pinky Beale in the mayor's communications office, ever attuned to opportunity, caught wind of the new trend and patched together a press release for IMMEDIATE distribution: "Mayor's LOVE THY NEIGHBOR Program Shows Stunning Results!"

While the general populace basked in the affirming glow of its newfound interest in the straight and narrow, the underbelly of the underbelly of San Francisco decided to tail the source of its troubles. A small undistinguished group of men began to gather every morning on the perimeter of Joyce Street with the intention of discreetly following Slater Brown as he made his way through the city. Every evening they would gather at the Mermaid Tavern, rub their sore feet, and discuss the situation. How oh how had this bespoke dandy turned up such good information — information their clients would just as soon not get turned up? The tailing first began when Slater Brown had left Moorpark. He hadn't noticed he was being followed, because the man only hung with him for one night. Duane Oswell had explained it all to his stepbrother at City Hall the following day.

"It's hard tailing someone around San Francisco when all the motherfucker does is get on a fucking bus and never get off."

The mayor listened carefully, head cocked. "And then what did you do? I know you messed this up somehow, Duane. Tell me what you did so I can figure it out."

"I did not mess this up. I followed him to the bus stop, just like you told me, and I sat three rows away from him so as not to raise suspicion, just like you told me."

"And?" asked the mayor.

"And I read the sports page cover to cover four fucking times, but after the bus done three complete round-trips I couldn't take it no more."

"The bus was obviously just a meeting spot . . . Did he talk to anybody? Did anyone slip him some paper? Did you see *anything,* Duane?"

"No, nothing. He just sat there, listening to music the whole goddamned time. Every once in a while he doodled something in his notebook. But most of the time, he looked like he was sleeping."

"Oh, sweet Jesus. I don't know what to believe," said the mayor, his face flushing grapefruit pink. "You're either fucking stupid, or we got ourselves a real situation on our hands. Some mysterious magician tools around listening to music and sleeping and somehow — some way! — he knows just about everything there is to know in the whole hell of San Francisco! If I had to bet, I'd take the 'fucking stupid' bet twenty to one!"

All two hundred and fifty pounds of Duane Oswell began to pout, as he stood humiliated in his red-and-white velour

213

sweatsuit.

"Well, I ain't fucking stupid," he said.

"Prove it!" screamed the mayor.

"Well, for starters I'm not the dumbass who sent me out on this assignment. If I'm stupid, that person must be stupider!" shouted Duane, pointing a shaky finger at the mayor as they reverted to a time-tested pattern of behavior that traced its origins to their early childhoods.

CHAPTER TWENTY

THE MORNING TRUMPET
PHENOM PLAYS FOR KEEPS

BY SLATER BROWN

San Francisco — Last night, at the Hibernian Hall, the city's finest chess player dispatched five worthy opponents in just under 40 minutes. That this victory was accomplished while playing simultaneous games was impressive. That the chess wizard was 23 years old was intriguing. That she was, in fact, a young female drove her competitors wild. In fact, after being defeated, almost all of her opponents complained of suffering from headaches, or stomachaches, or some other debilitating condition that had tragically diminished their abilities to concentrate.

"I don't have this toofache," said Herman Belcher, holding his jaw after the match, "sweetheart over there doesn't know what hit her." Mr. Belcher declined an offer to arrange a follow-up match. This reporter knows little about the ancient game of chess, but he looks greatly forward to learning more as he, and the City, follow the remarkable career of this astonishing talent.

Niebald crossed out "greatly" from the story and sent it to the copy desk for proofing. Before he left he turned to Slater.

"Let me give you a piece of advice."

"Shoot."

"When studying a woman, I find it wise to discount the shoes."

"Discount the shoes?"

"Yeah, see, shoes are an illusion. They're for promoting a quality — ambition, intelligence, sophistication — that may, or may not, be present. But you can't be sure. So the first rule when studying a woman is to discount the shoes."

"OK," said Slater, blinking slowly. Niebald was not in the habit of giving out advice, about shoes or anything else for that matter.

"Discount the shoes, but pay real close attention to the hair. Hair says everything about a woman: what she wants, what she

216

wants you to want, what she thinks about how she looks. If you pay careful attention to the hair, well, I don't think you can go wrong."

Slater considered this for a moment. The older reporter stood, his shirt half untucked from his large waistband, circles under his eyes. He'd worn the same trousers to work all week and his scuffed shoes begged for polish. Niebald felt Slater's eyes taking him in. He'd given more advice than planned. He felt a twinge in his diaphragm. Giving impromptu lectures to the paper's new star was not good for his digestion.

"Can I ask you something?" said Slater, looking over his shoulder. Motherlove and Maynard were in the far corner of the office, looking at a prototype of a future *Trumpet* that would include its first complete redesign and color photographs.

"Sure."

It was the first time they'd been completely alone for several months. Slater had been mulling something over in his mind for the past few weeks, ever since he'd found a shoe box full of his old yellow notebooks beneath his bed. Even as he'd pulled them from the box they'd seemed foreign in his hands, like long-ago presents from someone he could no longer remember. On the worn covers his handwriting cataloged unusual names he'd wanted to capture. He'd opened the first gently, the lined paper crackling in his hand. His eyes lit up as he scanned the pages, transported by his own handwriting to the time and place when they'd first been written. Ideas for characters, little snatches of dialogue he'd hoped to spin into complete stories, epigrams and epitaphs. One quote in particular had caught his eye:

"The problem is how to become what I wish I could, when I can't."
— James Agee

But even as one hand flipped through the notebooks, his other hand was busy pushing the shoe box back underneath the bed, pushing away the idea that he, Slater Brown, writer extraordinaire, was pursuing anything other than the one true path as provided by the overpowering light emanating from the Church of the Holy Pocket Radio. He stopped reading. Those old notebooks represented something he didn't particularly want to be confronted with. Or at least didn't want to be surprised by. But ever since his accidental discovery of them he couldn't shake the sense that, even though Maynard introduced him daily as the *Trum-*

pet's "big-picture guy," he had somehow gotten lost in the fog. He'd never felt lost before. He lowered his voice and leaned in a little toward Niebald.

"Do you think any of this will last?"

Niebald looked over at him with a raised eyebrow.

"What will last? Planet Earth, daylight savings . . . democracy?"

"No, no, I mean do you think any of this stuff I — we're writing for the paper. Do you think any of it will last?"

"Essh," said Niebald, dropping down into one of the fancy new orthopedic chairs that rolled around the office like bumper cars. "First off, nothing lasts. OK? And at the very bottom of nothing is what's written in a newspaper. Newspapers themselves might endure — this place has been around a hundred years plus — but the stories written inside them don't. See, news is just a catalog of what was important, what some poor schmuck thought was important at that time. But that doesn't last. This place, it's a magic lamp, passed from generation to generation. When you work for a newspaper, and let me tell you I've worked for a few, you get to be everywhere, get to see everything, but nothing we create ever lasts."

Niebald could see Slater was having

trouble understanding.

"But that's OK. We're not meant to write classics, we're meant to write news." He looked. "And the second thing is that nobody who ever tried to write something that lasted forever pulled it off. That's the main thing I want to tell you. It's impossible. Like trying to hit a cosmic hole-in-one."

Slater considered this carefully. Maybe what Niebald said was true, but on the other hand it seemed as if he were hitting cosmic holes-in-one on a weekly basis.

"Something like that just happens. You get out there, do what you're called to do, and let the rest fall where it may. Like falling in love," said Niebald, suddenly wistful. "You go with it."

"But surely you agree that writers have tried to create things that lasted."

"Kid," said Niebald, holding up two hands palms out, "you know a lot more about books than I ever will, but I'll bet you a month's salary that Shakespeare or Homer or any of those guys you think are such hot shit, none of 'em ever thought about lasting. And if they did they banished it from their minds because it's the kind of thing that drives even crappy writers bonkers."

He studied Slater Brown. He still wasn't

getting through.

"See, you don't *try* to do something that lasts, because then it just turns you into a self-conscious boob, twisting and turning, working so hard to figure out what might, or might not, survive that you let the true thing slip away right in front of you."

"The true thing?"

"The true thing is what you see, what's right in front of you, that doesn't need anything but for you to tell it, without you getting your mind thinking about how to make it last."

"Yeah?"

"Yeah."

Maybe, thought Niebald, maybe he *was* getting through.

"Look, everything's tits-up for you now, right? This is not the time to be worrying so much about what's going to last, what's going to survive. That's your pride talking. Just know this is your time, OK? To do with the best you can. Even the time we get isn't much to speak of. It's the strangest thing, but a man lives his life as if he's on unlimited time, and then one day he sees he's not. And it's almost as if the moment he realizes that time is limited, it begins to accelerate on him. It's the nastiest trick in the universe."

Poor Niebald, thought Slater, he really *was* getting older.

"I know a first-rate reporter like you," Niebald's voice couldn't help but dip into sarcasm, "can't help but notice in your wanderings around the city. There are some sad sacks out there, right? Some real wack jobs. Not everybody gets a shot. Some get a shot, they get scared, walk away. Some get a shot, they don't deserve it, but they get the shot anyway. Some deserve it, are ready for it, get up every morning waiting — they never get the shot. You . . . you got the shot, right? I've been in the newspaper business twenty-eight years and I've never seen anything like it. But you got the shot. Don't take it for granted is all. I know you hear an old man like me say 'Don't take it for granted' and your ears just about close over. But if you have an ounce of brains in your head, and I gotta believe you got about a quarter-ounce, then you should understand what I'm trying to tell you."

Slater was silent. Niebald mistook his pensiveness for dismay and opted for a condensed summary in the hopes that some of his wisdom would leach through Slater's consciousness later.

"Here's the deal, though. Nothing lasts. OK?"

He waited for Slater to nod before continuing.

"But this is your time."

"Time?"

"This is your time to get done whatever it is that's on your pea-brained mind!"

"But whatever I do, it won't last?"

"Exactly!" said Niebald, throwing up his hands with satisfaction.

In the next issue of the *Trumpet*, the complete story of Callio's chess match appeared on the front page above the fold in the "Goings On" column. The headline read "Phenom Plays for Keeps" in thirty-eight-point font.

Nowhere was it more carefully read than by the phenom herself. After her father brought it to show her Callio clipped out the story and taped it to the mirror in her boudoir, smiling to herself as she circled "city," "astonishing," and "Slater Brown."

CHAPTER
TWENTY-ONE

"Computers do exactly what they are told, and nothing more. They are limited only by time and memory. No computer ever asked to find the square root of pi decided to bake an apple pie instead."

Milo was ruminating again, alone in his laboratory. He was unusually agitated.

The humming noise from the red quantum computer was drowned out by six industrial fans he'd purchased to cool down the laboratory. They'd become a necessity, as the red computer ran hotter and hotter as it sifted day and night through the meteorological data Milo had downloaded on a T5 line from the National Weather Institute. One hundred terabytes of information. All the books in the Library of Congress added up to twenty terabytes, so this weather download was the last word when it came to a scientific understanding of how the heavens operated.

The computer was one of a kind, built with custom parts and a secret gate array that allowed cluster-node processing on what Milo liked to call "a very-high-order bit." Absent cables and monitor, the red computer weighed seven ounces and was the size of a matchbook.

It was capable of detecting and isolating patterns, any patterns, at a breathtaking rate. Feed it a map of U.S. population demographics and it could tell you within the hour who would vote Democrat or Republican, taking into account which hand they used to clip their toenails.

Tonight the red computer was feasting on billions of bytes of weather data, chugging through every meteorological factoid ever collected within the United States. Median earth temperature, greenhouse gas density, radiation spectrum, carbon dioxide levels, the diameter of the grapefruit-size hail that fell in Coffeyville, Kansas, in 1970, and the wild swings of the barometric pressure before and after Hurricane Heloise knocked down all the palm trees in Dade County in 1954. It was all there, a century's worth of weather data.

"Code!" yelped Milo as he scanned the numbers streaming past him on the computer screen. "Everything's just code! Even weather. Especially weather. Even a secret is just code for something hidden!"

As part of his thinking regime, Milo had gone back and read everything he could find pertaining to "the machinations of the heavens," as Sir Francis Bacon put it. He'd returned to Aristotle's *Meteorologica,* pausing to consume Isaac Newton's work on how heat moved within air and water, Anders Celsius's temperature treatises, and Nikola Tesla's ionic frequency papers. Not to mention Antoine Lavoisier, Evangelista Torricelli, Bernard Vonnegut, and several rare essays by Russian scientists on the topic of cloud seeding that had been buried in the basement of the Bodleian Library.

There was no publication about weather that Milo hadn't consumed, absorbed, and expanded upon until his mind, with its thousands of data points and circling hypotheses, zinging postulations and counterpostulations, became the neurological equivalent of a seven-day thunderstorm.

After several months developing his ideas with the help of the red computer, Milo had finally discovered how to reduce distinct weather events into pattern formulas. The breakthrough excited him more than anything he'd ever done before. Theoretically, he could reproduce independent, self-replicating, internally sustainable weather events as easily as he could make a dirty martini.

But even though he'd succeeded in accomplishing something wondrous — something previously thought mythical, *a feat none of Milo's historical peers had accomplished in the entire annals of recorded science* — not everything was coming together as planned. Which was why Milo was muttering in such concerned tones.

"Talk it out. Talk it out," he said before stopping and placing his right hand behind his back. He swiveled precisely on his heels and addressed the far wall as though it were a packed hall at Cooper Union.

"The universe is nothing but a gigantic formula, its equations strung out all over the place: in the air, in the trees, in the sunlight! My job, my responsibility," he shouted in tones that did not betray his flagging confidence, "is to chip off pieces of this galactic equation into little fragments so they can be replicated in the laboratory."

He looked with pride at his mobile creations. In one corner, hovering six feet above the floor, was a Key West rainsquall, while in the center of the room a New England hailstorm spat soft marbles of ice onto the floor. In the doorway, sulking, was a small patch of London fog created from scratch without benefit of any European weather data whatsoever. His main activity that morning had been checking and re-checking the windows and doors to make sure none of his weather packets slipped out into the wild. It had taken him ten minutes and the aid of an industrial-strength vacuum to keep the New England hailstorm from slipping outside via the furnace's intake duct. "I must remember to close the chimney flue," said Milo to himself.

But the first flush of inventor's pride was short-lived. There was still so much to do. So many new ideas about the weather arts were written in his notebooks, waiting to be tested. So many weather pattern formulas to reproduce.

"Hoarfrost, mud rain, supercell thunder-storms . . ."

His secretary, Alice, knocked lightly on the door, shuffling her feet as she approached to keep from slipping on the floor's wet surface. She carried an orange plastic lunch tray, a souvenir of the decade Milo had spent working as the chief weapons scientist at the Pentagon. On top was Milo's standard lunch, always the same: a Muenster cheese pumpernickel sandwich, a slice of banana bread buttered on one side, and a glass of apple juice served in a chipped teacup from his childhood.

"Here's your lunch, Milo," she said, looking for a place to put the tray down amid the mess of radiation monitors, barometers, aneroidographs, Geiger counters, Tic Tacs, spent batteries, and endless loops of electronic cords.

"Hmm?" came the reply as he worked out the divisible energy ratio of ball lightning in his head.

"Lunch, Milo," she repeated in an even, chipper tone. "And we need to talk about the backlog." She paused. "Milo, when can we talk about the backlog?"

The backlog was what the two of them called any piece of unfinished business, be it a phone call that needed to be returned, a pressing letter, a promise to deliver a speech, or any of the multiple board meetings Milo was required to attend in his elected position as world's most brilliant man.

"Can —" came the reply before a pair of unexpected integers flashing across the computer screen seized Milo's attention. Alice considered him for a moment. It was always a delicate dance, when to interrupt Milo with details from the external world and when to allow him his self-imposed isolation. The truth was he loved being alone, uninterrupted, unpressed upon. Technically, he was not antisocial, but she'd long ago learned his personality was not geared for the sorts of small talk the anchorman makes with the weather lady on the nightly news.

In addition to Milo's proclivity for solitude, Alice knew it was often several fortnights into these projects that his breakthrough thinking occurred. Early in her employment she'd had the unfortunate experience of insisting he take a call from the prime minister of India during a period when Milo was very close to figuring out how to build an optical calculator from frozen light. The call had gone several hours longer than expected and afterward Milo's concentration was shattered. He'd wandered around his laboratory for days, mumbling to himself like a master puppeteer who suddenly finds the strings to his marionettes hopelessly tangled.

"Can it . . . wait?" finished Alice, instinctively knowing what Milo had been about to ask. She narrowed her eyes and ballparked the things waiting for his attention: 340 phone messages, over 5,600 e-mails, two boxes of handwritten letters, 123 invitations to speak at conferences, countless solicitations for money, and two requests for pro bono services from Third World nations trying to develop their telecom systems from scratch.

"Yes," she said, gently closing the door behind her, careful to keep the Key West rainsquall from moistening her blouse. "Of course it can wait."

"Altocumulus *stratiformis,* cumulonimbus *incus,* cirrus *radiatus . . .*" Milo spoke each Latin cloud name with precision. He had created them all and more within the temperature confines of his weather chamber.

But still . . .

There was nothing more dangerous to a fully concentrating mind than failure. Failure, even the intimation of failure, instantly closed the gates of possibility and snatched new ideas from the precipice, where they were poised to make intuitive leaps above the abyss.

He pinched the bridge of his nose in an attempt to refocus his mind. In the center of the laboratory chamber a cumulonimbus with the first promising spike of a tornado tail was warily circling a miniature waterspout as if to pick a fight. The sight of his two creations intermingling only caused him more frustration. Failure flitted through his mind again like a delirious night bat.

"All well and good if I want to tour county fairs every summer as the crazy professor who can make the steam rain!" he shouted in despair. "But you can hardly alter the course of human history with these little buggers!"

Principally it was their size that bothered him. Or, more specifically, their lack of size. He'd envisioned great sheets of thunder that would descend upon enemy cities, wreaking havoc and knocking out phone lines before a military attack. Or a phalanx of snowstorms that could be sent out in advance of the Winter Olympics with the synchrony of a Swiss train. Talk about just-in-time delivery! Not to mention weather that could deluge a midwestern drought! It would be a *symphony* of weather: lightning, rain, and wind, creating an awe-inspiring music that would seize the world's attention.

But at the present moment he found that instead of creating a symphony, he was a soloist playing a kazoo. He'd tried everything. He'd changed the pattern formulas. He'd refined the ingredients, including using melted Tibetan snowpack flown in at great expense. He'd gone over his calculations again and again, but there was something limiting the size of the weather packets.

Was it ionic? Or atmospheric? Or was he up against a fundamental limit of reverse engineering?

Round the clock the red computer scouted for patterns within the meteorological data that would allow an even deeper understanding of his problem.

"Everything's a pattern," said Milo to the empty room. "Everything's . . ." His voice trailed away.

Yet if everything was a pattern, why couldn't the world's most brilliant man, aided by the world's most powerful computer, figure out mathematically, or scientifically, with pattern formulas, or higher calculus, or late-night REM-based intuition, how the hell to get the little buggers larger than a hula hoop?

"How," wondered Milo, as the red computer hummed obstinately along beside him, "can I check a computer's intuition?"

CHAPTER
TWENTY-TWO

The consumption was approaching Gil-gameshian proportions. Scandinavian meatballs, bison jerky, toasted coconut snowballs, Lobster Eugenia, terrapin soup, suckling pig, pails of Bolinas clams, soft-shelled Chesapeake Bay blue crabs, calf's-head stew, scaloppine, scungilli, fat squid fried with vinegar, Shuan Yang Rou, filet of beef Richelieu, chocolate truffles, cornmeal fried chicken, rack of lamb, ravioli, koshari, soufflé à la Rothschild, quails en croustade, and finally, for dessert, champagne and orange water jelly. The mayor of San Francisco consumed all of this and more over the course of just two weeks.

"It's official," said William Heck to the inner circle called together on short notice. "We've got ourselves in a real pickle."

"Shhhh!" hissed Duane Oswell. "Are you crazy?"

"What?" said William Heck, squinting.

"Easy on the food references, Holmes," said Duane, jerking a thumb toward the mayor's chambers and lowering his voice. "You said 'pickle.' "

Everyone nodded solemnly in agreement.

"First things first, we gotta get him out of here," said William Heck.

"To where?" asked Duane.

"I've made some calls. We're going to take him to the Mayo Clinic for psychological evaluation, blood work, and —"

"Whoa, whoa, whoa, Romeo," said Duane, raising his palms. "Back the fuck up. We're gonna send a guy's got trouble stuffing his face to a place called the Mayo Clinic? I mean, Christ sakes, why not just send him to the BLT Hospital while we're at it?"

William Heck waited until the nervous laughter died down before walking calmly over to Duane and punching him in the nose as hard and fast as a prizefighter accused of pederasty.

"Listen here, fucknut. I don't need a lot of interjection out of you right now. Just go get me a couple of horse tranquilizers so we can get the big man the health care he deserves. Be sure to get the same kind we slipped that fellow debated the mayor a couple of years ago. What was his name?"

"Senator Stevens," said one of the men.

"Right, you remember what I'm talking about?"

"I tink so," said Duane, holding his nose.

"Good. OK, fellas, let's put this plan into motion," said William Heck, extracting a pocket silk from his suit and handing it to Duane with a pat on the back.

In due course the horse tranquilizers were procured from a local racetrack veterinarian who owed Duane a favor. To get them to the City Hall kitchen during rush hour, Duane clamped the portable siren he carried in the glove box atop his 1976 Ford Gran Torino and swerved into the oncoming traffic pouring down Van Ness. Once safely delivered, the tranquilizers were stirred into a serving of Nesselrode pudding sent over on short order from the Ambassador Café. All the mayor had wanted to eat for the last two days was Nesselrode pudding. He'd even taken to calling someone "Nesselrode" if they did something that pleased him. But it had only taken one tentative taste from the end of the monogrammed sterling silver spoon before the tainted pudding was pushed away.

"Tastes . . . weird," he said, smacking his lips like a wary cat. "Bring me some of that double chocolate Bavarian brownie pie that's left over from last night. And put some crème fraiche on top."

Bix Butterfield hadn't been so difficult to engage. Shortly after the mayor had given his orders he'd been spotted coming out of a fancy dress party on Nob Hill and, after a spirited conversation with Duane Oswell and several of the mayor's men, was stuffed headfirst into an extra-large canvas duffel bag, thrown into the trunk of an official Town Car, and driven with police escort to the cargo dock at the airport, where he'd summarily been air-shipped to the New York Public Library, C.O.D.

The story of this expulsion, told expertly by Duane, put the Oswell brothers back in each other's good graces and even stopped the mayor's gluttony at City Hall for precisely seven hours and twenty-three minutes, which was how long it took before the mayor read Slater Brown's most recent story in the *Trumpet*.

There on the front page was an article suggesting that several of the mayor's biggest donors had met secretly in the back room of Mermaid Tavern to discuss how to bring impeachment proceedings against Tucker Oswell.

"That's it!" he shrieked. "Now it's personal. Now it's *fucking* personal. I tried to live and let live. I tried to let those pissants go around with their free press and their silly little rumors and innuendo. But this shit has got to stop," he said, scooping up the last honey-soaked square of baklava sitting on his desk. "The time has come to issue a punitive blow directly to the enemy," he screamed. "William Heck, get in here!"

For well over a hundred years City Hall had sent weekly advertising to the *The Morning Trumpet,* favoring its back pages with announcements of new zoning ordinances, bidding projects, or business contracts.

"Hit 'em where they live," said the mayor with a wink and a nod to William Heck as he delivered the order to cancel the long-standing advertising contract.

"Now we've got their attention. Next we cut the little fucker's ears off!" he shouted as he tucked into a steaming platter of spicy Shanghai dumplings recently delivered by bicycle messenger.

William Heck returned to the anteroom outside the mayor's office, where the staff waited out their boss's shouting like men outside a jail cell. He did not need to be reminded whose ears the mayor was talking about.

When Doris Lester, the *Trumpet's* circulation manager, caught wind of the cancellation order she was beside herself.

"Triple!" she told Maynard Reed in the hallway. "We can sell the new ad space for triple the price the city's been paying all these years!"

CHAPTER
TWENTY-THREE

The tides come upon San Francisco four times per day, lifting and lowering the city's skirt with impunity. On a low tide, red and purple and orange starfish cling to the waterfront's pilings like embedded gems. On high tide, the water laps the doorways of the lowest houses as a reminder that the city survives at the ocean's pleasure. Out on the Bay, chartered fishing boats weave as packs of seagulls follow them like chattering thread.

For their first date, Slater and Callio went to Fisherman's Wharf and rented a small rowboat from the Neptune Club. All manner of ill-dressed tourists swirled around as they stepped gingerly into the wooden rowboat, using each other for balance. Slater stowed the picnic basket he'd brought in the bow, and the tender made them sign a faded waiver before throwing two beat-to-hell orange life jackets into the bottom of the skiff and pushing them away from the dock with a practiced kick. Slater smiled broadly, his brown fedora tipped back on his head, as he leaned into each stroke with casual authority, hoping to impress with speed, not effort. The little boat jumped across the water as they made their way beyond the shelter of the piers.

He'd requested the date in writing, of course, writing on exotic rice paper, for which he'd paid an exorbitant sum for five sheets in Japantown. But he had followed up with a phone call. In fact, he'd followed up with a phone call so quickly Callio hadn't even had time to open her mail yet. But when Slater Brown's voice materialized on the other end of the phone she either recognized it, or had been expecting it. Either way she was not surprised. She had been tracking his arc through the city's firmament as keenly as anyone.

"I'll pick you up at your house," said Slater, trying to get off the phone before he said something stupid.

"Do you need the address?" asked Callio, sensing his urgency.

"No," said Slater.

Shit! Now she would think he was a stalker.

"Yes, yes, your address would be perfect."

■ ■ ■ ■

Out past the Golden Gate Bridge, the tip of
the fog's long finger showed itself for the
first time all day. Northward across the Bay,
the sun lit Raccoon Straits with bright yellow bands so that the whole waterscape
looked like the world's largest oil painting.
Between strokes Slater glanced at the map
he'd been given at the dock and occasion-
ally adjusted course. After narrowly missing
a tacking sailboat full of Australian extro-
verts — "G'day, wanker!" they hailed him
— and almost capsizing in the wake of a
Hong Kong container ship, he pulled the
little rowboat into the leeward cove of
Alcatraz Island, where the water was calm
and the beaches empty.

He brought the battered oars gently inside
the boat, careful not to let them drip on the
ankles of his passenger. Callio watched with
amusement. She wore a long black scarf
around her head and large sunglasses in the
manner of an old-time movie star at a world
premiere.

"This is . . . highly original," she said, folding her hands around her knees.

"Well, I could have taken you to dinner,
and we would have made all sorts of small

talk," he confessed, stopping to check her expression. "Or I could have taken you to a movie, but the problem with movies is you can't talk and we would have wasted all of our time not saying anything. So I decided to test out the old adage, 'If you want to get to know someone, spend some time alone with them in a boat.' "

As he spoke, his nervous hands made quick half-circles, trying to unravel a ball of invisible string. He still had trouble looking her in the eye for more than a moment.

"Who told you that?" she asked.

"This old lady I know," said Slater, smiling.

From the wicker picnic basket in the bow he retrieved cucumber sandwiches with watercress and French mustard, two packets of crushed potato chips, a pair of exquisite Templeton plums he'd paid two dollars apiece for at the Farmers' Market, and a petite magnum of French champagne. Callio waved off the champagne, saying she had a ranking chess match to play the next day, but Slater made such a show of how good it tasted by smacking his lips together and pronouncing it "Frounch" champagne that she held out her glass and took a few sips, which instantly flushed her pale cheeks and made her shy smile more fluent. For dessert he produced an assortment of Italian pastries from Generosa's.

As the boat spun in lazy circles, trapped in a gentle eddy, they were too busy studying one another between bites of food to notice the way the light tattooed their reflections onto the surface of the water. "So," said Slater, gathering up the waxed paper from their sandwiches, "tell me about chess."

"What do you know?" asked Callio.

He remembered his match against Mrs. Cagliostra.

"Nothing really. I take that back, almost nothing. I know you roll dice at the beginning to see who goes first."

She narrowed her eyes.

"That's backgammon," she said before realizing his jest.

"How did you beat those men last week?" said Slater, unwrapping two biscotti and popping them into his mouth.

"It was easy."

"But how?"

"They were no match for me."

"But I read their biographies — they weren't world champions, but they were strong players. Respectable opponents."

"Humppff," she said, looking away and shrugging her shoulders. She'd picked that

244

up from her father; he used it whenever he heard something he could not be bothered with.

"They were not strong. They were memorizers."

"What's wrong with that?"

"There are two types of chess players in the world: the intuitive chess players, who use a library of learned moves plus a deeper instinct, and the memorizers, who obsessively read about past games with the intention of remembering a string of moves that will outlast their opponents' ability to produce a string of countermoves."

"And your opponents?"

"Memorizers. One and all."

"And you?"

"Let's just say my intuition has never failed me," she said, staring at him. He avoided her gaze by squinting, as if the sun were suddenly in his eyes.

"How do you beat a memorizer?"

"Simple. You just have to outlast him. Play long enough without suffering too many casualties, until he's run out of memorized moves and is on unfamiliar ground."

She paused to make sure he was following. "Then you crush him."

He glanced at her. Part of her beauty was simply poise. Every gesture was well constructed, like that of a stalking heron. Even the selection of which potato chip to eat was done with just the right degree of selectivity. But it wasn't the poise or the beauty that shook him most. It was the eyes. Or rather what was behind them, suggesting knowledge that dwarfed his own understanding. Not just about chess. But everything. They were the eyes of a much older woman, and in them he saw an answer to a question he was not yet capable of asking.

Few men can stare into the eyes of a beautiful woman for long without being compelled to speak, for they mistakenly think that by speaking they will prolong the spell. Fewer still can remain silent if the young woman herself does not, almost willfully, break the silence. But Callio drew silence around her the way a soloist is enveloped in a cloak of music. Her long sojourns into the intricacies of chess, and its interior movements, had taught her that silence will reveal all things: all insecurities, all flaws and hidden cracks, all necessities of human nature. They looked at each other this way until Slater could stand it no longer.

"What time is it?" he asked, though he knew she did not know the answer and he couldn't have been less interested anyway.

She shielded her eyes to look at the sun and pronounced it somewhere close to two o'clock. The silence was broken.

After they'd finished lunch Slater lowered the oars into the water and swung them out from behind the shelter of the island, pointing the rowboat toward the city. It took him thirty seconds of rowing to realize something had gone terribly wrong. The tides had shifted and what had been a gentle tug of water moving inward from the Pacific was now a sizzling rip moving outward. He looked across the flat surface of the Bay at the city's shoreline. It was so close you could hear the clang of the trolley bell on Hyde Street, yet there was no chance of making it across now. He looked as casually as possible toward the Golden Gate Bridge. It was not as far away as he'd hoped. After they'd been swept underneath it the boat's next stop would be where — Russia?

Callio trailed her hand in the water, looking over his shoulder. The city hovered behind her like a white cake sparkling in the sun. Off to the left the fog was sneaking in from out in the Pacific and was swallowing up the Golden Gate Bridge. Slater nonchalantly swung the boat back around, digging the oars into the racing water, and returned to the island's protected cove.

"The current is fierce, no?" said Callio.

"Hmm?" mumbled Slater as if he hadn't quite heard her.

"What should we do?" she asked, checking a smile before it spread.

"Let me get situated," said Slater as purposefully as possible. "And then I'll row us back to shore."

By situated he meant taking off his jacket, rolling up his shirtsleeves, and cracking his knuckles in a professional way before sitting down to thrash the Pacific into a white froth.

"I would prefer not to," she said just as he sat down to begin.

He looked at her and then dropped the oars with a clunk. Was she quoting Melville to him? Oh sweet Jesus, was she quoting Melville to him? The water lapped up against the boat like laughter.

"OK," he said.

"I would prefer to talk instead."

It takes six hours for the tides of San Francisco Bay to switch from ebb to flood. Six hours is a long time at a family reunion, or flying in an unpressurized cockpit, or standing in line at a blood bank. But six hours in an eight-foot rowboat with a young woman who has the limitless capacity to cause you to forget to draw breath is considerably less time.

While in the boat Slater Brown did something totally out of character. Perhaps the tight quarters were to blame. Or perhaps it was a mild case of heatstroke. But little by little he found himself revealing to her things he'd shared with no one. He did it all in ecstatic language that burst out of him without calculation and was often in sentence fragments two thoughts ahead of what he was thinking, as happened when he asked what she was doing for dinner.

"But I'm in a boat with you," she reminded him.

He should have been embarrassed, but he was off again. He told her stories of his great adventures in the city. Of things he'd heard and written, of people he'd met, and how he'd learned to read people by the way they walked. Callio was quiet as she listened. She marveled at how his mind worked, the darting eyes and the quick attention that moved like a delirious lightning bug. She'd never known anyone so perceptive in such an original way. She studied him the way she studied a chessboard, but her eyes were soft and when she saw an opening, she did not take it.

"Tell me, Slater Brown," she asked when he finally paused, for she sensed the depth of his ambition, "where are you on the shelf?"

"Shelf?"

"Yes, where will your name be on the library shelf? What company will you keep?"

He flushed. "That's a good question."

"Where is it?"

"I'm not sure."

"Come on, where are you in the great pantheon of literature?"

She was teasing him. He was almost certain she was teasing him.

"I have no idea."

"I don't believe you."

"I don't know."

"I still don't believe you."

He looked into the distant fog for a moment, wondering if he could change the topic.

"Below Balzac and above Chekhov," he said finally in a low voice.

"Wonderful! That is very good company for you. A Frenchman and a Russian."

He looked to confirm that she was teasing him and when he saw that she was not, a tremendous pressure found its release from deep within his chest, like a buoy cut far beneath the surface. It was the pressure of keeping your secrets secret. Once it was out there in front of her, his heart roared. He could finally talk! To her! This was real!

Little by little Slater was aware of something new. For the first time in his life he had the feeling that finally and forever everything was going to be all right. The effect this had on him was instantaneous. His breathing smoothed. He stopped picking at the ragged nail on his left thumb. The mysterious tightness in his stomach vanished.

The fog moved in, shrouding the boat in a milky haze and revealing only two silhouettes. Even the lineup of tourists scanning the Bay with silver-faced binoculars at Ghirardelli Square could not see them. Three hours into the conversation they grabbed the side of the boat for stability and moved toward the center where their shadows touched once, lightly, and then a second time more intently. Slater noticed that her lips tasted of honey and almond and wondered how she did that. He'd already forgotten the biscotti they'd eaten for dessert.

Beneath them the boat seemed to levitate. Every few minutes as they kissed Slater slapped the oars on the water just to confirm they were still of this world.

As the temperature dropped and the fog

overtook them completely, he bundled her up in his jacket. She told him in quiet tones about chess and what she dreamed for herself. "I want to play chess at the highest level of my ability for as long as I possibly can," she said. She even told him about a new opening she was developing. Not one bit of it made sense to Slater as he lay there, head in her lap, but he remained very quiet as he listened so as to assure her he was paying attention.

They might have floated away that afternoon to another world. It's been known to happen. All the elements were in place. Inside the eight-foot rowboat the universe was perfectly balanced. It was only a sound — always a sound — that reached out to the celestial rowboat, returning it to the world of time and tides.

"Did you hear that?" asked Slater, cocking his head in the fog as the current shifted again beneath them.

"The foghorn?"

"Yes, but closer, listen closer."

Past the surfers at Fort Point, past the clam diggers at Baker Beach, the Mile Rock foghorn sounded off like a belligerent, exuberant opera star.

"Hue-mannnnnnn."

"Huuuuuueeeeee-mannnnnnnnn."

"Huuuuuuuuuuueeeeeeeeemmmmmmaa-
aaaaaaannnnn."

CHAPTER
TWENTY-FOUR

The mayor's office was starting to smell like the rooted-out cave of a hibernating bear two weeks past spring thaw. It was now official custom for people entering the offices to hold their mouths in little o's in order to avoid breathing through their noses.

The honorable Mayor Oswell was always in the same position, propped up in his stuffed leather chair with a half-dozen decorative pillows jammed like cotton balls along the sides. Rumor had it that he slept in the chair because it was too much strain on his knees to leave the office each night.

William Heck stalked the office with a pinched expression, and it wasn't simply the smell. He had one too many problems and not enough time to solve them. The mayor had gained a gastronomical amount of weight since he'd started gorging himself and there was growing concern he might slip into a diabetic coma. Doc Little, Oswell's family doctor, had visited earlier in the day, stepping past the line of delivery boys before closing the door for privacy. Afterward he'd pulled William Heck aside.

"How long's this been going on?"

"About six months."

"Well, I can't diagnose it as binge eating because that suggests it comes and goes. Does it come and go?"

"No, mainly it just comes."

"That's what I was afraid of."

"What's the prognosis?"

"Well, you gotta stop him somehow."

"Harder than it looks."

"I can see that," said the doctor as a tray of piping hot hand-rolled Dutch crullers with powdered cinnamon and melted French butter passed them.

"My guess is something's happened to trigger a deep reaction in his psyche. He feels vulnerable. He feels unprotected. At some elemental level he's decided he needs protection."

"Like a suit of armor?" said William Heck.

"Exactly."

"We could have something made."

"No, no. Psychological armor. You can't buy him protection. He's decided to protect himself."

"How?"

"How do you think?"

"Well, if he needs protection he's always got Duane and me."

"No, see, he's protecting himself by *eating*," said Doc Little slowly.

"Oh," said William Heck. For a moment, his biggest problem had been on the verge of being solved by an open-minded welder with a chain-mail template.

"Any idea what's behind it all?" said the doctor.

"Just a few," said William Heck.

"Well, you better figure out how to get to the bottom of it. He keeps eating like this, his heart's gonna explode."

"How long we talking about here, Doc?"

"I don't do hypotheticals, but I don't think you've got another —" Just then a steaming platter of special-delivery meatball marinara from Mama Luigi's Italian Kitchen passed them on a cart. "— another six weeks to play around with."

"What do you suggest we do in the meantime?"

"How does he feel about salads?" asked the doctor as he put on his jacket.

CHAPTER
TWENTY-FIVE

In the days and weeks after the rowboat, Slater and Callio spent as much time together as possible. This was both easier and harder to do with a blind father trending toward monomanical thoughts about female world championships. Easier, because sometimes out of sight really was out of mind, but harder because of the strict training regime that Havram enforced. But no matter how rigorous Callio's schedule, she and Slater managed to meet every day at four P.M. for a walk in the Presidio, or for stolen kisses beneath the eucalyptus trees in the Japanese Tea Garden, or they would meet at their favorite spot, the Conservatory of Flowers, a fantastical folly made of white glass that sat like a Victorian spaceship in the middle of the city. In a side room there they watched a flock of Amazonian butterflies flit above a grove of wild orchids.

On Friday nights, with Havram's permission, they went out on the town. Private dinners, charity events, box seats at the ball game. At the Hummingbird Ball, lunch with Slater was listed in the silent auction at five thousand dollars and the city's favorite couple was seated prominently next to the stage. Each table had a custom ice sculpture of a Bay Area motif by the famed artist Franz Schwanz. The sculpture on their table was of fog, which they made sure to have their photographs taken with while wearing wry smiles.

Across the way Slater spotted Brooke van der Snoot among a group of women clustered around a ten-foot-tall forty-gallon chocolate fountain shaped like the Coit Tower. She had just returned from yet another island vacation, her skin a deep brown and her hair the color of corn silk. When she looked up she caught his gaze, which she acknowledged for a microsecond, before making an effort to snub him by spearing a strawberry with a fondue fork and dunking it in a cascade of melted chocolate.

Callio and Slater lasted thirty minutes into the gala, speaking to the people who stopped by their table, including Callio's many chess admirers — she was the subject of a class at Berkeley that semester studying feminine power and board games — and Judge O'Sullivan, who stopped to shake Slater's hand but whose real interest seemed to be in learning when Slater was next going on vacation.

"You can use my lake house in Tahoe," he said with something approximating a smile. "Stay the entire autumn if you like." Slater nodded and demurred until Callio pulled him away.

By the time the houselights dimmed and Gloria van der Snoot began the silent auction, they were both slightly twitchy. Callio kicked Slater under the table.

"How good a secret agent are you?" she asked, her black eyes flickering with mischievous intent.

"Pretty good," said Slater, speaking into his cuff links.

"OK, test number one. What's the fastest way out of here?"

"Follow me," said Slater without missing a trick as he slid out of his chair and underneath the cover of the linen tablecloth. He waited for her before they carefully crawled past their dinner companions' legs toward the apron of the stage. While underneath the platform Callio grabbed him by the ankle, pulled him toward her, and kissed him hard on the lips. When Slater attempted to draw her closer she wiggled away. "Just as I suspected," she said, giggling as she crawled rapidly toward the stage door, "you just failed test number two: Never get distracted during an escape."

It was a crisp night. They paused to look up in the sky where the moon rested calmly, slightly fuzzy at its edges, as if it had been rolled in very fine baker's flour. "I love this place," said Slater, almost to himself, as he surveyed the way the streets looked in the moonlight. "Like a sister and a mother and a beautiful girl all wrapped into one, I love her."

Callio looked over in surprise, then kissed him again. The way his mind worked never failed to delight her.

"Where should we go?" she asked, burying her nose in the nape of his neck.

"Hmm," said Slater, snapping out of his reverie.

"No stalling," said Callio, "you know this city, and apparently love this city, far better than anyone. Take me to your secret spots and tell me everything about this woman you love so much before I get jealous."

Twenty minutes later they were in the corner booth at TK's.

"Can we get two rum punches over here?" said Slater to Whilton's overall astonishment. Not only was Callio the most beautiful woman ever to grace TK's Bar & Simmer, she was just about the only woman anyone could ever remember *being* in TK's.

They drank their overpoured drinks, then ordered another round. She was wearing an English driving cap and a black scarf wrapped around her neck. Slater thought she looked like royalty trying to keep a low profile.

"Tell me something, dear one," she said, leaning toward him.

"Like what? What's your pleasure?" said Slater as they collapsed into laughter onto each other's shoulders. Everything was funny now. Whilton looked over from the bar in disgust.

"I don't know, tell me something I don't know." This too received a gale of laughter.

"Well," said Slater, rolling his eyes back up in his head, searching for something. "I'm the luckiest man in the world." She nodded. "And I have the luckiest job in the world." She nodded again. "And I've learned more about human nature since I started working at the *Trumpet* than I've ever known in my entire life." She was watching him closely now. "And," he said, pausing for effect, "if I'm not mistaken, I think most days of the week I'm being tailed."

"What?" Callio frowned. "Are you kidding?"

"I kid you not," he said with a small burp.

"By who?"

"By whom?" he said, laughing and pulling her close.

But Callio was not laughing. "OK, joker, who is tailing you?"

"I'm not sure; it might be a mistake. But every day when I get on the bus I just have this creepy feel—"

"Bus?" she said, interrupting him. "Why do you get on the bus? You live eight blocks from your office. You take the bus to work?"

He looked at her carefully. In the background was the overexcited commentary of a televised cricket match. It wasn't the booze that had loosened his tongue, he told himself, it was the feeling that shot up between them. It was a feeling that courted secrets because it too was a secret. Something that no one else knew, or if they knew, they only knew a tiny bit of it. He knew something of secrets. He'd kept his own, and those of the city, for a long time now. On more than one occasion he'd been tempted to tell Motherlove and Niebald (and even once, Mrs. Cagliostra) what had happened to him, but each time he rationalized that there was enough uncertainty in his life; why add to it? Who could know what their reaction might be? It was better, safer, not to tell. But this was different. He trusted her. Of course he could. He cleared his throat.

"I have something to tell you," he said, waving over two ice waters from the bar.

And he did. He told her about the pocket radio, and the bus, and the judge's bet, and what it was like to be the funnel through which the entire city flowed. It poured out of him — all of it — in a way that revealed the toll that secrets take on psyches. She listened to him patiently, carefully. When he was finished, the cricket match was over and Whilton was asleep at the bar, one hand wrapped protectively around the cash register. Callio took Slater's hands in hers and looked at him with her dark, wise eyes.

"Slater Brown."

"Yes."

"You should stop this."

What was false inside of him rubbed up against what was true.

"What are you talking about? Stop what? Stop writing?"

"No, not stop writing. *Start* writing." Her face flushed. She could see the stubborn dimple in the middle of his forehead growing deeper. He moved away from her.

"How is transcribing what you hear real writing?" she said, pressing on. "You're the city's stenographer, a court reporter at best. How is that really writing?"

"Court reporter!" he yelped, standing up. "You tell me what court reporter gets invited to fancy balls, gets asked to lead the Chinese New Year's Parade, gets treated like royalty?" His face had flushed too, a deep crimson. "I'm, I'm a big deal now!" he said. Callio did not answer, nor did she flinch from his gaze as he delivered a five-minute lecture on the subject of writing before segueing into a very comprehensive list of all the writers who had found their footing at a newspaper before going on to bigger things. "I suppose you would tell Dickens he's a court reporter too!" he shot back, laughing darkly to himself.

She looked into his ricocheting eyes. "That's not what I meant," she said. In her gaze he was faced with the reflection of his own behavior, and having nowhere to go with it, he started to lecture her again. She waited two minutes before holding up her hands in truce. "I just want to tell you one thing."

"What?" he said crossly. He had already ripped up their cocktail napkins into nervous ribbons and was presently tying tight knots in the stem of a maraschino cherry.

"What attracts me to you is not what you hear on a bus, or how badly people want to shake your hand, or the prospect that someday there may be a Slater Brown Avenue in this fair city, or any of the other things that give you pleasure. I'm interested in everything else. Don't you see that?" He waited. She looked at him, trying to engage him below the surface where he currently dwelled. She could see how hurt and confused he was. And she could see — with feminine clarity — that a full explication would have to wait for another day.

"Whenever you decide to write, I'm sure it will be wonderful."

Slater Brown, man-about-town, looked at her. With masculine clarity he sensed the conversation had more depth to it, but they were coming up against Callio's midnight curfew and Havram accepted no excuses for being late.

CHAPTER
TWENTY-SIX

"Motherlove, Niebald. Get in here!"

"Yes, boss."

"Look!"

"What the hell is it?"

"Move over a little, I can't see."

"I don't know."

"Get a picture of it."

"It's an umbrella."

"Where's the camera?"

"Umbrella? What the hell kind of umbrella is that?"

"One of those clear ones so you can see what kind of day it's going to be."

"Since when does an umbrella float forty feet above the ground?"

"It ain't an umbrella. It's a —"

"Battery's dead."

"In what?"

"In the camera."

"I got it. It's a rice maker."

"A floating rice maker! What will those

Chinese think of next?"

"That ain't rice, you bonehead," said Niebald, squinting as he studied the apparition. "That's snow."

The newly discovered snowstorm hovered, like an orphaned jellyfish, in front of Maynard's window.

"Wow."

"What should we do?"

"About what?"

"About the snow!"

"There's not enough to shovel."

The three men fell silent as the strangeness drifted in front of them.

"This has front page written all over it. We gotta get out in front of this before the *Sun*s get ahold of it."

The three men looked at one another. "I'll get him," said Motherlove, trotting off to summon Slater from his office.

"Kid," said Maynard, pointing out the window as the snowstorm quietly proceeded with its business. "You see that? That's a snowstorm. You see this?" he said, pointing to a calendar on the wall. "That says August. You have any idea what it's doing snowing in August?"

"That's not the point, Maynard," said Niebald, trying to remain calm. "The point is what the hell's it doing snowing in San

267

Francisco, period."

"That too," said Maynard.

"Think you can help us out with this?" asked Motherlove.

Slater stared at the strangeness on the other side of the window as it began to produce perfectly formed snowflakes not five feet away. He'd never seen anything like it.

"Help you with what?"

"C'mon, you gotta be kidding me," said Niebald. "Use the old Slater Brown touch to find out what's going on."

Slater put on his poker face and shrugged.

"Maybe it's some secret government experiment," said Motherlove.

"This has aliens written all *over* it," said Maynard.

"Or El Niño's revenge!"

Motherlove and Maynard shared a laugh.

"Wait a second, hold on. I know that look fifty miles away. What're you thinking, Niebald?" asked Motherlove.

"I'll give you a leg up, kid. The guy to start with is Milo Magnet."

"Good idea," said Motherlove. "Remember that time we saw him speak? He's the smartest man in San Francisco. Kinda guy who messes around with stuff no one can explain. You must have come across him out in the city."

Not only had Slater not come across Milo Magnet, he'd never even heard the name.

"Not that I recall. Who is he?"

"He's this genius-type guy."

"Dabbles in esoteric stuff."

"Black magic," Motherlove said with a laugh.

"You should check him out. He's not the smartest man in the city, he's the smartest man in the world," said Maynard.

"I thought you held that title," said Niebald. Motherlove raised his hands between his two colleagues. They'd been sniping at each other more than usual lately over what new initiatives were worthy of the *Trumpet's* new cash reserves. "Milo Magnet would be a good starting point for you. See if he knows anything about this weather stuff."

"If not, dimes-to-doughnuts he knows who does," said Niebald, rubbing his neck.

"OK," said Slater, nodding. "Where can I find him?"

The three men looked at each other as if they were having their legs pulled.

"Find him?" said Motherlove, momentarily baffled. "Just use your contacts."

In the end it was not that difficult to find Milo Magnet. Slater asked Alistair, the

Trumpet's librarian, to look up Milo's address in the official unlisted-address phone book. Every newspaper, bail bondsman, and bookie in San Francisco paid an annual subscription fee in order to have an updated copy hand-delivered by bicycle messenger every ninety days.

Slater had taken the number 11 bus out to Twin Peaks, listening carefully along the way for stories on his pocket radio. For the first time, only low-level static filled his ears.

Milo Magnet lived on the edge of the edge of the city, and thus on the edge of the continent, in a house of modern architectural design composed of interlinking gray concrete blocks. On the exterior, intermittent patches of brown ivy grew over a sign that told of the building's former owners: St. John's Episcopal Church. The heavy gates at the end of the long driveway were ajar, and after confirming the owner of the house by flipping through the mail in the mailbox Slater passed through and walked to the front door.

If Alice had answered the door she would have dispatched Slater Brown right away, but she was running errands, which included picking up Milo's laundry from the dry cleaners', mailing some packages, and purchasing six ounces of silver iodide in

Chinatown for a massive thunderstorm experiment Milo hoped to initiate later that evening.

It was by chance, then, that Milo, having left the confines of his laboratory in the back of the house, where he could not hear the front doorbell, was in the kitchen heating up a cup of hot chocolate when he heard the rap on the door. He looked through the peephole, but it was fogged over from all the temperature vacillations going on inside the house. Cracking open the door to see who it was, Milo realized this was the first time he'd spoken to anyone other than Alice in over six months. He pulled a palm-size device from his pocket and held it to his larynx. He'd developed it years ago for the FBI. Using dual synthesizers it could instantly transform any voice into any other presampled voice. In this case he had selected Alice's.

"He-llo," said Milo in Alice's voice, squinting into the sunlight. Behind the crack in the door Slater Brown could see only darkness.

"Hello, I'm looking for the inventor Milo Magnet."

Oh, dear, thought Milo, the kid looked to be yet another MIT undergrad who'd impulsively dropped out of school and driven cross-country to share with Milo his solution to Fermat's Last Theorem, or the Sinnerton-Dyer Conjecture, or some other centuries-old unsolved math problem in the hopes of entering the genius pantheon ASAP. How many times had he been forced to explain the students' errors before sending them back to school with promises of staying in touch? The first couple of times he had even paid for their return plane tickets, but after the seventh or eighth time it had become just plain annoying.

"He's not here," said Milo wearily.

"When do you expect him back?"

"Can't be sure. One never knows. Who's asking?"

"Slater Brown." It was at times like this when Slater was especially glad for his notoriety.

The door closed several inches. "Slater Brown," he said, "from *The Morning Trumpet.*"

The door closed further, leaving barely enough room for a sheet of paper to pass.

"Please tell him I'm interested in talking about a story."

"He's not available for media inquiries right now," said Milo, his synthesized voice sounding suspiciously like a female Stephen Hawking. "Please call ahead next time and shut the gate behind you," said Milo, smiling as he closed the door. That had been kind of fun.

"Tell him I'm here about the weather," said the voice on the other side of the door.

By the time Alice returned from her errands Slater Brown and Milo Magnet had made each other's acquaintance and were sitting in a pair of faded canvas beach chairs in the laboratory talking like old friends.

During their conversation Slater couldn't help but sneak glances at his surroundings. The laboratory was a mess, the desk cluttered with research books and doughnut boxes and stained with brown double-helix rings from cappuccino cups. Milo wore gray stubble on his chin and had the gaunt look of a man ten pounds shy of his natural weight. Around his neck was a brass medallion with the words "Cryogenius Inc." etched into it.

"What's the medal for?" asked Slater.

"Ah, yes, this is a very interesting company that freezes people after they — what's the proper euphemism? — kick the bucket. The idea is to keep you frozen until advances in reanimation technology are developed."

"Sounds . . . expensive," ventured Slater.

"I don't know. I'm not paying for it. They

are only freezing geniuses at the moment. Very clever, isn't it? Like a long-term advertisement. Anyway, I didn't sign up for the full-body freeze, which would allow me to be reanimated in toto, but rather for the cranial freeze, which means they freeze just my head."

"But why?"

"Why? Connections, my dear boy. Connections!" said Milo, patting the thatch of silver-blond hair on his head. "I'm not particularly interested in being reanimated at some future point in human history. Can you imagine the trouble people in the future will have caused for themselves?" He shuddered. "But I do think my ideas, *my connections,* might be valuable, even invaluable, and so I donate my brain not to science exactly, but to the future."

Slater thought about this for a moment.

"And if I'm not mistaken, when you say reanimate you mean . . ." He drifted off.

"Ahhhhh," said Milo, settling into his chair. This young man did not speak science as a first language. His initial fears had all but dissipated. The secrets of his laboratory were safe, and consequently he was growing more enthusiastic about the young reporter with each passing moment.

■ ■ ■ ■

All current weather events in the laboratory, including a beta-fogbow and a new batch of Montana hail, were in the midst of natural dissipation by the time Slater first knocked on the door. The only weather still operating in the chamber was a Shanghai blossom shower, which Milo had shooed into the closet, where it thumped meekly before draining out the crack at the bottom of the door. "Just a leaky radiator," said Milo, waving it away when Slater glanced in that direction. Milo locked his eyes onto Slater's, indicating that the young reporter had his full attention.

"Mr. Brown. What beat do you usually cover for the newspaper?"

"Oh," said Slater, stretching, "I'm a bit of a generalist myself."

"Really? How delightful. I fancy myself a bit of a generalist too," said Milo. "What story are you most proud of writing for the august *Morning Trumpet*?"

"Well, let's see, that's a hard one. There's always the first story I did, about the voting scandal."

Milo's face betrayed no sign of recognition. Slater waited with his head cocked to one side until it was clear Milo would have to say something.

"I must have been out of town," he said finally.

"Then there was the story about the blind bank robber."

"Right," said Milo absently, as his thoughts wandered back to the beta-fogbow.

"I guess my absolute favorite is when I wrote about the chess match. I don't know if you know this or not, but San Francisco's in possession of a bona fide genius."

"Really?" said Milo, perking up. Like most geniuses, nothing annoyed him more than news of company. "I'm all ears."

"The finest chess player in the country, if not the world, lives here."

"Ah, and what is this fellow's name?"

"That's just it," said Slater, rapping the arm of his chair with his knuckles. "It's not a man. It's a woman. Ms. Callio de Quincy."

Just saying her name aloud produced a familiar buzz across the top of his head.

"Interesting, and what makes her such a talented chess player?"

"Well, she's undefeated. Perfect record. Plus she has a first-class mind. Total recall. She can see six, seven moves ahead of her opponent, and she has this incredible intuition, this, this ability to understand what's going to happen before it happens. She sees patterns others don't. It's quite amazing. Do you play chess, Mr. Magnet?"

Milo nodded noncommittally.

"See, understanding patterns is the secret to winning chess."

"I see," said Milo Magnet, concealing his amusement at being on the receiving end of a lecture on the value of patterns. "You sound like a true admirer of her talents, Mr. Brown."

"Oh, no," Slater waved with false bravado, "just a reporter's native curiosity at work, sir."

"Well, I can only imagine a busy reporter like you, working for one of the city's finest newspapers, doesn't have time to waste on an old fuddy-duddy like me. What can I assist you with?"

Slater straightened in his chair and pulled out his notebook. Technically this would be his first in-person interview.

"I was told you were the man to see when something needed to be explained."

"Please explain," said Milo, smiling.

"Yesterday we saw something, looked like a kind of toy —"

"Yes?" said Milo. "I like toys. What kind of toy was it, Mr. Brown?"

"A toy snowstorm, I guess. I know it

sounds far-fetched. But there it was, spinning around like a plate on the end of a stick in downtown San Francisco."

"Stick?" said Milo. "What kind of stick?"

"No, see, there wasn't a stick. The cloud, whatever, it was forty or fifty feet off the ground. An honest-to-goodness snowstorm in August."

Milo put his fingers together to signal the onset of maximum concentration.

"Tell me more. How big was this snowstorm?"

"Well, hard to say, but I don't think it was any bigger than a card table. That was what made it so strange. You have a beautiful day, not a cloud in the sky, and then along comes this little snowstorm, just minding its own business." He studied Milo's face.

"What do you make of it?"

Milo stared back at him unblinkingly.

"I mean, I can't say for sure what it was. Maybe the description is slightly off. Some of the other fellas thought it might be a floating rice maker, but I didn't see it that way —"

"Others?" said Milo finally. "What others saw this snowstorm?"

"The fellas at the paper. Niebald, Motherlove, Maynard. They run the place."

"I see, the four of you witnessed this

strange display, and then you," said Milo, fixing a knowing eye on Slater, "were dispatched to get to the bottom of it."

"Something like that."

"Well," said Milo after a deliberate pause, "you're in luck." He glanced over at the closed closet door. "I can help with this weather story you're working on. In fact, I can think of several people to contact who would most certainly have firsthand knowledge of something like this. Bernard over at Livermore Labs would be a good place to start, and then there's always Hawkins down at DARPA. In fact, this is just the sort of stunt he would delight in playing . . . Anyway, the bottom line is yes, I can help."

Slater Brown was stunned. How hard had that been? The gates to success did not simply swing in the breeze for him, they appeared to have been taken off their hinges and put aside so he could drive past in a chauffeured limousine.

"Thank you, Mr. Magnet, I don't —"

"Please, it's Milo. And don't mention it. Happy to help, happy to help. I would, however, like to ask one favor."

"Anything, of course," said Slater.

"I've been thinking of arranging a little test for one of my malfunctioning prototypes. Ideally this test would allow me to study the computer's intuition in an algorithmic environment." He watched Slater's face for comprehension. "Let's just say it would allow me to iron out some software wrinkles."

"That sounds interesting," said Slater Brown.

"It occurs to me that you could help me with this."

"Me?" said Slater. "I'd be happy to help — what kind of test?"

"I was thinking of something that would allow my computer to show how it makes decisions in an open environment. One which cannot be manipulated by me."

"I don't see what I can —" said Slater.

"Something that will allow my computer to be surprised and reveal how it . . . thinks."

"But I —"

"An exhibition match, Mr. Brown! Between this malfunctioning computer of mine and your friend."

"Huh?"

"A chess match, Mr. Brown, between my box of rocks and your friend who so brilliantly plays the game of chess. I believe her name is Ms. de Quincy."

Slater considered this for a moment. He couldn't see why Callio would object to such an offer. "Sure, I should think she'd be happy to straighten out your computer for you."

"Excellent. My computer's very good, but a match against your friend would be the perfect way to test the computer's architecture. Especially if her intuition is all it's cracked up to be. Plus it will garner excellent exposure for her. Put her on the map, so to speak," he said. "Think of it as a win-win-win."

"Deal," said Slater, with the faraway eyes of a fight manager who senses a first-round knockout.

"Good, this would be of great help to me. And of course I will be only too happy to help you with your weather story. I'm assuming you'd like to keep this an exclusive?"

"Absolutely," said Slater, unnerved that he hadn't thought of that himself. "Yes, of course. An exclusive would be perfect."

CHAPTER
TWENTY-SEVEN

In the weeks leading up to the chess match all manner of details had to be arranged, starting with who would organize, publicize, and pay for the competition. One by one the pieces fell into place like a jigsaw puzzle.

Once the *Trumpet* and then the two *Suns* wrote about the "chess challenge," as they were calling it, backers came forward with checkbooks in hand. But each and every one of these potential backers was politely turned away until it became public knowledge that Gloria van der Snoot herself had underwritten the entire match, including a fifty-thousand-dollar grand prize to the winner. "I've always loved chess," she told a reporter from the *San Francisco Sun.* "The back-and-forth part reminds me of my first three marriages."

In truth she was more than a little bored with the standard social scene, and its endless repetition of fancy balls interspersed by gala fund-raisers seemed more wearisome than usual this season. It was time for something different to enliven her spirits before she took her annual trip to Greece.

Gloria van der Snoot's first order of business was to move the match from where it was originally intended to take place, the gymnasium at Galileo High School, to the most grand and central location she could manage on short notice: the Rotunda at City Hall.

"CHESS MATCH SHOOTOUT," claimed the *Sun of San Francisco*.

"CITY HALL BRAWL," shouted the *San Francisco Sun*.

"BEAUTY AND THE BEAST," blasted the *Trumpet*.

"In order to accommodate the working people of this fine city," said Mayor Oswell in his weekly radio address, "the chess match-up will start promptly at eight P.M." He was feeling particularly good about all this. The event would be the perfect opportunity for him to reposition himself as the city's natural leader.

Milo wanted the match to start immediately, the next day if possible, but Havram, no stranger to tournament contracts, haggled and counteroffered on every point until the match was postponed by two weeks just to get everything ready.

All the activity sent Slater Brown into a wild-eyed panic. He understood all too well that he was the fulcrum flipping this unlikely event into being. Or perhaps it was the intensity of the attention the match was receiving around the city that unnerved him. The week before the match he presented himself at the de Quincy residence, where he found Callio in the backyard reading a murder mystery.

"What are you doing? This is not chess," he said, sweeping her into his arms as she squealed in surprise. "You've got to practice."

"You sound like my father," she said as he lowered her to the ground.

"But this is important. The New York papers are sending reporters to cover this and —"

"I am preparing for this match the same way I prepare for all my matches."

"But this is different!"

"How would I know? I've never even seen your friend's computer. Nobody has. How can we know what it's like until we see it? There are no records of other matches to study. This computer is not internationally ranked. This computer has no legacy to protect, or research to promote. This is not something I can prepare for. I'm just going to do what I normally do."

"Which is?"

"Read comic books, eat bonbons, and write poetry."

He kissed her even harder than usual, knowing such excesses were forbidden in the house.

"I need to talk to you," he said. Behind them a door slammed and Havram appeared, head cocked to one side, listening. Slater held his finger to his lips, but Callio would have none of it.

"Yes, Father," she called out sweetly, "I'm right here."

"Are you alone?"

"No," she said, clamping a hand across Slater's mouth.

"Well, then, it's time to finish up your lunch and get back to practice. I have some more matches for you to study."

"But I thought you agreed I could have the afternoon off —"

Havram cut her short.

"I've just received a fax from that awful woman sponsoring the event. She's met my terms. All of my terms. We cannot take any chances. You must be totally prepared. Nothing less will do." Slater wiggled his eyebrows in agreement even as Callio kept her hand stretched across his mouth.

"Very well, Father, I will send my guest on his way."

"Excellent," said Havram as he stood waiting at the back door.

The following morning Slater returned. In his satchel he carried a half dozen Belgian bonbons, a book of Sufi love poetry he'd found at the bookstore, and a seven-page letter he'd stayed up all night writing, apologizing for his behavior at TK's. He lifted the heavy brass lion's paw that was the door knocker and brought it down three times. Havram opened the door with a scowl.

"Yes, yes, I'm blind, not deaf. Who is it? If you're proselytizing, we're not interested."

"It's me, Havram."

Havram's scowl grew darker. "Me who?"

"Slater. Slater Brown."

"Oh," Havram said, pausing to wipe his nose with a handkerchief pulled from his shirt pocket. "My daughter is busy, I'm afraid. Interrupting her would be deleterious to her progress." Ever since Slater had brought news of the chess match against Milo Magnet's computer, Havram acknowledged Slater even less than usual. For him, it was inevitable that people would want to challenge Callio's record. Why should he be grateful for their appetite?

"Would you give her this, then?" said Slater, pressing the package with the letter and gifts into Havram's hands. The blind man ran his fingertips over the box, lifting it to his nose for a sniff.

"She doesn't like chocolate," he said, thrusting the box back at Slater and slamming the door.

The evening of the match, City Hall glowed from inside with the white light of a blacksmith's oven. The mayor had closed traffic for six blocks so the overflow crowd could watch the match on large television monitors placed outside on the green lawn adjacent to City Hall. Scalpers circulated, selling standing-room-only tickets inside the Rotunda for two hundred fifty dollars apiece. Pickpockets trailed behind, noting which pocket people kept their money in.

In preparation for the mayor's welcome speech a special podium had been built to hide his girth, which had then required a specially reinforced stage to bear all the weight. But when it came time to get him out of his office (for the first time in many months) a problem was discovered: He couldn't fit through the office door.

"Get an ax!" shouted the mayor as his men pushed and pulled in a vain effort to squeeze him through the entryway. "Call maintenance and get an ax to widen this damn doorway. This is insane. When did they put a new doorway into my office?" he shouted as the men grunted around him.

"It's the same doorway it's ever been, boss," spat William Heck between clenched teeth.

"Bullshit!" shouted the mayor. "I could fit through the old door. This is a new doorway and somebody's going to find himself in a lot of trouble just as soon —" With a mighty shove he was pushed into the antechamber outside his office.

"Pheww!" said the mayor, wobbling a bit on his feet as he smoothed his waistcoat.

"Call maintenance and cancel that ax order."

The men around him dared not move. Each was in the process of grasping the unavoidable fact that there were four more doorways to battle with before they could deliver the mayor to the Rotunda and the reinforced podium.

"What say you deliver that speech tonight by speakerphone?" said Duane Oswell, dabbing sweat from his forehead.

"What say I transfer you to the Septic Inspection Department, Duane?" asked the mayor.

"All right, boys, let's keep this train rolling," said William Heck with a snap of his cuffs as he moved behind the mayor and gently guided him toward the next opening.

Slater Brown was pacing in the hallway leading to the Rotunda. The BBC had requested an interview with him after the match; the president of the World Chess Federation was there, drawn by rumors that Callio was a future world championship contender; and just that afternoon another in a series of recent faxes had arrived from Bix Butterfield promising the moon and the stars:

"Always at the center of attention, eh? Come to New York. I'll arrange a parade in your honor. Which do you prefer: red or blue ticker tape? Ciao, Bix."

Slater was rereading it when Maynard Reed rushed up to him.

"I want an exclusive on this. Tell us what went on backstage before the match."

"Not a chance, boss," said Slater, smiling.

"Well, then tell us what she's been doing to get ready."

"Reading comic books, eating bonbons,

and writing poetry."

"C'mon, don't pull my chain. And I want you to describe the match, too. What it feels like sitting in the front row watching beauty and the beast battle it out in front of the whole city. Make it vivid. Make it exciting. Make it appeal to the youth market —" Maynard paused. This was a particularly important night. The very next morning, after a thirty-three-year hiatus from the competitive newspaper scene, *The Morning Trumpet* would once again become a daily newspaper. They'd run the numbers and double-checked the accounting, and with the current state of growth there was more than enough revenue to pay for all projected expansion. It had also been decided that an increase in frequency should be met with an increase in price. It wasn't "right," as Maynard argued, for a newspaper as hot as the *Trumpet* to still charge fifteen cents per copy. "We gotta charge four bits if we want to play with the big boys," he said. Everyone nodded, tugged along by Maynard's economic reasoning. They voted. It was unanimous. The next edition of the new and improved daily *Morning Trumpet* would cost twenty-five cents. "And that's still a bargain!" Maynard had said when he'd announced the new plans amid the popping of champagne corks. Everyone had lifted a glass to Slater Brown, who had been inexplicably absent.

"Who am I kidding?" said Maynard. "You know what to do! Tell your lady friend good luck," he said before landing a hearty back slap that left Slater breathless.

Ten minutes later the crowd filed in and settled into their seats. The great domed roof of City Hall was lit with special lights that bounced off the gilded filigree so that the effect was that of standing on the floor of the world's largest Fabergé egg.

The spotlight roved around before settling on Callio, sitting poised and beautiful in the center of the stage. Her eyes were calm and her hands steady as they rested lightly on the edge of the table. Across from the chessboard, almost comically small, was the red computer. Before the match, Milo had propped it up on several books covered in green velvet so that it could be seen by the crowd from all angles.

As the ushers steered people to their seats, Milo made last-minute adjustments in a back room. "Let's just take it slow, shall we?" he said, gently turning the red computer on. "No need to show off here at the very beginning." His plan was to remain offstage, watching the computer's decisions on a remote monitor, in the hopes that he could catch a flaw in its calculations that would allow him to finally understand how to create larger weather packets.

In the hall the lights were lowered until only the circle of the stage was illuminated. As the lights went down, the crowd grew quiet. In the back, a young man who had traveled all the way from Chicago by bus to see Callio play spontaneously shouted, "I love you, Callio!" to the general amusement of the audience. Slater waited until the noise settled down before responding "I love you more!" which tripled the volume of laughter as the spectators craned their necks to point out to their neighbors who he was and where he was sitting. If Callio blushed she did not show it.

Finally they were ready to begin. Slater took out his yellow notebook and began to write:

The fluttering of a silver dollar tossed high in the air settled the first question: Who goes first? Callio wins! Sorry. Callio wins.

The referee of the match, "arbiter" in chess parlance, is a well-dressed man wearing a burgundy waistcoat. His sole job is to move the computer's chess pieces after it has flashed its instructions onto the monitor mounted on the table.

Callio moves first, decisively and with great authority.

The computer is thinking. Computer moves.

Callio takes one of the black thingies away from the computer. Think it was a bishop but can't be certain.

Computer makes another move, but slowly.

Callio takes her time. She's studying each possibility.

What a pro!

Crowd gasps. Not quite sure why.

Crowd gasps again. I'm leaning over to ask the person next to me.

Callio has apparently just brilliantly demonstrated something called the Steinitz attack!

Milo Magnet is nowhere to be seen. He's probably already in the parking lot waving down a taxi.

Clock reads 8:49 p.m.

Am getting thirsty.

Callio appears calm. Makes deliberate move. Takes off one of the bigger pieces from the computer's side. Crowd approves. They are clearly with her!

Flurry of activity across the board. Everyone holds their breath.

Shout goes up!

Hold on —

She's won!

Callio turns and bows slightly to the crowd.

(Must tell her not to do that again as a fellow can get a pretty good peek.)

She is smiling. Even Havram is smiling.

She looks very confident going into the next match.

Where shall I take her for a victory dinner? Must apologize to her for everything I said at TK's. Her victory here tonight will be a victory for Intuitionalists the world over!

Time: 9:10 p.m.

Second match is starting.

Computer moves a pawn. Callio counters. Flurry of activity. Shout goes up!

She's —

Here Slater's notes ended, for in fact Callio had not won; rather, her king had been snatched from the board with such rapacious instincts that even the oldest grand masters in the audience had never seen anything like it before.

Callio seemed oblivious to the loss. It was a fluke, she told herself. Just as her undefeated record was a fluke. She put it from her mind as easily as emptying an ashtray. As she sipped from her water glass she sought out Slater's face in the crowd and when she found it she winked at him. He fought the urge, but he could not contain himself and he smiled. The feeling from the rowboat

294

returned to him — finally and forever, everything was going to be all right.

For the third and final match, the audience stood in order to get a better look. Not a sound was heard in the hall.

From the beginning Callio exercised great discipline, making each move with deliberate calculation as she drew on her years of playing and reading and thinking.

Even so she became more and more agitated with each passing move. From the front row Slater noticed a fine sheen of perspiration on her forehead. "It's the lights," he mumbled to himself. "It must be the lights."

Out front of City Hall the crowd grew silent as they watched the final match played out on the Jumbotron screens. Even the circulating pickpockets and souvenir vendors selling "Beauty and the Beast" T-shirts paused to watch the action above them.

Each time the computer collected a piece from Callio's side of the board, a collective moan went up. Havram's composure was starting to fray. His companion, respected Grand Master Hendrik Filchnik, president of the San Francisco Pawn chess club, whispered each development into Havram's ear, but the reporting only served to darken the blind man's scowl.

In his back room at City Hall, Milo Magnet hovered over a computer monitor obsessively studying the readouts of the decision tree the red supercomputer was generating.

"Excellent. Good. Bravo!" he called out as he watched the two players clash against one another across the board. These were exactly the data he was looking for to help him with his weather packet dilemma. The girl genius seemed to be handling herself pretty well, all things considered, but they were only operating at fifty percent. Now that he had the first segment of information he was looking for, it was time to accelerate the red computer's abilities.

"Now," he said, tapping a string of commands into the keyboard. "Now we go to seventy-five percent power and see how our genius handles herself."

In the main hall the tenor of the game changed almost instantly, although nobody could place it exactly. It was a feeling about momentum, and momentum being famously elusive, it passed even the most careful observer until it was too late. Earlier Callio had done her best to quickly meet and neutralize each of the computer's attacks — King's Gambit met Steinhowser Defense — but she now spent more and more time between moves. Slater noticed that her left foot tapped against the side of her chair.

The computer made decisions at twice its earlier rate, and the strangeness of some of its choices, and the quick confidence with which it made them, baffled everyone. The shouts of incomprehension that greeted earlier moves by the enthusiasts in the crowd were now muted. Either there was a bug in the computer's software, causing it to behave erratically, or it was operating on an entirely different level.

Soon enough the answer was clear. One by one Callio's pieces began to disappear from the board. For the first time a wrinkle of doubt appeared between her eyes. She paused to wipe her forehead with the napkin the arbiter had laid at her elbow. The expression of frustration on her face had morphed into that of a tourist trying to speed-read Egyptian hieroglyphs. When she glanced again at Slater there was no wink.

The computer responded to Callio's alarm by increasing its attacks, taking rook, knight, and queen.

As each development on the chessboard was whispered into Havram's ear he began to twitch, balling his hands into fists until he could contain himself no longer. He stood and addressed the game, not ten feet away.

"Attack! My dear. Danish Gambit! Concentrate. Capablanca's Counter. Attack! Now! Do it!"

His advice, coming as it did two or three moves behind the red computer's lightning-quick decisions, was jumbled and useless. One by one the arbiter lifted Callio's few remaining pieces from the board. She couldn't have felt more alone or over-matched if she'd been floating on a wooden plank in the middle of the Pacific. Even with his primitive understanding of the game, Slater Brown knew things were not going well. He stood on his chair, hoping he could give her a look of support, but Callio's eyes did not leave the board. It was her turn to move, but for once she couldn't decide what to do. Like a skater on spring ice, each motion put her deeper and deeper into peril. She paused for a moment, studied the board one final time, and buried her face in her hands.

When Havram was told this, his sightless eyes bulged out as he stood and marched straight for the chess table. He did this so quickly and unerringly that it took everyone by surprise.

"Mischa," he called out, for that was his private name for her, "do not give up! Do you hear me?"

He was not addressing her directly, but projecting his voice a little off to the side and into the empty air to the right of the table.

If this had been anything other than an exhibition match, Havram's shouting and interruptions would have been objected to and the game stopped. But the red computer only whirred away, oblivious to the scene unfolding around it. Its only issue at hand was to anticipate and counter whatever desperate move its weakened opponent would try next.

Perhaps Havram sensed how dominant the computer really was, even sensed that there would be no rematch. No return to glory. Perhaps he even understood that the computer was not operating at full speed. In the press area next to the match the telephoto lenses whirred faster than ever, capturing the images that would festoon the next day's stories.

"Mischa," Havram called out to Callio, even as he caught the faint sound of his daughter's crying. "Please, calm yourself. Just take a deep breath. This can be overcome. You can overcome this. We have come a long way and we have a long way to go. This is nothing to —" But Havram could not see what the others already knew.

"Checkmate," said the arbiter with finality.

The stunned silence that followed was broken only by the sound of a pair of hands clapping from the upper balcony. The crowd arched to see a jubilant Mayor Oswell standing at the brass railing. Unable to squeeze through the last doorway leading to the main hall, he'd decided, in the manner of a French monarch, to survey his people from above.

The source of his delight was easily traced to the stricken face of Slater Brown. This gave the mayor a pleasure so intense that it surpassed that of every gourmet morsel he'd eaten in the last six months. From deep within his twinkling eyes something he'd been searching for had found its way to the surface: His enemy was finally wounded.

As the silence was broken, so too was the spell of the spectacle. Slater was out of his seat like a shot.

"Ladies and gentlemen, we have a winner," shouted the arbiter.

Havram lifted his cane to smash the computer monitor, but he was standing five feet away and all he managed to do was slash the air until security guards led him off. He twisted and turned out of their hands like an unhappy newborn.

"Cheated! They cheated!" he shouted over his shoulder. None of his escorts volunteered to explain to him what had just happened.

At first the crowd was quiet, which quickly changed to bafflement as soon as Havram exited the stage, and finally suddenly angry, as crowds often become when they cannot work out their bafflement quickly enough.

A photograph taken at the time reveals only the blur of a streaking comet as Slater Brown made his way across the marble floor. He did not say a word as he bent to put his arms around Callio. "So strange," she said to him, her hands pressed against her face. The only way he could think to help her, with the hot glare of the television cameras approaching and the eyes of the audience still trained on her, was to get her away as soon as possible. He picked her up in his arms and moved toward the fire exit, not registering his own labored breathing, nor her weight in his arms, as he ran through the intricate marble hallways leading out of City Hall. Finally, after asking two stunned janitors standing next to their mop pails for directions, he bolted for an open doorway and the fresh air outside.

Even as he carried her, his mind began to reel, careening over each recent detail, looking for a thread, anything, something that would reveal it all to be a mistake, or an accident. Finding no such thread, he told himself it wasn't so bad. Unexpected, sure, but not irreparable. Something would happen to remedy the situation. He just needed to regroup.

As the crowd poured out of the front doors of City Hall, they were greeted by the beginnings of a rain shower that would otherwise not have merited mention but for the fact that each and every drop was chartreuse.

∎ ∎ ∎ ∎

BOOK THREE:
THE BEGINNING

∎ ∎ ∎ ∎

CHAPTER
TWENTY-EIGHT

From the moment the three of them had come home from City Hall, Havram had been at Slater's throat. It was all Slater could do to get Callio into bed without a confrontation erupting. For her part, perhaps to naturally balance her father's foul mood, Callio projected good spirits. Slater had even made her laugh with his impersonation of the mayor.

"Ark, ark, ark," he said, flapping his arms like seal flippers as he mimicked the mayor standing in his shiny black tuxedo, belly pressed against the banister railing.

"Do you know that last week there was a two-point-one earthquake in San Francisco?" he asked her. "Turns out it was just the mayor getting up to use the bathroom!"

Even as Callio giggled beneath a down comforter he couldn't help but notice how fragile she looked. The way her arms lay next to her body and her feet made a tiny tent out of the bedspread.

"Thank you, thank you. I'll be here all week," said Slater, bowing slightly. But the lighter the mood became, the darker Havram's face turned until finally he stormed out of the room, slamming the door.

Slater exhaled. For the first time in what seemed like a long time they were alone together.

"How do you feel, my love?" he asked. He marveled that even after her tough night she could still summon a smile. "I have so much I want to tell you. I have so much I *need* to tell you," he said, holding her hand as he kneeled next to the bed.

"Good," she said a little sleepily as her head sank into the pillow and her eyes closed. "Stay here tonight."

"I don't think that's such a good . . ." but Callio's eyelids had already begun to flutter as she slipped into a deep slumber. Their conversation would have to wait until morning.

"I'll ask if I can stay in the guest room," he said, leaning over to kiss her cheek. "I won't be far."

As he tiptoed out of her bedroom he heard a noise and turned. At the top of the stairs he saw a shadow tapping slowly down the hallway toward him. It was a grim sound on a rainy night, and the combined effect caused him to pause for a moment before announcing his presence. Did he really want an encounter with Havram at this late hour?

"London, Berlin, Davos," the soft sounds from the sightless man spilled forth in incantations as precise as a prayer. "St. Petersburg, Vienna, Barcelona. They will all welcome us with open arms," he continued as he made his way down the hall. Slater stood silently, his back to the wall, as Havram passed. When Havram was only inches away he paused, sniffing the air. Slater lost his nerve.

"Havram?" he said. The figure spun in Slater's direction with the confidence of a man with perfect eyesight.

"Yes, fool, I see you are hiding again, as usual," said Havram.

"But I wanted to ask —"

"Ask what? Ask what else you could do for my family? Nothing. You have ruined enough lives for one night."

Though he knew the man was blind, Slater couldn't help but look away.

"But Havram —"

"Not only her beautiful past, all of her victories, all the stunning success. But her future as well," said Havram, speaking

307

beyond Slater, as though addressing a jury. "Does the fool have any idea how much work perfection takes?"

Slater could feel himself being pulled into the older man's irrational rage like a leaf on the edge of a tornado. He wiped the spittle off his face.

"But this is just one match. There will be others."

"Others?" said the dark silhouette. "There is only one perfect record," said Havram before reaching out for the contours of his bedroom door and moving inside. "As far as my daughter is concerned, Mr. Brown, you are quite correct; she will meet others." In the darkness Slater heard the click of the bedroom door locking between them.

He took a deep breath. It hadn't seemed like an ideal time to ask if he could stay in the guest room. He walked down the hallway to the bathroom and opened the window that led to the roof. It did, however, seem like a very good time for a smoke. He crawled out onto the slate roof on his hands and knees.

The rain had stopped and the night sky was temporarily clear. Above him the stars of Orion's Belt winked, oblivious to the tumult beneath them. His hand rummaged around in his coat pocket until he found a cigar, which he lit. It was a remnant of a forgotten dinner party where he'd undoubtedly been the guest of honor. As he sat there blowing tiny geysers of smoke into the blue darkness he thought of how suddenly everything had shifted. It hadn't taken long. And the end result had upended the world he had come to depend on, the world he had created. The thought of it filled him with a disquiet he hadn't known since his earliest days in San Francisco. But what did it matter how quickly things had changed? When he had been alone in the room with Callio the electric hum between them had come through so clearly it had made his heart swell until it was as taut and full as a spinnaker on a spring day. Let's keep this in perspective, he told himself. *That* was what mattered most, he thought, as he blew another smoke ring toward the moon. She, not the writing, was the true thing Niebald had tried to tell him about.

In the morning he could begin setting everything back into motion, but right now, tonight, there wasn't anywhere in the world he would rather be than on this roof, smoking a cigar, with Callio safely inside. Even the *Trumpet* was a distant memory.

"No one can see me," he said, blowing another smoke ring. "And no one can hear me," he said, following it with another. "And I can't hear a thing. Not even a story," he said, fingering the pocket radio through the fabric of his jacket, reflexively drawn to its reassuring weight.

Through the open window below came the sound of Havram shuffling, making his final rounds before going to bed. The blind man's finely tuned senses soon perceived the new draft. His footsteps drew closer to the open window, drawn by the scent of a lit Montecristo. Slater sat frozen in place as Havram stuck his head out the window, turning left and right like a bomb-sniffing dog at the end of his leash. Finally, the blind man retreated back inside the house. Slater let out a breath of relief.

Crack!

The window was shut with the force of a captain closing the hatch on a submerging submarine. The noise, and its intention, made Slater jump, and he slid several feet down the roof before catching himself. The orange-ended cigar fell from his fingers and tumbled off the roof before its cinders exploded into sparks on the sidewalk below.

Slater put his hands down to steady his position. The slate tiles were slick from the earlier rainstorm, and except for the dormer, which he was now straddling, his options were few and far between. He could sleep on the roof (was that what Havram wanted?), or he could climb up to the chimney, slide down the far side, and jump onto the top of the garden shed in the backyard. He looked up at the chimney.

Each step up the slate roof felt as if it would be his last. Four times he slid back to the dormer and had to begin again. Below he could hear the unmistakable sounds of Havram shutting and locking every window in the house. In five minutes the place would be as secure as a bank vault.

Finally, he reached the spine of the roof, where he hugged the brick chimney and looked down the other side. To his horror it was a steeper incline than he had anticipated, and the garden shed was set farther away from the house than he remembered. It was not within jumping range. Especially in the dark.

Across the city yet another fork of lightning lit up the sky and the wind began to rustle the eucalyptus trees. Very slowly it dawned on him that this was not an ideal night to be hugging a chimney in San Francisco. In the darkness above him a wrought-iron weather vane twisted into the outline of a black king chess piece squeaked.

As the gusts multiplied, it began to slowly spin.

As Slater shifted his weight to look for other escape options he accidentally knocked the pigeon grate off the top of the chimney. Stooping to pick it up, he was faced with the chimney's wide-mouthed opening. He peered down into the darkness before glancing back at the angled roof in front of him. There was no way he could navigate the roof's slick surface without falling three stories to the street below.

"You could die," said Slater aloud, startling himself with the sound of his own voice. But as the unattractiveness of his position slowly dawned on him, so too did the only solution.

"It would sorta be like Santa Claus," he whispered, psyching himself up until the only question to be resolved was the angle: headfirst or feetfirst? And what about circumference? As big as the chimney mouth appeared to be, he knew he'd need to be as slender as possible. He looked down at the suit he'd worn to the chess match. It was bespoke, requiring three sittings and two tailors, made with special Belgian silk. His shirt was Egyptian cotton, his cuff links mother-of-pearl. All one of a kind. Irreplaceable. There was no question that if he went

312

down the chimney the suit would be ruined. Plus, he told himself, the finery only added to his bulk. The suit would have to go. That was all there was to it. Slater stepped neatly out of his clothes, folding everything up, careful to button his pockets so that his wallet and keys were secure.

First, a test. He picked up his custom-made calf-leather shoes imported from Bologna and dropped them down the dark opening, counting as they fell down the chimney. One . . . two . . . three . . . *clunk* went the shoes as they hit the floor of the fireplace below. "Ladies and gentlemen, the flue is open," he said, before lifting up his carefully folded suit, pausing to inhale the smell of the private-label Caribbean after-shave on the collar of his shirt, and dropping the clothes down the chimney. "Think of it as a dress rehearsal," he called after the bundle.

Across the city the lightning intensified, initiating the start of a new rainstorm. He couldn't be sure, but the lightning looked red. Above him the squeaking of the weather vane had become seriously annoying. It was time to go. He'd made up his mind. Feet-first it was.

At the last minute he had retrieved the pocket radio, clenching the strap between his teeth. He couldn't leave it behind. Not yet.

As he slung a leg up and over the lip of the chimney the faintest smell caught his nostrils. Acrid and familiar. Slater looked down. "Oh, for the love of God," he said when he saw the source of the smell. Forty-seven feet below a small fire was crackling itself into a larger fire, fed every few moments with another stick of bone-dry almond kindling. Havram had been busy, for in the center of the fire sat Slater Brown's clothes, engulfed in flames. He watched as long as he could before the smoke forced him back to reality on the roof. Above Slater the black king pivoted raucously in the buffeting winds and the rain began slapping hard against his exposed body. Quite unexpectedly he would have all night to ponder the lightning's changing colors.

CHAPTER
TWENTY-NINE

The weather had turned completely feral. To Milo's great surprise, the person who knew the most about this was his own sweet Alice.

"Milo," she said the moment he walked in the door from City Hall, her face ashen, "there was nothing I could do." He had been stuck in traffic, sitting in wet clothes, for two hours in the post–chess-match traffic.

"About what?" he asked, searching her face as a panicked thought whisked through his mind: Had he misjudged Alice? Only now, on the cusp of his greatest triumph, was she showing her true colors? He studied her carefully. She seemed about to crumble.

"Tell me everything," he said. Behind them a low boom of thunder rattled the house before illuminating the walls with the force of ten thousand flashbulbs.

"It was a bird," she said, biting her lower lip.

"A bird?" said Milo, eyes darting side to side.

A bird, she said, had flown into the large plate-glass window in his study. "It made a huge, terrifying crash. I was in the front hall when it happened and I thought we were being robbed. So I grabbed a butcher knife and ran in there" — God bless you, Alice, thought Milo — "and there was this pile of bloody feathers lying at the foot of your desk, and, and —" She broke down. Just typical, thought Milo; never was a woman as prone to falling to pieces as when it involved the death of a small animal.

"I think it was a delirious pelican," said Alice, tossing her head in the direction of the carcass, still unable to look at it directly.

"No," said Milo, already nudging the dead bird's head with the tip of his shoe, "it's much stranger than that. It's a short-tailed albatross, *Phoebastria albatrus,* extremely rare, known mainly for inhabiting Japanese ports. We are certainly outside of its normal range. Some call it Steller's albatross. It has a huge wingspan, nearly seven feet. If I'm not mistaken this was the bird that served as Coleridge's central symbol in *The Rime of the Ancient Mariner.*" Alice listened politely

316

before raising her hand to pause the ornithological dissertation.

"Don't you want me to tell you what happened?" she asked. He took in the shattered look on her face. For heaven's sake, he thought, Alice was no Judas. As he gave her a stiff hug, the wind from the storm rushed through the opening in his office, gathering up all his papers and abandoned correspondence into a white cyclone that, for a moment, obscured the two of them from each other's view.

"And all the weather packets are gone," he said, finishing the story for her.

Alice nodded. "I don't know what to say. I feel so . . ." He patted her awkwardly on the arm as his mind raced to reconstruct what had been going on in the laboratory before he'd left for the chess match. He had made only incremental progress on the size issue and the weather packets had still never attained a size larger than a Ping-Pong table, but a big breakthrough had come when Milo had figured out how to construct weather formulas previously beyond his reach. In the last two weeks alone he had created fog flakes which had existed quite happily next to the fax machine for three days, two batches of self-replicating mud rain contained in the shower, some mediocre hoarfrost, one failed attempt at Scotch mist, and, the jewel in the crown, the ultimate weather packet: corposants, otherwise known as Saint Elmo's fire.

The albatross's derailed flight plan meant that all of his hard-won weather packets were out in the world now, operating independently. The simple weather formulas he had discovered in his laboratory were capable of exhibiting extraordinary complexity in the outside world. What combinations they would enter into, and what the final results would be, was beyond even the comprehension of Milo Magnet. "Alice," said Milo, "I have no idea . . ." He trailed off as his gaze turned out over the Pacific.

"No idea what, Milo?" said Alice.

"I have no idea what's going to happen next."

The irony, if there can be irony about a man losing his private stash of weather, was that Milo had gained remarkable insight by watching the red computer's processes at the chess match. His observations and records promised to yield tremendous results when applied to the weather packets. But with the constantly changing developments going on outside, Milo was unable to focus on his work in any sustained way. The first and most pressing problem was that he was besieged with reporters' inquiries. By phone, letter, and e-mail they bombarded him day and night. Almost all of them contained some variation of "I just need two minutes of your time. If two minutes is too much, two seconds will do." Some nut had even hacked into his fax machine, sending lewd images of a computer being sacrificed on the altar of a female body.

Milo was not without blame for fanning the flames of this intense interest. Before he'd left City Hall the night of the chess match, after the crowds were swept away by security, he'd unplugged the tiny red quantum computer and dropped it into his shirt pocket. Three reporters apiece from the *San Francisco Sun* and the *Sun of San Francisco* appeared at his elbow.

"What do you think of the girl, Mr. Magnet?"

"Oh, I sincerely hope she can recover. I imagine losing an internationally publicized chess match to an opponent who has never played the game before is quite a strain on a young mind. I guess every perfect record meets its match sometime. But it does show us precisely why computers are more reliable than human beings, doesn't it? When computers break, you either reboot them or replace them."

"What are you working on now?" asked the reporters as they followed Milo to the arched doorway.

"Well, I've shown you the power at my disposal tonight, but not the purpose of the power." It was precisely the sort of quote that made newspapermen weak in the knees, as it implied intrigue, intention, and lots of follow-up.

"When? Where? How?" came the queries like darts from a blowgun as Milo buttoned his trench coat.

"No comment, boys. Not yet," he said, making his way confidently out the revolving doors and into the colored rain. Milo registered this new information with immediate alarm, looking up at the heavens as the freakish deluge came down through the light of the streetlamps like something out of a drive-in movie about Armageddon. This wasn't part of his plan. More important, how on earth had this happened? It took Milo an extra moment before he could reinstate some semblance of a poker face, aware that the trailing television cameras were still filming his every move.

But when it became clear that it wasn't going to work to pretend there was nothing unusual about chartreuse rain, Milo opted for Plan B, which involved breaking into a crazy-legged sprint for his chauffeured car, which sat idling in the handicapped spot in front of City Hall. The pack of shouting reporters was on his heels immediately, its size doubling every ten feet, but Milo managed to make it to the safety of the backseat before any of them could catch him. As they pressed their faces up against the glass windows of the Lincoln Town Car and shouted questions about the weather, Milo couldn't help but blurt out the first thing that had popped into his mind.

"At least it's finally bigger than a hula hoop!" he shouted as he was driven away.

CHAPTER THIRTY

"I've been thinking," said Mayor Oswell, sitting like a groomed peacock in his favorite chair. He was in an exceptionally fine mood. It was as if last night's strange weather, coming as it had on the heels of the glorious chess match, heralded a new cycle of good luck for his administration. All morning he'd gone around imitating Slater Brown's face the moment Callio lost the match. "Poor little golden boy got hurt," he said, sticking out his lower lip.

"You've been thinking?" said William Heck in a neutral tone so as not to disrupt what he and the others had taken to calling "The Mood" from its delicate perch.

"Yes. It's time we swing into another gear around here. We've been playing too much catch-up. Too much defense. Not enough offense. Especially — and I know I don't have to remind you of this, William — especially with the coming election." The election was still a long way off in the distance, but the fact that the mayor was thinking about it at all suggested a return to form.

"What'd you have in mind?"

"Well, you know how much fun Gloria had putting together the whole chess thing. She was as excited as a teenager. Talked my ear off about it. It occurred to me that perhaps really old wealthy dames simply need to be spoon-fed projects to keep them from thinking about things like varicose veins and their impending deaths."

William Heck knew from experience that the mayor was simply practicing the proposal's surface logic on him to see how it sounded when spoken aloud.

"I think you're onto something, boss."

"Exactly, so I've been casting around for a new project that befits her interests, something that matches her financial position, and especially, and this is of paramount importance, keeps her engaged with the community in a way that is in perfect accordance with her temperament."

"Wow," said William Heck, "like what?"

The mayor pursed his lips to evoke maximum certainty.

"Like buying *The Morning Trumpet*!"

"It's for sale?"

"As my grandpappy used to say, 'First we ascertain you're a whore, then we establish the price.' "

"I didn't know Gloria wanted to buy a newspaper," the mayor's chief of staff said, circling from another direction.

"She doesn't. Not yet. But give me an hour over lunch. It makes sense from all angles. Book me the private room at Le Tab and it's a done deal. What do you think?"

William Heck inhaled slowly. The mayor rarely, if ever, asked what anyone thought, and when he did it was either a trick question, or it meant His Honor was unsure of himself. Either way, it was not an avenue William wished to travel.

"It's a fine idea, boss. Truly inspired. Wish I'd thought of it. Only problem I can see is the van der Snoot yacht left the harbor at seven this morning."

"For where?"

"Greece."

"Greece!" shouted the mayor. His eyes darted around the desk as he groped for the platter of petite éclairs, or the basket of double-fudge brownies, or the bowl of extra-large pineapple jelly beans normally within reach. But they'd all been swept away, part of "Operation Aorta," the special-op code name that William Heck had outlined at the morning staff meeting. Wounded, the mayor's furtive eyes were left to focus on a steaming bowl placed inconspicuously at his elbow. He drew it toward him with the long-armed sweep of a ravished orangutan before pushing it away.

"For Christ sakes. Get this soybean noodle crap out of here."

"It's not soybeans, boss. It's tofu, with injected beef flavor," said William Heck, cribbing a glance at the box in the grocery bag in front of him. "I'm told it tastes a lot like prime rib."

"You're told! You're *told!* Please. I'd rather lick hubcaps."

"The doctor says it'll be good for you."

"I've been *good!* For nearly three whole days." He slid the bowl of tofu noodles over the edge of his desk and into the trash can below. "As a human experience, it's overrated."

The mayor caught William Heck's worried look.

"Oh, don't get all hangdog on me. Tell the good doctor I'm off the sweets. Tell him I haven't so much as looked at a bowl of chocolate mousse. No crumb cake, no Russian taffy, and my adultery with Charlotte Russe is but a memory in the mirror," said the mayor, batting his eyes for effect. "Tell him I even took a short walk yesterday to exercise myself. *But!* Tell him I'm not eating any more bean sprout smoothies or arugula yogurt or broccoli kebabs, or any of the other flimflam the two of you keep sending over. My spirit cannot sustain such infidelity!"

There was nothing to do but shrug. William Heck placed the offending items back inside the grocery bag. Operation Aorta had officially ruptured.

"What would you like for lunch?"

"Hmm," said the mayor, smacking his lips. "You know what sounds really good? Something I haven't indulged in in a long time?"

What could possibly have fallen outside the mayor's indulgences? Ten-to-one odds said he wanted either a goose liver pâté sandwich from Christophe's or a pulled-suckling chipotle burrito from Agua Caliente's in the Mission.

"How about a good old-fashioned PB and J, extra crunch!"

The mayor's chief of staff peered into the bag of groceries he'd picked up that morning from the health food store. It didn't seem like the right time to ask if organic almond butter and wheatgrass jelly would do the trick.

"I'll just step out and get the necessary

ingredients."

"Capital idea, guv'nor," said the mayor in his best cockney accent. His disposition seemed to be improving with each passing moment. "And while you're out, pay a little visit to our friends over at the Department of Transportation and see how Duane's acclimating as the new director. First, be sure to tell him how proud we are to have him back in the City Hall family. That's important. Take my word for it. Duane needs to feel appreciated. And then, of course, tell him how grateful we are that he accepted the position. Finally, tell him his big brother has been working on a new 'Fresh Air' initiative. Tell him federal regulations have changed. Mention that the Global Warming Index is up! Tell him we're investigating that weird rain that fell the other night. Tell him," said the mayor, spreading his arms luxuriantly and cracking his fat knuckles behind his head, "that I've got an idea of how to stop that reporter once and for all. We'll be in touch shortly."

CHAPTER
THIRTY-ONE

The morning after the chess match, in the early light, as the city was still coming awake, a cold, pale figure had walked the streets in his bare feet. Even the buses were not running yet. The figure's stride was deliberate, though tempered by the desire to avoid stepping on broken glass and bottle tops. In his hands he carried a small pocket radio, his only companion from the harrowing night he'd just survived. His escape from the confines of the roof had come at the hands of Mexican gardeners, who had come early to clear branches from the elm tree next door that had been blown down in the storm. They'd extended their aluminum ladder to the nearly naked figure standing on the roof and held the bottom while he climbed down. Too dazed by present circumstances to pay full attention to the strangers, he nodded politely in thanks and headed down Pacific Avenue.

At the junction of Van Ness, where the pale figure would have been expected to turn left toward home and a dry and warm change of clothes, he inexplicably turned right and began walking southward.

Twenty-two minutes later he was in the Mission District, on his way to San Jose's Taqueria Espectacular. The thought of returning to speak to Answer Man hadn't occurred to him until dawn, when he'd been shivering on the roof. But of course he should explain to Answer Man what had happened to him since he'd last sought his counsel. It was a strange story, to be sure, but would it really be that strange to Answer Man, who had, after all, initiated it? The thing was, Answer Man hadn't told him what to do each time the story had turned strange, and Answer Man hadn't fallen in love with a beautiful woman in a park, and he hadn't ridden around on buses listening to other people's stories and reporting them as if he owned them somehow. And above all Answer Man hadn't set into motion a chess match that had caused severe pain. He and Answer Man had a lot to talk about.

During his sleepless night on the roof he had replayed all of these things, turning them over in his mind as if they were domino pieces and he only needed to match

329

them up properly to figure out how to win the game. But each time he tried to come to a satisfactory conclusion about what his next move was, he realized he needed counsel, some kind of guidepost, some synchronistic coincidence to help him know for sure. The thing about synchronistic coincidences, he'd realized, is that you didn't see them unless you needed them.

He came to a stop in front of San Jose's Taqueria Espectacular. Owned by the Wong family since 1972, it was most famous for having the best horchata in the city, but the sign in the window now told a different story: "Shabby Chic Antiques — 1/2 price." The taqueria was *vamos.* There wasn't even a handwritten sign announcing a new location. Nor was there mention of Answer Man, not even a forwarding address. The pale figure took in the situation and kept on walking. In the gathering fog even the streetlights seemed muted and wanting power.

At Market Street and Third he encountered other manifestations of the strange new weather. He sat down on the curb at Lotta's Fountain to take it all in. All up and down the boulevard enormous balls of gray fog bounced gently, west to east. He couldn't help but think that it looked like a parade in reverse, each sphere holding its shape with mysterious grace. As he watched them, he barely remembered to breathe. It seemed like another lifetime when he had stood on this very corner and looked up at the light bathing the city, before he had made up his clips, before he had discovered the power of the pocket radio, before he had discovered his power. Before.

Then it came. For the first time in a very long time it came back. First it was just a tiny half-turn south of his sternum; then a ripple below his navel. In an instant his stomach curled up into a churlish knot. But it was not the knot that was the trouble. It was what accompanied the knot. Like many grand edifices, Slater Brown's newfound identity collapsed far quicker than anticipated, hollow as it was. And with the collapse came a sickening sense that he'd made so many wrong choices it was foolish to single out just one.

For the first time ever it occurred to the pale figure that there were things that hadn't occurred to him. It was as if he had finally stumbled into the smithy of his soul, only to find a dark cave incapable of producing even an echo.

As another rolling ball, as big as an elephant, passed in front of him he could see exactly what needed to be done. Before —

331

how many times before? — he had known this question was approaching him, but lacking an answer he had simply pushed it away, back into the darkness. This time it would be different. He knew that now. The old expression floated back into his head, this time charged with a completely different current: *make happen.* He rose without hesitation and stepped directly into the ball of fog, disappearing. On the curb, left behind for the city's many scavengers, sat the pocket radio, its headphones neatly wrapped, its batteries freshly replaced only two days earlier.

CHAPTER
THIRTY-TWO

"This is a regular Book of Revelation," said Niebald, squinting into the dawn. They were shorthanded, but they'd pulled an all-nighter and finally put together tomorrow's edition of *The Morning Trumpet*. Now every five minutes someone would look nervously out the window to see what weather oddity was currently shaping up outside.

"What do you see?" said Motherlove, rushing to the window. Just visible in the outer dark was the love child of a rainstorm and a fog patch, which explained the raindrops made primarily of fog falling very slowly from the sky. Some were as big as marbles, others the size of garden peas. That afternoon, Pier 39 had been attacked by two dueling waterspouts that had bounced off the structure like exuberant teenagers until they'd collapsed the corner of the building. These and other climate curiosities were still being spotted on an hourly basis and phoned in by citizens from around the Bay Area. The mayor, thrilled with the chance to do something decisive, had declared the situation a city emergency and soon schools and businesses announced they were officially closed.

"The global warming invoice we've all avoided paying has finally come due," stated a rush press release faxed out by the mayor's communications department. Pinky Beale worked the phones as if it were campaign day. There were so many outdoor photo ops for the mayor, the biggest challenge had been navigating around town in the horrendous weather.

But at the *Trumpet* there was only the adrenaline buzz of a big story to work off, coupled with the paralyzing fact that their star reporter was missing in action. That morning Maynard Reed had flown to a broadcasting conference in Indianapolis, lured there by reports of investors clamoring — he'd actually said "hot to trot" — for a chance to launch Trumpet TV.

"That turd ain't got the memo," said Niebald. They sat next to each other, on the fifth floor of the Trumpet building, looking warily at the sky for ten minutes before Motherlove spoke.

"Have you called the kid?"

Silence.

"I left him a message."

"Well, call him again."

"It's not going to make a difference; his landlady said he hasn't been home since his girlfriend got crushed by the laptop."

More silence.

"What about her house?"

"I tried there. I keep getting a busy signal."

"Must be off the hook," moaned Maynard.

"You think he's there?"

"Where else?"

"Well, I say we just go over there and get him."

Silence.

"When?" ventured Niebald.

"Right goddamned now!"

They let that sit for a moment before looking outside, where the sky had turned a light shade of burgundy as the setting sun over Ocean Beach filtered through the visiting weather.

"Something tells me he's out there as we speak trying to get the story for us. Let's give him a little more time. We owe him a little more time."

They settled back and continued looking out the window as if it were a television screen from another world.

CHAPTER
THIRTY-THREE

The quirkiness of the weather continued, which meant that the reporters only chased Milo harder. It was an international affair now. The national cable news programs had shown a thirty-second video clip of a dwarf tornado made of sleet vandalizing Fisherman's Wharf and soon the phones lit up with calls from Birmingham to Bellevue. It was a slow news cycle and the words "San Francisco" and "Milo Magnet" were on the news crawl every nine minutes. Some young prankster had even attached a GPS device to the bumper of Milo Magnet's car so that every time he or Alice went out they were trailed by a line of automobiles so long his progress through town looked like a funeral procession. A pair of Swedish journalists calling themselves Piers and Hans, who claimed to be filming a documentary for European television, were the worst of the lot. Twice Alice had found them digging through Milo's garbage.

"And what are you doing?" she said upon first discovering them.

"Jah," they'd said, squinting simultaneously, "we are lucking for contact lens?" The final indignity came during Milo's annual prostate checkup (at fifty-nine, he was in a high-risk class), which was interrupted by a clutch of reporters (including Piers and Hans) tapping on the glass window of the examining room. Even lying on his stomach, Milo had managed a furious grunt of protest, punctuated only by the sound of the doctor snapping on his rubber glove.

The cumulative experience was so annoying it forced Milo to accelerate his next plan.

"Two steps removed and three steps ahead." He whistled to himself as soon as all the pieces came together in his head. Was he responsible? "Can't say," he said to Alice, when asked. "Too many variables. Far too many variables." That became their code phrase for the next several days whenever a question with no ready answer appeared: too many variables. Unlike most people, after having a chance to think about it, Milo didn't exactly see the strange flowering of the weather as necessarily a bad thing. It was proof of concept, he told himself. But just like a recipe for a delicious cake, if you added too much flour, it would taste bad. Same with the weather. Despite the easy analogy, the task now was to figure out how to correct the pattern formulas so that he had more control over his invention in the future. He had proof of concept, but not ownership of concept. Yet.

What he needed was more time.

But time was, of course, in short supply. It wasn't just the reporters who bothered him. The governor — the governor! — had called last night to ask if he had any knowledge of what was going on. And he wasn't exactly polite about it, either. What nerve. After all Milo Magnet had done for the world's fifth-largest economy, to get a phone call in the middle of dinner from a dippy first-term *governor,* demanding in headmasteresque tones "what he knew," and "what could he do." Just like clockwork, thought Milo, the first whiff of a photo op and the politicos turn all command-and-control.

What was happening on the ground didn't really matter, thought Milo. People, particularly on-the-ground people, were not going to solve a situation like this. The only way to solve something like this was for Milo to go where no one could follow. Where he could get a more instructional vantage point. No phones. No e-mail. No faxes. No governor. He was already thinking of it as a kind of working vacation. The silence beckoned him. There was a much better chance of figuring out the weather dilemma from up above, but there was also an overriding need to get out of town: There was a better-than-average chance everything was about to get really weird.

To announce his new plan, he did the most unexpected thing possible. He called a press conference in the center of the polo fields in Golden Gate Park.

"But why?" asked Alice in exasperation when she heard the news.

"The best way to achieve the kind of anonymity I want is to make my departure highly visible. That way they'll know I'm really gone." Alice looked outside at two photographers belly-crawling across the front yard in full camouflage. Maybe it would really be for the best if Milo disappeared for a little while.

The morning of the press conference he climbed atop a ladder and addressed the throng. "Ladies and gentlemen," he said. "I leave you today to pursue the greatest challenge of my career. If I succeed I will enter the pantheon of scientific greats: Pythagoras . . . Newton . . ." He paused to let the reporters catch up to what he was saying. "And me!"

Behind him, dwarfing the crowd of reporters, was the gargantuan red material of a partly inflated hot-air balloon. After taking a handful of questions, Milo stepped clumsily into the capsule, catching his ankle just so on the metal frame and collapsing with a yelp inside. The hot-air balloon began to buck like an impatient stallion in the morning wind. The aluminum capsule was watertight, contained enough food and water for sixty days, and could climb 60,000 feet into the upper reaches of the atmosphere. "It can go as high as the troposphere," he told reporters with glee.

A considerable portion of the evening prior to Milo's launch had been devoted toward what to call his craft. At first he thought of calling it the *Fox & Hedgehog* after his favorite Greek poem. But Alice pointed out that you couldn't name a single hot-air balloon two names. Attempting to narrow it down to one of the two reignited a long-standing internal debate.

"Am I a fox or a hedgehog?" he asked Alice the night before the trip.

"The fox knows many things, but the hedgehog knows one big thing," recited Alice from memory. That usually did the trick when the topic came up.

"Do you think, dear Alice, that I know a little bit about everything? Or a lot about one thing?"

"Milo, I don't understand why you worry about this."

"Well, I do. I can't decide for myself. Which is it?"

"I think you're a fox disguised as a hedgehog."

"Brilliant!" he said, relieved of the old struggle.

"But I think you should name the balloon something else."

"What?"

"Well, you understand things from a certain elevated perspective that others don't."

"True."

"And you don't flit around from thing to thing but rather make careful decisions before deciding where to land."

"Right," said Milo, his face brightening.

"Well, it all reminds me of a bumblebee."

Milo turned the word over in his mouth as if it were Swahili for "genius."

"The bumblebee has a kind of detachment as it studies the world below."

"Simply, absolutely perfect," he said as he stared at Alice with renewed admiration.

■ ■ ■ ■

After takeoff, *The Bumblebee* rose like a returning pearl diver into the sky. Milo waved from behind the small round glass window of the capsule long after anyone could see him from the ground. Once he'd unpacked his things, and done some calisthenics to keep limber, he unwrapped the red computer, which was swaddled in a thick hiking sock to protect it.

As the capsule made its way upward Milo began hooking up all his equipment, including a powerful radio transmitter he hoped to use to enlarge his weather packets at high altitude. Finally, he would be able to implement some of the observations he'd made at the chess match. As a test run he turned everything on: red computer, pattern-formula generator, hydrogen lung, radio transmitter.

Nothing.

The capsule was buffeted by the winds, and Milo muttered to himself as he checked the cables, rebooted the computer, and turned the radio-frequency modulator higher. Unbeknownst to him, 4,500 feet below, every automatic garage door in San Francisco received the radio frequency from

The Bumblebee and began opening and closing simultaneously. From a certain altitude it looked as if the entire city of San Francisco was winking good-bye.

At 10-1/2 New Montgomery, things were getting twitchy. Motherlove had developed a tic in his left eye, which made it appear as though he were jeering at everything anyone said. Most immediately this had the effect of nearly causing a fistfight with Niebald every couple of hours. "You mock me again and I'll knock your teeth out," Niebald shouted at two A.M. as the two men went over the front-page stories they had both just finished writing.

The long-planned increase in the *Trumpet*'s printing schedule, from weekly to daily, had been laid entirely on the shoulders of the veteran newspapermen. They wrote like maniacs, generating fifteen thousand words a day between them and trying every trick in the book to fill up the pages of empty newsprint. The cartoons had been enlarged to four times their normal size, the fonts for news stories bumped up, margins expanded. They'd even resorted to running a header called "From the Archive" above stories culled from the stack of memorable *Trumpet* scoops from years past (this explained the photograph of Winston Churchill on the front page), and all the very best of B. Franklin's letters to the editor.

Anything to fill up the blank pages of newsprint they had come to see as a kind of desolate desert they could never quite cross. Single-day newsstand sales were already plummeting as readers noticed that Slater Brown's byline no longer appeared on the front page. Or any page. The *San Francisco Sun* and the *Sun of San Francisco* circled like giddy vultures.

After a week of this, with Maynard still away, no sign of their star reporter, and nobody to help them investigate the crazy weather, Motherlove and Niebald both collapsed, falling asleep at their desks. The current edition of the *Trumpet* looked like a printer's error, with whole blocks of paper left blank. The idea of running Spanish translations of the stories next to their English counterparts as a way of soaking up the blank space hadn't gone anywhere, for lack of a translator who would work for free.

The radio on the windowsill played a fugue by Bach as Niebald and Motherlove's snores settled into syncopated rhythm. Outside it was so foggy the weather's motives were impossible to read.

As the clock edged toward morning the

fax machine in the corner chirped, fell silent, and then came to life, rocking back and forth until a one-page memo spilled onto the ground. Motherlove rubbed his eyes and walked over to retrieve it.

"Hum, wha — can't you see I'm sleeping?" grumbled Niebald, rubbing his eyes.

"This just came through. Read it."

It was a one-paragraph letter from Gloria van der Snoot's lawyer making an offer to "buy all business, trademarks, spin-offs, and real estate associated with *The Morning Trumpet*. Terms and price to be negotiated by close of business Friday."

"Friday?" mumbled Niebald in disbelief. "It *is* Friday! They can't mean by close of business today?"

"Or do they mean next Friday?" asked Motherlove.

Niebald and Motherlove were many things, but one thing they weren't was businessmen.

The mayor had convinced Gloria to buy *The Morning Trumpet* while her yacht was refueling in Santiago, Chile. However, the ship-to-shore phone connection had been particularly bad, and for the rest of her three-month sea voyage Gloria was under the impression she had purchased the "Corning Crumpet," which she assumed was a new bakery supply store.

"The mayor has simply become obsessed with pastries," she told her companions. But it really didn't matter to her what it was that he wanted her to buy. The amount of money they were talking about was a rounding error to her, and besides, she had a feeling that Tucker Oswell wasn't going anywhere and keeping him close was in her best interest.

"We better call Maynard," said Niebald.

Maynard's return, the next afternoon, was not a happy affair. His trip to Indianapolis had been energizing, as he'd been, for the first time in his professional life, courted, feted, and schmoozed by potential investors who told him in reverential tones they saw the *Trumpet* as a "media property" that could be spun out "into a multicontent digital delivery platform." Whatever it was, it certainly sounded more exciting than producing a daily newspaper. When he first got the panicked call from Motherlove he was petulant, like a child pulled away from a particularly fun play session by parents who insisted it was time to go home.

By the time the revolving doors emptied Maynard into the lobby of the *Trumpet* building, he'd incubated himself into a state of paranoia that during his absence everyone had been talking about him behind his back. Everyone *had* been talking about him behind his back, but Maynard only worsened the already weird vibe in the air by cornering Niebald and Motherlove one by one and saying "I heard what you said about me" in a conspiratorial voice meant to trick the questionee into confessing all sorts of hideous comments.

This poisonous atmosphere lasted until Sunday evening, when they were all sitting in on an executive staff meeting to discuss Gloria van der Snoot's offer. In front of Maynard lay a sheet detailing the current operating costs of the *Trumpet* compared to the current rapidly vanishing advertising base. "Guess what, guys?" said Maynard. "It turns out nobody is particularly excited about advertising next to blank pages. Go figure!"

While they looked at the columns of numbers for the hundredth time, a strange sensation filled the air.

"Hey, look at you screwballs!" shouted Niebald, pointing at his colleagues.

"Look who's talking!" shouted Motherlove.

Inexplicably, all three men's hair stood on end. Even Maynard Reed's heavily oiled coif stood limpidly in the air. They smiled at one another, and not the half-smile smirks they had recently been producing for each other, but real, generous, gasping smiles. It was funny seeing your colleague's hair stand up on end. The tension in the room had finally broken. This lasted right up to the moment the building was rocked by a violent clap that knocked out the lights, shattered the windows, and threw the men to the floor in a deafening panic.

"It's the Russians," shouted Maynard, as his ears rang and his eyes filled with dust. "It's the Russians or the Chinese. That was a surface-to-air missile. I read all about it in *Soldier of Fortune* magazine. Get ready," he said, covering his head with his hands, "they travel in pairs." Niebald and Motherlove crawled cautiously to their feet. Every desk had been swept clean and broken glass crunched underfoot.

Niebald wrinkled his nose. "Smells like lightning to me," he said as the bitter smell of burnt electricity filled the room. Seventeen thousand feet above, Milo Magnet fiddled regretfully with the knobs on the control panel in front of him.

The *Trumpet* had taken a direct hit, but the roof remained unscathed and the sandstone building had not allowed a fire to take hold. The only lasting casualty of the lightning strike wasn't discovered until the next day, when Niebald noticed that the "Sound of News" clock on the outside of the building had been struck. The clock still told time, but oddly enough, only in reverse.

CHAPTER
THIRTY-FOUR

At the de Quincy mansion it was quiet. No one came or left. The morning after the chess match the Peruvian housekeeper had been told her services would no longer be needed. Calls made to the house by the director of the International Chess Association inquiring into Callio's availability to play in a series of important ranking matches in Europe continued to be answered by a busy signal.

After two entire days with no discernible weather crisis, the mayor lifted the city emergency status, schools reopened, and the transportation system returned to full service. The only new development was that all the strange weather had drawn itself into a giant cloud of vapor hovering on the Marin side of the Bay. The astonishing vision of circular snowstorms and miniature tornadoes careening down Market Street like out-of-control go-carts had ceased. All that remained was the black ball, which seemed to have gathered in the middle of the Bay for the sole purpose of deflating itself. Even its color had gone from a shiny, menacing black to more of a brown before ending up in its current state, which was being described by the papers as "pale ocher." A motorboat filled with graduate climatology students from Stanford had driven through the vapor ball in order to take samples. Upon reappearing through the fog they reported that if you listened very carefully inside the cloud you could hear tiny popping sounds.

Motherlove's tic had taken over the entire left side of his face. It was so bad that Niebald had gone out and bought his friend a red bandanna, which he tied around Motherlove's neck and drew up under his nose to hide the physical disintegration. Above the bandanna fold Motherlove's eyes darted nervously.

Every morning they met for the regular staff meeting and tried to come up with fresh solutions to the problems, which were many and multiplying. The most recent edition of the paper looked like it had been composed by Pablo Picasso in the midst of a vicious hangover. The entire front page contained nothing but the name of the newspaper, with two little stories on the bottom about the historic rainfall for the Sierra Mountains, written by Niebald, who had typed it out using large blocks of text from the *Encyclopædia Britannica* for quotes. The center of the page was nothing but a giant bald spot. Just looking at it made Motherlove sick to his stomach, but they'd slipped behind the printer's deadlines and there was nothing more to be done.

"Contest!" shouted Maynard. "We need to run a contest! We'll ask our readers to write the stories." Niebald and Motherlove just stared at him, their heavy-lidded eyes at half-mast.

Every morning the three men — principal shareholders in "The Morning Trumpet LLC" — voted on Gloria van der Snoot's offer, and every time they voted unanimously against it.

"Well," said Maynard, looking out the window of his office onto the clear afternoon. "Tomorrow's Friday. I guess we should vote on this once and for all. The time has come for us to seriously consider the offer." He paused and looked again at the latest issue of the *Trumpet* as if he were speaking at an open-casket funeral. "What do you fellas say?" Before they could answer, the door to Maynard's office opened. A young man wearing blue jeans, a heavy sweater, and a baseball cap stood in the doorway.

"Can I help you?" said Maynard to the stranger. His colleagues turned.

"Yes," said Slater Brown.

Ten seconds passed. They stood speechless. It wasn't just the surprise, or the shock of recognition; it was that Slater looked different. That he wasn't dressed in his usual finery was obvious, but there was something else there too. Some new quality just beyond the reach of a journalist's quick description. Motherlove broke first, leaping and hugging him around the neck. "I knew it! I knew it! I knew it!" he shouted. Niebald, addled by lack of sleep and the overall pressure, twitched through a short nervous breakdown before rising to his feet and joining Motherlove's celebration, hopping up and down, their arms around Slater's shoulders. He waited for them to stop before stepping back and pulling a piece of paper from his pocket.

"Oh, boy, do we ever need a story from you," said Motherlove, forgetting to remove the bandanna from his face as he took the paper.

"I'm going to take you out for the biggest steak dinner you've ever had," said Niebald, beaming at his long-lost protégé. Mother-love turned his attention, almost reverentially, to the paper in his hand. He looked at it so long it was clear he was reading it twice. He looked up at Slater.

"No offense, but this doesn't exactly have the same pop as your earlier stuff." Mother-love handed the sheet to Niebald.

"I know," said Slater, "but I need you to print it."

Niebald took his time reading the story. He looked up at Slater. Starry bewilderment exploded in his eyes.

"This isn't exactly news."

For the first time they noticed what was different about Slater. It wasn't the clothes, or the weight — although he did have the hollow-cheeked look of a young man who had come up against himself and learned something. It was his eyes, which burned with an intensity they hadn't seen before. Even his first story, his career-making story for the *Trumpet,* hadn't brought out such palpable focus. "I don't know," demurred Motherlove, looking at his colleagues for guidance.

"Run the story. Just print it. You owe me that. You all owe me that."

Motherlove and Niebald looked at each other and then back at Slater and then at the sheet of paper.

Maynard, who had hung back slightly, was running the numbers through his head. The move to take the *Trumpet* back to daily circulation had all been predicated on the fact that Slater Brown would be generating more stories, not fewer. His absence, plus the increased price, had been a calamity for the paper's finances. They weren't running in the red, they were swimming in it, and soon they would have to make a decision from the options at hand.

"Gentlemen, given the state of the paper's finances, and the speed at which we are capable of writing, and the fact that Slater Brown does have a dedicated following, why don't we see what Mr. Brown's fans think of his story rather than just what we think?"

"Very well," said Motherlove, "but we print this, you gotta do us a favor." He wasn't thinking just of the next edition of the paper (which happened to mark the anniversary of the Mayflower Compact, which they were reprinting in its entirety), but of the edition after that, and beyond. Somehow they had to keep the *Trumpet* going.

But Slater Brown had closed the door behind him, leaving the three men to wonder if they'd just had a group hallucination. The only proof to the contrary was the paper in Niebald's hands.

They printed Slater Brown's story in the very next issue of the daily *Trumpet*. It was the long letter he had written to Callio, the one he had tried and failed to deliver in person to her. It concluded with a passage that none of the three newspapermen could make much sense of though they had, as promised, run it above the fold on the front page. The headline read:

A LETTER TO CALLIO DE QUINCY

. . . Of the many kinds of happiness available in this world, I have known only two. The first was the unfolding of a long-anticipated dream of mine. I wanted to write, but more important I wanted to be read, like nobody else before me. And I was. I see now that what the public loves, in part, about a famous person is not so much what the person has done, but that the person has had his dream come true. That's why they want to know you. To have your autograph. To touch the hem of your jacket. You are the living proof they lack in their own lives. The happiness of notoriety can, if you let it, transition your soul. I let it. And there was nothing quite like it in the world.

My second happiness is because of you. Once witnessed, like all natural things, this state of bliss appeared to have been in the cards, predestined. But it was not. And it would be a mistake to think so. Because to believe that it was written in the stars would absolve the two people from thinking they needed to do anything about it. It just *is,* they could tell each other. But they would be wrong because things that seem inevitable must also be turned toward. Now that I have seen even the faintest outline of this possibility, I know I must give chase as if my life depends on it. Because it does.

After confirming it had been printed in the newspaper Slater Brown secluded himself at Mrs. Cagliostra's cottage and waited for a response.

At City Hall there were whoops of joy when the "fucking happiness" story, as it was known thereafter, came out. It confirmed what they'd long hoped for, which was that once and for all, their enemy had finally gone off his rocker. In the glow of celebration, William Heck had been able to get the mayor to commit to reduce his calorie intake to seven thousand per day. "It's a start," said Doc Little when he came in to take the mayor's blood pressure.

The big news, however, was that a new plan to rehabilitate the mayor's image was under way. A political consultant had come in to assess the current polling data and advised the mayor to "reach out to the community and engage in their stories."

"Reach out?" said Tucker Oswell from behind his desk when the report was read to him. "That's what we paid fifteen thousand dollars to some schmuck from D.C. to tell us? I'll tell you what I'm going to do, I'm going to reach out and wring her pretty little neck!"

"Hold on, boss," said William Heck, "she has some action items down here at the bottom. Ah, this is a good one. She says research shows the fastest way for a beleaguered incumbent to gain traction with voters is to do simple things: Open up City Hall for night tours, have monthly town hall meetings, take strong stances on crime and education, and remember to call people on their birthdays."

"Wait a second," said the mayor, nodding his head approvingly. "That last one is pretty good. How hard would it be to get me a daily list of everyone's birthday in San Francisco?" William Heck smiled as he handed over the already organized list, prioritized into two columns: names and addresses of those who had voted for the mayor in the past, and those who hadn't.

"Get me a phone," shouted the mayor as William Heck moved in behind him, softly pressing a phone to his ear. "And get some of these people on the line. I don't want to wait around all day."

"The first fifty are already holding for you, Mr. Mayor," said William Heck.

"Hello, hello," said Tucker Oswell as he squinted at the paper in front of him. "Is this Marjorie Shields? Well, madam, this is the mayor of San Francisco and I wanted to take the time to wish you a very happy birthday. Oh, seventy-six, well, that's not old at all." The mayor looked up at William Heck and winked. "Especially if you take good care of yourself . . ." It was all his chief of staff could do to keep from shedding tears of joy.

One week after the birthday blitz campaign had been initiated, Tucker Oswell's internal polling numbers were up twelve percent.

At TK's Whilton polished the redwood bar with lazy circles of his wipe rag. The worst of whatever it was that had been afflicting the city seemed to be over. As proof of this, the long-standing suicide betting pool was back to its usual flow.

"The lovers are humping and the jumpers are jumping," said Whilton to Moon and Rocco and the rest of the residents. Two suicides off the Golden Gate Bridge in just the past week had put everyone in a better mood (one had survived, which paid double).

To commemorate this, Whilton reached up and rang the brass bell next to the cash register — it hadn't clanged since Nixon won his second term in 1972 — and bought a round of drinks on the house.

It had been three days and he had heard nothing. His mind raced with irrational fears, trumped only by negative projections. She hated him, she had been brainwashed, her father was selling her into white slavery. It was as if he'd sent an S.O.S. into the void. It never occurred to him, as indeed it never does occur to the sender, that the recipient

360

simply had not come into contact with the message.

Mrs. Cagliostra was his only link to the outside world, and she gave him wide berth, leaving hot meals on a tray outside his door and shooing away unwanted visitors.

She did not even tell him that the papers were reporting that the announcement of a new owner for the *Trumpet* was imminent. "Trumpet Squeaks By?" said the *Sun of San Francisco;* "Trumpet or Dump-it?" said the *San Francisco Sun.*

That afternoon when the mail came Mrs. Cagliostra almost threw out a postcard that had wedged itself into the pages of a ladies' hosiery catalog. But something about the watercolor sketch of a small rowboat on the front prompted her to save it. She slipped it underneath Slater Brown's door.

On the back was written: "Wednesday. Flowerpot. Midnight. Very quiet."

It was unsigned.

CHAPTER
THIRTY-FIVE

He parked the car two blocks away. Two blocks because one block seemed to be pushing his luck. For all he knew, Havram had trained his already good ears to pick up on the sound of the Riley Imp Roadster's antique muffler. So two blocks it was. Above him the moon shone clearly, like a spotlight from another universe, as Slater stepped lightly down the sidewalk as if hoping to leave no trace on the ground.

The key was right where the postcard said it would be. At precisely midnight he fished it out from beneath the fake rock in the cast-iron pot of geraniums and slipped it into the front door lock. Inside he could hear the antique grandfather clock begin to clang midnight and he took advantage of the sound to turn the key in the lock. As he stepped forward to open it Slater had a flicker of intuition: Havram was on the other side, waiting unblinkingly for him. Once he'd imagined it, his mind ratcheted up the stakes until chills of dread raced through his body: What if Havram had sent the postcard? The writing had been so faint he couldn't tell if it had been hers. What if this was a trap? *It was a trap.* He paused in limbo. The door was unlocked, but not yet opened. There was still time to change course.

Sometimes the body does what the mind cannot, and Slater watched in horror as his hands rose up to gently push the door open. He would have to face whatever darkness was on the other side. He waited on the threshold for his eyes to adjust. There in the middle of the grand hall, sitting quietly on the first step of the stairs, a lit votive candle had been left for him. A five-story lighthouse could not have lifted his heart as much.

He stooped to pick up the candle and climbed the stairs two at a time. On the second landing he quickly passed Havram's bedroom door, noting with relief the sound of deep slumber coming from within. His heart beat at a rate in keeping with a hurdler halfway through the hundred-yard dash. Her door was opened slightly. He took a deep breath and stepped inside.

She was sitting very still and very straight. Around her head was a corona of golden light, the sum result of the many candles lit around the headboard. As they looked at each other Slater decided he would never ask God for another favor for the rest of his life if he could just be allowed to cross the open room. When they did get their arms around each other, and their lips touched, they grabbed each other as tightly as if they had just been asked to jump overboard and the other was the only known life jacket in the world.

In for a penny, in for a pound, he told himself as they snuck out. There was no way they could talk the way they needed to within the confines of the house. He took her to a hidden café on a side street that ran parallel to the late-night hustling in North Beach. They made their way quickly through the crowd, hoping to remain unrecognized. The heavy November fog helped. Callio flipped up the collar on her jacket and drew her scarf tight around her face.

In front of the café was a single empty table beneath a heat lamp. Behind the cash register an old Frenchman dozed, the smoldering cigarette between his fingers nothing but ash. The silence between them was as comfortable as ever, as it suggested an uninterruptible conversation for which spoken words were only punctuation.

As they sat there he felt himself gathering up his forces, for he knew this was the time. If he waited, there would be other times, but something told him they would never be as good.

"I, I want to talk about us — about next," he said finally.

"Good," she said, folding her hands in front of her. "Me too."

"I want to talk about getting, getting out of here," he said.

"Here?" said Callio, glancing at the snoring Frenchman. "But we just arrived."

"Not here. I mean *here*. I mean out of our current situation and into something more —" He suddenly ran out of words. This hadn't seemed so hard five minutes ago. Callio saw he was binding up and she stopped him.

"Write it down for me," she said, steadying him with her gaze. From the way she tilted her head Slater understood something.

"You didn't see my letter to you in the paper, did you?"

Callio shook her head slowly, her eyes widening.

He drew a rumpled newspaper from his pocket. "I didn't know any other way of

365

reaching you."

The Frenchman appeared unbidden at their elbows with two tiny cups of espresso and a pair of cookies cut into a tiny moon and star.

"Merci," said Callio with a polite nod before turning back to Slater. She raised her eyebrow.

"May I read it?" she said, reaching for the newspaper, but at the last moment Slater drew it closer to him as what was true in him rubbed up against what was false.

"Come," she said, sending her hand through the gates of his arms until her fingertips touched the newspaper. "Let me read it," she said as her eyes locked onto his. The electric hum between them intensified into a great cloud of charged energy until it blew out the lightbulb behind the bar. *"Merde!"* said the Frenchman under his breath as he began to fumble toward the utility closet. Slater Brown let her pull the paper from his grasp very slowly.

She read it once, twice, three times before she looked up at him.

"Slater Brown," she said, "this is beautiful." She took his hands in hers. "There is glorious happiness ahead of us."

He looked at her, wide-eyed. Every ounce of him believed her.

"Together?" he said, just to confirm. She lowered her head slowly and touched it to his in a gesture of silent affirmation.

After taking a long, looping drive around the city to show her Coit Tower rising through the fog and the new Navy battleship in port, he pulled to a stop at a quiet place beneath the Golden Gate Bridge.

"Let's talk about our next move," said Slater, putting his car into park.

"Let's," said Callio.

"What if we just keep driving?" he said, sitting forward and putting the car in gear, hoping she wouldn't stop him. "We could be in Denver this time tomorrow." But she only laughed. There was no reason to rush things now.

"Things are going to take some time," she said, her eyes suddenly serious. "My father is very angry. He has threatened to take us back to Turkey. It would kill him to live there now; he has no connection to that place. But in his state of mind he wants to control everything by sweeping all of the pieces from the table rather than recognize how things have changed."

"What are you going to tell him about us?" asked Slater.

"I'm going to wait for the right moment.

He has a hot head, but he will calm down."
She didn't sound entirely convinced, but he
let it go.

"What do you have in mind to do next?"
she asked.

"Well, I once had this crazy theory about
all the things you were supposed to have accomplished by the age of twenty-nine," he
said, smiling at the memory of it. "And now
I see that my life," he looked over at her,
"our lives are going to go beyond what I
had imagined."

She thought about this for a moment.
"You're forgetting something else."

"What?"

"You now have something you never had
before," she said.

"You?" he asked, hoping to beat her to
the punch.

"No," she said, smiling as she stared into
his eyes. "You now have a story."

It was nearly two-thirty when they pulled
up in front of the de Quincy mansion. He
could not bear to say good night outside, so
he carried her up the steps in his arms. If
Havram was listening for footsteps, it would
be better if the echo of only one pair hung
in the air.

As they made it back to her room without
incident he lowered her gently into bed and

turned to click off the bedside lamp. It was time to go. He had pushed their luck far enough.

"Slater," she said after the room went dark. "Come closer, I want to tell you something." He leaned down until her warm breath tickled his ear.

"I've been giving our next move some thought," she said very quietly. Before he could protest, or pretend to protest, he felt her hands around his waist and himself tipped into bed with her. There was a muffled squeal, followed by the shucking of clothes as quickly and efficiently as if they had been on fire. Finally there was only the contented sounds of two people who have discovered with great delight that they fit perfectly within each other.

Something woke Slater Brown an hour after dawn. At first he wasn't sure what it was. He looked over at the clock. The alarm hadn't gone off. He looked at Callio, her breathing soft and measured beside him. Outside, rain ticked against the window. He knew he should leave now. There was so much to be done. The sound came through again. It was the front doorbell.

He pulled on his pants as he ran over to the bedroom window to see who it was.

"Sweet Jesus!" he shouted as he looked down at the front door. Callio was resting on her elbow, blinking.

"Who is it?"

"Stall your father. Don't let him come downstairs. Tell him it was a wrong address!" said Slater, running from the room. As he passed Havram's door in the hall he could hear the agitated tapping of the walking stick making its way around the bedroom. He took the stairs three at a time before skidding to a halt across the marble floor at the front door.

Underneath the alcove two men stood pressed tightly together in an attempt to stay out of the morning drizzle. Slater opened the door and stared at them.

"Well, hey there!" said Motherlove. One of his eyes had a broken blood vessel, and his face was the color of egg yolk. "Look who's here."

"What are you doing here?" said Slater in a hushed tone as he stepped out onto the porch and pulled the door behind him.

"Ah, we were just in the neighborhood and thought we'd —"

"It's six-thirty in the morning," said Slater. He didn't bother to ask why Motherlove was still wearing a bandanna across his face.

Niebald elbowed Motherlove. "C'mon, Bob," he said out of the corner of his mouth.

"Any chance we can step inside for a second, get out of this weather?" asked Motherlove, ignoring his partner.

Slater shook his head. "This isn't my house and the owner's a little —"

"Say no more," said Motherlove, holding up his hands in mock protest. "We just wanted to check on you is all. Lay eyes on you. Haven't heard from you in a coupla days, and —"

"Seven days," corrected Niebald.

"Seven days, and I just wanted to make sure everything's OK. That you're, you know, OK?"

"Everything's fine."

The sound of the raindrops hitting the tin roof above them forced everyone to raise his voice in order to be heard.

"WELL, THAT'S GOOD. THAT'S WONDERFUL NEWS. AIN'T THAT GREAT NEWS, NIEBALD?"

Niebald nodded his head in agreement and elbowed his partner a third time.

"WELL, YOU ASK HIM, THEN!" snapped Motherlove. "AND STOP DIG-GING ME IN THE RIBS."

Niebald turned to Slater and the younger man noticed for the first time how tired and drained he looked.

"KID, WE, I, . . ."

"HE'S TRYING TO SAY HE MISSES YOU!" cracked Motherlove nervously.

"KID, WE WERE WONDERING IF YOU HAD —"

"NOT TO PUT ANY PRESSURE ON YOU," said Motherlove, suddenly serious.

"WE WERE W-WONDERING," stuttered Niebald, "IF YOU'D GIVEN ANY THOUGHT AS TO WHEN YOU MIGHT BE COMING BACK TO THE PAPER?"

Slater cringed. Behind him the front door was shut forcefully and he heard the ominous sound of double locks snapping shut. Havram was up. He tried to put it from his mind.

"DON'T GET US WRONG," continued Motherlove, on a roll. "EVERYTHING'S FINE DOWN AT THE PAPER."

"THE PAPER'S GONE TO SHIT," said Niebald, almost simultaneously.

"WHAT YOUR FRIEND AND MENTOR IS TRYING TO SAY IS THAT WE COULD USE YOUR HELP. NOT TRYING TO TAKE YOU AWAY FROM THIS, OF COURSE. BUT I'M SURE WE COULD FIGURE SOME WORK SCHEDULE OUT — THREE-QUARTER TIME, OR HALF TIME . . . OR QUAR-

TER TIME . . ." He read Slater's face like a safecracker, trying to decipher the right combination.

"OR WHATEVER AMOUNT OF TIME WORKS FOR YOU. BUT THE POINT IS IT WOULD BE GREAT IF YOU COULD COME BACK AND PUT A LITTLE PIZ-ZAZZ INTO THE OLD *TRUMPET*."

"YEAH," said Niebald, brightening at the sound of it.

"IN FACT, YOU BETTER COME BACK SOON," said Motherlove, elbowing Niebald in an overly jovial way meant to avoid the fact that they were still waiting on an answer.

"YEAH," said Niebald. "SOONER'S ALWAYS BETTER."

Finally they stopped talking and smiled like Seventh-Day Adventists still hoping to be invited inside.

"FELLAS," shouted Slater over the rain, which thundered down around them like a kettledrum orchestra, "I'M NOT COM-ING BACK."

The two men reacted as if struck in the solar plexus. Their heads drooped down-ward and they suddenly took an intense interest in the eyelets of their soaked shoes.

"THIS ISN'T. THIS ISN'T THE RIGHT TIME IS ALL. EVERYTHING'S

CHANGING. EVERYTHING'S DIFFER-
ENT NOW."

Though the essential information had
been shared, the three of them stood there,
shoving their hands deeper and deeper into
their pockets, as if searching for words to
keep the conversation going.

Finally Motherlove stuck out his hand for
a shake, but Slater mistook the gesture and
they ended up in a clumsy hug, each man
clapping the other around the shoulders as
if putting out a small fire. The harder Slater
squeezed Motherlove the stronger he felt
the older man trembling beneath his over-
coat.

He watched as they turned out from
underneath the awning and walked slowly
for the front gate. They did not even bother
to open their umbrellas. As soon as they
had disappeared Slater felt a wave of exhaustion come over him. It was as if a magic
spell had been cast, or broken. It was hard
to tell. He could feel himself getting bigger
and bigger and then smaller and smaller and
he felt the need to sleep for days and days
and months and months and years and
years. He didn't even give Havram the
satisfaction of trying the locked door.

CHAPTER
THIRTY-SIX

The fog ball lingering in the middle of the Bay had reduced itself to the size of a small house. The meteorologists who had gathered from around the country to observe it predicted that it would completely dissipate within the week. Pinky Beale, the mayor's press secretary, was preparing a press release in which the mayor would announce that his "Fresh Air" initiative was, if not completely, then ninety-five percent responsible for stabilizing the weather. The press release would contain a paragraph near the bottom, which nobody would bother to read, explaining that the mayor, "after listening carefully to his constituency," had decided to work with Duane Oswell at the Department of Transportation to take the appropriate environmental action necessary to deal with the aberrant weather in the future. This included replacing all the electric buses in the city, and their accompanying wires, with new, state-of-the-art automatic solar buses.

"How can we be sure that the carbon footprint from our electrical buses isn't responsible for causing our unstable weather? The answer is we can't. Which is why I've proposed a quick and fair plan to do whatever is necessary to bring our weather back in line with historical patterns." For the mayor the best part was that these new buses didn't require drivers, being programmed to run routes by a central computer. In this way he eliminated the human element that he was certain was behind Slater Brown's ability to locate stories. The bus drivers *must* have been the ones passing the young reporter all those tips.

Two weeks later, on the front steps of City Hall, the mayor unveiled the first evidence of this transportation change. It was in the shape of an enormous abstract blob of molten metal, perched on a wooden pedestal. To some it looked like a flying saucer; others mistook it for an oversized bedpan. But to Tucker Oswell it looked like what he had expressly commissioned it to be: a giant ear. Slater had seen it for the first time on his way down to the *Trumpet* building. He'd pulled his car over and walked up to the metal disk, rotating on a steel pivot in the gentle breeze. He ran his hand over the metal folds of the nine-hundred-pound ear. At the bottom a plaque read:

This sculpture was created from the recycled wires removed during the recent transit upgrade to solar-powered buses. No longer will the most beautiful city in the world be covered by a net of unseemly wires just to serve the needs of our electric buses. The sculpture was chosen as a way to honor the citizens of this green city, where, as a forgotten reporter once wrote, "Every voice should be listened to."

Slater winced. He was the forgotten reporter referenced. He'd written that sentence not three months earlier in the *Trumpet.* All too quickly the mayor was trying to write him out of the story.

Behind him he heard a group of loud voices. Glancing over his shoulder he saw a phalanx of men, arms swinging as they speed-walked out of City Hall. In the center of the pack was the shiny face of Tucker Oswell. He was dressed head to toe in a red velour tracksuit and was on the second of the day's five miniexercise regimes. Around both wrists he wore copper bracelets recommended to him by his new personal trainer. His waistband was a Velcro belt with four water bottles attached to it. Having salved the wound that had caused such exuberant eating, he'd turned his compulsive nature toward physical exercise with the publicly stated goal of becoming America's healthiest mayor. Pinky Beale had been drafting the press release all morning. Right now the mayor was out with his posse for a power-walk before lunch (chickpea salad) in advance of his two-hour Pilates class that afternoon. He was so busy talking — about plans for a mega shopping mall in the Presidio — that his group breezed right past Slater Brown. Ten feet later the mayor wordlessly held up his hand, the universal symbol to stop. He had sensed something. Duane Oswell, who was in the front of the pack (and wearing an identical blue velour tracksuit), missed the signal and kept right on walking, arms pumping, all the way across Van Ness Avenue and around the corner. The rest of the group stood perfectly still, like bird dogs waiting for the covey to flush. Slowly the mayor turned in little half steps toward where Slater was standing. His group turned with him, tensing as they did, as they could see the mayor's mood had shifted.

The mayor licked his lips. Slater stood relaxed, hands in the pockets of his jeans.

"Should we wrap it for you?" asked the mayor, nodding toward the giant sculpted ear. "Perhaps put a little ribbon around it so you can take it with you?" The mayor's men chuckled as they settled into a half fan around him, like the outer feathers on a peacock's tail.

"I must say it is *quite* appropriate that I should come across you just as you were coming across our newest sculpture," said Tucker Oswell. "You know there are going to be ten of these, planted around the city?"

Slater said nothing.

"Ah, well, you're the only person in the entire city who could appreciate how delightfully meta this particular moment is for me!"

The more Slater held his tongue the louder the mayor became, leaning forward on the balls of his feet, as if shouting into a great abyss.

"The tide has turned, my young friend. First your lady friend abandons you — so sorry to hear about that — and now your clandestine spy network has been dismantled. I knew you were getting your scoops on those buses somehow. It was just a matter of time before I figured it out. Try finding a story now!"

The mayor's eyes were shielded by the wraparound mirrored sunglasses favored by triathletes and little beads of sweat appeared on his forehead. It didn't matter to Slater, of course. He'd already made his decision — the pocket radio was long gone. But there was something about the mayor's confidence, the joyless self-confidence of a bully, which alerted him to the truth. So he pounced.

"Yeah, well, that was pretty smart how you figured out how I was getting my stories from the bus drivers," Slater said with a hangdog shrug. The corners of the mayor's mouth twitched with a cruel smile.

"Well," he said, "I *am* a professional, young man. And sooner or later a professional always ends up on top."

Slater grinned. It was just as he'd suspected. "Mr. Mayor," he said slowly and quietly, which caused the mayor to lean even closer toward him. "You don't have the foggiest idea how I got those stories, and you're no closer today to understanding than you were yesterday, or you'll be tomorrow. But rest assured, I've put mechanisms into place that will effectively track your activity very carefully for the duration of your term. So play nice. Or we will be seeing one another again on the front page of the paper." The two men stood staring at each other for a full minute, the mayor using every bit of his intuition to ferret out the truth. It was impossible to tell if Slater Brown was bluffing or not.

From all the way down the block a loud voice boomed, "HEY, BONEHEADS!" The group turned. It was Duane Oswell, who had circled back once he realized that he'd lost his pack. "Come on, we've got to keep our heart rates up!" he said, pointing at the enormous cardiovascular watch strapped to his wrist. From across the street he couldn't see who the mayor was talking to.

That night as Slater lay in his bed he couldn't fall asleep. He'd tried calling her but the phone didn't even ring busy, there was just some weird message saying "This number is no longer in service." Havram must have gone berserk when he'd realized that Slater had spent the night with his daughter. There was really only one thing to do. In the morning he would go over and demand to see her.

"I *demand* to see her!"

"I demand to *see* her!"

"I demand to see *her!*" he said, practicing aloud.

The clock beside his bed read three A.M. He turned out the light and put his head down. As he was drifting off to sleep a multitude of sirens invaded his dreams. He tossed and turned in his bed as the sounds grew louder. A few minutes later came a knock on his door.

"Slater? Slater, get up. That's not a normal fire," said Mrs. Cagliostra on the other side of the door. "The dispatcher said it was a five-alarm." For years Mrs. Cagliostra had kept a police radio, turned low, next to her bed. "Must be a big one."

He scrambled to put his clothes on. The first thing to do was to make sure she was safe.

"I demand to see her!" he continued practicing as he dressed and began running from the cottage gate toward the center of the city.

He could hear the fire engines wailing in the distance and then he saw one, like a beast in the fog, swerving around the corner with a dozen men hanging on to the side. He ran as fast as he could and caught the tail end of the truck just as it turned onto Broadway. Several men on the back turned to help him climb aboard.

He caught his breath as the fire truck roared through the city. He had no idea where he was going and nobody on board volunteered a word. A man in front of him simply pointed toward the glow coming from Japantown, where a thick line of fire was billowing in the night air like a giant orange-and-black sail.

Passing Fillmore Street, an old lady stepped out of the thick smoke carrying her rescued possessions: a birdcage in one hand and a silver punch bowl in the other. As the driver jerked the big steering wheel to the left to miss her, Slater lost his grasp, and then his footing. As he fell off the truck he watched in slow motion as the men reached out to grab him. But it was too late and he hit the street hard, tumbling three times before coming to a stop against the curb. By the time Slater sat up, the wailing truck had vanished into the smoke.

Broadway and Baker, where he'd landed, was two blocks from Callio's house. He set off in a run, taking a shortcut up the Lyon Steps. For a moment a breeze blowing off the Bay ruffled the eucalyptus trees and restored his senses.

Her street was quiet, although there was smoke coming from the house next door. Slater looked up at Callio's bedroom window, half expecting her to be keeping a lookout for him, but the shade was drawn tight. Slater reached the front door and grasped the lion's paw that was the brass knocker. As he touched the brass he felt a curious tingle in his hand, although he couldn't place the sensation.

He released the knocker silently and grabbed the double handles. The doors swung open into the anteroom, which was quiet and dark, and he unconsciously let out a small breath of air he'd been holding.

The house was safe. She was safe. No sign of fire. He glanced around the dim room, letting his eyes adjust to the light and taking in the giant paintings on the walls (which had always intimidated him), and the signs of opulence and comfort, and the general idea of interesting people being reflected by interesting things, until something caught his eye.

He walked over to a small antique table. Two chess figures sat on top a piece of stationery, a black queen and a white pawn. On the light blue paper was a typewritten note.

Dear Slater —
Best of luck to you in your life.
Please do not follow me.

It is better that way.

Sincerely,
Callio de Quincy

In his shock he chuckled. Havram was clearly behind this. The signature underneath was not her handwriting. Just a strange squiggle, the best a blind man could manage on short notice. He read it again, quickly searching for other meanings. Although it was the work of a childish mind, the implication was real. The sightless bastard had either lured her or taken her away. But where? She had said Havram had no roots in Turkey. Would he take her to New York?

Then it came back to him, Havram's muttering names of European cities to himself when he thought he was alone in the hallway that night. It sounded exactly like the list a bitter, fevered mind would construct for the purposes of staging a chess comeback tour.

For a moment Slater Brown's heart raged with the kind of passion Havram had flashed like a knife during their battles. As his rage overtook him the giant painting hanging above the double staircase fell off the wall in a great slicing stroke. It sounded as if somebody had ripped a gigantic piece of paper in half. The painting, a springtime scene of an eighteenth-century Parisian ball, landed with a crash on the marble stairs before tipping over the railing and falling ten feet to the floor below at his feet.

Slater's first instinct was to try to put the painting back together, but as he looked at the pile of torn canvas and splinters another painting fell, sweeping a pair of Chinese palace vases off a table before ruining itself on the marble floor.

He stared motionless at this phenomenon. Was it a trick meant to scare him?

Above his head the great crystal chandelier inexplicably dropped from the ceiling as easily as if someone had thrown an anchor overboard. He braced himself for impact as the mass of twinkling crystal fell toward him, but the chandelier stopped short, swinging slightly side to side, as if ruffled by a mere breeze.

Slater ran upstairs to her room. Part of him expected her to be sitting in there, oblivious to the nightmare, waiting for him to come take her to lunch. He pushed her door open, but the room was empty. Clothes spilled out of her drawers and a handful of jewelry was left behind on her dressing table, including a silver necklace he'd once given her. He scooped it up so fast he almost missed what had been intentionally left underneath. It was a postcard. He flipped it over. On the front was a photograph of Moscow's Red Square, on the back an announcement about an upcoming international chess tournament. She had left it for him. He was certain of it.

From all over the house he could hear crashing, as if it were falling apart piece by piece. Halfway down the stairs he stopped at the place where the first painting had fallen and ran his hands lightly over the blue walls. They were warm. Above his head were two black spots where the enormous nails supporting the painting had been fixed. But the heads of the nails were gone, shorn off by the weight of the painting.

"Strange," muttered Slater. He snatched a piece of the splintered frame from the stairs, pushing the end of the nail into the wall before pressing his eye to the nail hole.

It was as if he'd opened the grate on a smelting furnace. The inside of the house was on fire. Behind him the last of the paintings fell to the ground. The iron nails holding them had lasted as long as they could before melting in the blistering heat.

As the internal fire started to warp the paint, a giant brown scar appeared on the wall in front of him, like the smile of a specter.

CHAPTER
THIRTY-SEVEN

San Francisco, more than any American city, understands the focus required to beat back a raging fire. The Great Fire of 1906 had permanently etched into the souls of all who ever loved the city the rare peril they faced by living so close together.

Even as they fought the fire — schoolchildren with garden hoses standing next to pensioners with wet towels wrapped around their heads — the rumors began to circulate. Motherlove was the first to make the connection in print. In the hours leading up to the fire, no fewer than ten people had seen great flashes of red lightning coming from a silver vessel hovering over the city at midnight.

"I'm telling you right now, it was those damn UFOs started this," said Edgar Schilling, who insisted he'd seen a series of lightning balls coming from a silver UFO "with a parachute on top of it." Others said more of the same, although each description was slightly different, and no one could agree where in the city the fire had first started.

After twelve hours the blaze looked to be beyond them. The fire department was fighting the conflagration in no fewer than a dozen locations, with a new front being called in every ten minutes. Each of the city's forty-two fire stations was fully deployed. On WGGB, every man, woman, and child was requested to report to the bucket brigades forming along Lombard Street. Most had tears in their eyes, not from the smoke, but from the sinking feeling that their city was doomed.

At nine P.M. a strange mist enveloped the city, cooling everything and everyone down. By ten-thirty the mist had turned into fog so thick the men running the fire hoses couldn't see the fire itself. At 11:17 P.M. the fog produced the most surprising sequence yet — even for a city on fire from UFOs. Hail the size of quail eggs dropped from above and was greeted by the inferno with an angry hiss. By sunrise the fire was out. Soon after, the entire populace collapsed from exhaustion.

So too did the sleep-deprived genius, floating high above it all, who had spent a panicked twenty-four-hour period doing everything in his power to keep from setting the entire West Coast ablaze.

In the days that followed, Slater kept himself busy packing, stopping once to drive past the de Quincy mansion, but all that remained was ash. He'd decided not to try to say good-bye to everyone. The encounter with Mrs. Cagliostra had been hard enough.

"Whadd'ya mean you're going to leave? You can't leave now. Where will you go? How will you survive?"

"That's the problem," he said, "I can't survive here."

She looked at him, just as she had the moment she'd first laid eyes on him, and she understood.

"You should go, then. Go and find her. And when you do, I want you to promise me something."

"What?"

"I want you to promise me that you'll bring her back here and have a whole bunch of babies. In my day we didn't have time to wait so long before having babies."

"Thank you, Mrs. Cagliostra," he said, leaning in to kiss her cheek.

"Call me Aurora," she said, clutching him with surprising strength.

■ ■ ■ ■

That afternoon, a giant shadow loomed over the green grass on Crissy Field. At long last, and with much anticipation, *The Bumblebee* was coming in for a landing. Waiting for it was a full scrum of reporters who had gathered in the parking lot of the Palace of Fine Arts. As the hot-air balloon began its soft touchdown the mass of journalists began running toward *The Bumblebee,* shouting questions long before they could possibly be heard.

Although it is hard to judge a moving crowd, there were easily one hundred reporters, not to mention cameramen, photographers, and gaffers, pulling their equipment behind them as they cantered across the grass. As they drew closer, the balloon's position changed. The capsule door opened, but its pilot did not appear. Instead, a large bag of trash was pushed out just as the gas jets roared to life, jerking the balloon into the sky. This caused an existential crisis among the media who couldn't decide if they should stay and tear through the bag of trash looking for leads, or if they should try to catch *The Bumblebee* outright before it slipped the earth's grasp. A couple of younger reporters did manage to catch the trailing ropes from the capsule and hold on to it for a good long while, writhing as the apparatus rose upward, shouting their questions into the wind before finally being dropped, with a splash, into the Bay.

On his way out of town Slater Brown stopped at the *Trumpet* building. Motherlove and Niebald were in high gear, flitting around the newsroom, and there were several new faces he couldn't place.

"We're out of the tunnel," said Niebald in a voice hoarse from conducting all of the interviews they'd been running about the fire. His face was taut, and he looked like he'd lost ten pounds, but his eyes burned bright from the wave of adrenaline newspapermen feed on when in close proximity to big news. The fire was certainly big, mysterious news. And so was Milo Magnet. Perhaps the most mysterious ever. Niebald and Motherlove could not help but be amped by their proximity.

Paradoxically, the fire, and the mystery of it, had breathed fresh life into the *Trumpet.* That, and the fact that the day they were to sign the papers to officially sell *The Morning Trumpet* to Gloria van der Snoot — they'd finally voted for it when Slater had turned them down — an unexpected offer had come in asking if the *Trumpet* building's "air rights were available for liquidation."

"What's that?" said Motherlove when Maynard had brought in the fax.

"Liquidation means 'do we want to sell,' " said Maynard.

"Not that, you zipperhead, what does 'air rights' mean?"

"Oh," said Maynard in a knowing tone (he'd just had it patiently explained to him on the telephone by lawyers), "air rights are promises from buildings to their neighbors that they won't build their top floors any higher than their current location." This was particularly valuable in downtown venues where fancy hotels often wanted to make sure the views from their penthouse suites remained unobstructed. The fancy hotel going in behind the *Trumpet* wanted just such a guarantee and was willing to pay handsomely for it.

When Motherlove told him the news, Slater just smiled in admiration. Despite the obstacles to its existence, the *Trumpet* would endure. As it should be. The two men walked down the Hallway of Fame toward the newsroom.

"What are you going to do next," asked Motherlove, "career-wise?"

Slater looked at him. "Not sure. I'm going on a trip first. And then I'm going to read every book I own. All the way through." The older newspaperman nodded, wondering to himself why this distinction seemed noteworthy.

"I almost forgot," said Motherlove as they walked into his office. He went over to his desk drawer and pulled out a packet tied with string. Slater recognized the wrapping paper as an old *Trumpet* comic strip.

"When we heard you were leaving we wanted to give you a little something to remember us by." He held up his hand. "No need to open it now."

The sound of chair legs hitting the floor came from behind them.

"Open it," said Niebald.

Slater slipped the string from around the paper. Inside were three double-spaced typed pages. At the top it read:

The Sounds of San Francisco
A literary excursion
by Slater Brown.

"We saved it for you. We thought you might want it for your archives," said Motherlove. Slater read the first page and then reached out to clasp Motherlove's hand in his own, but the short-tempered journalist simply nodded at him before looking out the window. Their only hug was behind them.

It took just ten minutes to clear out his office. All the pads of paper and notes and gifts and invitations to parties (including Gloria van der Snoot's eightieth birthday next spring on Alcatraz) he left in a box by the garbage chute. Niebald walked him down to the street. Slater turned up to look at the *Trumpet* building one final time. The rush of the good-bye surprised him as the distant tumblers of the present moment clicked into place and quietly, firmly, ushered what was happening into what had happened.

He was being released, and he knew it. From Motherlove, the *Trumpet,* San Francisco, even his own curious notions of who he was and what he wanted. It was all happening at the same time, even as he stood there, flesh and blood. Above him the *Trumpet* building was dirtier than ever, the faces of the eight sculpted muses staring down at him stoically.

"I wonder who the ninth muse was?" said Slater to himself as he stared one last time at the building's facade. Niebald turned his eyes upward.

"The ninth? Wasn't the ninth the muse of poetry?" he said absently as he squinted into the sun.

"Ah," said Slater. "How perfectly appropriate. The muse of poetry." They stood there in silence, looking upward.

"Calliope," mumbled Niebald to himself.

"What'd you say?"

"Calliope was the muse's name," said Niebald.

A perfect roar filled Slater Brown's ears and his knees went weak. He reached out to steady himself on Niebald's elbow. As synchronistic coincidences go this was hard to beat. All this time and he'd never put together the fact that his Callio was named after one of the immortal muses. Was named after? Or *is,* he thought to himself. Was named after? Or *is.*

"Wow" was all he managed to say.

After collecting himself, he realized it was time to share something with Niebald. A secret for a secret.

"You know how I found all those stories, don't you?" he said.

"Listen," said Niebald, mistaking Slater's candor for doubt. He grasped Slater's hand in his own and pumped it up and down. "It's a gift, kid. It'll come back in all due time. Sure as turkeys fly it'll come back.

But right now, just concentrate on the true thing right in front of you." He winked, as if the true thing required no further explication.

And then just like that Niebald backed away. There was a deadline to file, and a town hall meeting about rebuilding all the structures damaged in the fire, and all the other mysterious details of the lightning to track down and print. Slater did not want to let go of Niebald's elbow, but the swirl of the city forced him to release it as she spread her hustle and bustle between them.

As he was about to raise his hand to flag down an approaching taxi, he stepped back off the curb and onto the sidewalk.

The afternoon light, flickering over the street in solid bands, was the same as ever. So too was the afternoon crowd, milling around, "like fish," he thought, patting his pocket for a yellow notebook. Then, as if called, he turned.

From within the crowd, as if born there, came a vision. From the moment Slater laid eyes on the slope-shouldered boy, or young man, it was clear who he was and what he wanted and why he was there.

The boy was walking not without purpose, but not with purpose. There was no meeting at the other end of his amble, no romance guiding his footsteps. His eyes were cast up, and then side to side, and then down at his feet as he sponged up everything around him into the notebook he held — not yellow, but purple.

Slater watched, his mouth half open, as the young man, with a patina of baby fat around his cheeks, swaddled tightly in a dark blue Navy peacoat from some Midwest discount surplus store, passed obliviously beneath his nose. As the apparition crossed his path, Slater held his breath. Somehow he knew that if he and that boy touched, it would set off a cataclysmic explosion that would render moot the universe's concept of cause and effect. They were not supposed to touch, or meet. It was a miracle he had seen the boy at all.

As Lawrence, or Tom, or Will, or Evan, or Max, or whatever his name was passed slowly by, Slater realized that this was the moment when the perfect thing happens to let those who are paying attention know that one story has concluded, just as another begins.

On instinct Slater Brown spun tightly behind the boy's shoulder and looked down at his open notebook. He couldn't help himself. There wasn't much time; an empty cab had pulled up against the curb and was waiting. But he wanted this last look, just this last look into whatever numinous mirror he had discovered.

EPILOGUE

Three years later, on a warm spring day, as the cherry blossoms were blooming and everyone was out in full force, a young journalist, Fernando Parrado, wandered about, working on a story about the city's thriving café culture.

He was tired, having nearly walked his feet off. A good quote had been hard to find. His editor, Javier, had specifically asked for a good one and so he delayed returning to the offices empty-handed. Finally, at the end of a long side street, he spotted a young couple sitting very closely together in front of a café. They did not look like locals, which in his experience went some way toward guaranteeing a good quote.

As Fernando approached he noticed the young woman was writing notes in the margin of an unbound manuscript of some kind. Perhaps it was a doctoral thesis. Or a novel. From where he stood it was hard to tell. The young man was intently staring at a pocket backgammon set, rolled out between them. Two or three times he made a move on the board before changing his mind and returning the pieces. Something about the quality of their solitude kept Fernando from interrupting. The photographer, less sensitive to such nuance, snapped some photographs which accompanied the story when it ran in *El País* the next day. The caption read: "Two visiting *turistas* enjoy each other's company in the Barcelona sun."

ACKNOWLEDGMENTS

The author wishes to thank Frederica Friedman, Kerri Buckley, Zoe Rosenfeld, his fellow writers at the Grotto, and most especially his wife, Lindy Fishburne, for the sharp eyes and sharper minds they brought to every aspect of this book. And special thanks to the San Francisco Police Department for recovering this manuscript when it was stolen from the author's car.